January Gilchrist is a Brisbane-based mystery author, boy mum, and former performing arts professional. She holds a Bachelor of Creative Arts, majoring in Literature and Performing Arts, was longlisted for the 2019 Richell Prize, and her debut thriller, *The Final Chapter*, is inspired by her time at the Varuna Writers' House. Balancing her time between writing, running a Pilates studio, and raising two sons, January draws on her varied life experiences to create authentic, nuanced characters. Fascinated by puzzles, especially the mysteries of human behaviour, January explores the stories we tell, the secrets we keep, and the truths we hide – even from ourselves.

THE FINAL CHAPTER

January Gilchrist

FICTION
HQ

The Final Chapter
© 2025 by January Gilchrist
ISBN 9781038971135

First published on Gadigal Country in Australia in 2025
by HQ Fiction
an imprint of HQBooks (ABN 47 001 180 918), a subsidiary of HarperCollins*Publishers*
Australia Pty Limited (ABN 36 009 913 517).

Gadigal Country
Level 19, 201 Elizabeth St
Sydney NSW 2000
harpercollins.com.au/hq/

This edition published 2026

HarperCollins acknowledges the Traditional Custodians of the lands upon which
we live and work, and pays respect to Elders past and present.

The right of January Gilchrist to be identified as the author of this work has been
asserted by her in accordance with the *Copyright Act 1968*.

All rights reserved. Apart from any use as permitted under the *Copyright Act 1968*, no
part may be reproduced, copied, scanned, stored in a retrieval system, recorded, or
transmitted, in any form or by any means, without the prior written permission of the
publisher. Without limiting the exclusive rights of any author or contributor, or of the
publisher of this publication, any unauthorised use of this publication to train generative
artificial intelligence (AI) technologies is expressly prohibited. HarperCollins also
exercises its rights under Article 4(3) of the Digital Single Market Directive 2019/790
and expressly reserves this publication from the text and data-mining exception.

HarperCollins*Publishers*
Macken House
39/40 Mayor Street Upper
Dublin 1, D01 C9W8, Ireland

This is a work of fiction. Names, characters, places, and incidents are either the product
of the author's imagination or are used fictitiously, and any resemblance to actual persons,
living or dead, business establishments, events, or locales is entirely coincidental.

A catalogue record for this book is available from the National Library of Australia
www.librariesaustralia.nla.gov.au

Printed and bound by CPI Group (UK) Ltd, Croydon, CR0 4YY

For Linda—
You shared stories with the world.
Now you're part of one.

The Blue Mountain Herald

Police have sealed off a section of the Blackheath area of the Blue Mountains National Park, including the grounds of Thorne House, after a body was discovered on the track to Govetts Leap.

This comes on the back of reports that police were called to Thorne House, now a writers house called Rhamnusia, to investigate the suspicious deaths of two as yet unnamed individuals, believed to have been staying at the house.

Detective Sergeant Michael Tomlinson said today, 'We cannot reveal the identity until next of kin have been notified. However, we can confirm that the police force have cordoned off part of the area near Thorne House, while we undertake further investigations, after two people were found deceased.'

Police were unwilling to confirm if and how the three deaths are related.

Locals told *The Sydney Informer* that they're not surprised.

The property, set on the edge of the state forest where Australia's most vicious serial killer, Byron Jackovic, hunted his victims, is the site of the tragic passing of the Thorne family, and is widely believed by the people of the town to be haunted.

A resident, who wishes to remain anonymous, said, 'The locals won't go anywhere near it. Too much bad luck. It's not right, what went on up there. It's not right.'

Day One

Desley

The taxi pulls to a stop at the side of the road. Overgrown trees crouch over a faded sign:

RHAMNUSIA. WRITERS HOUSE.

'There you go, love. Up there.'

Desley squints. The taxi's window is grimy and paints everything with a ghostly hue. The driveway is long, winding, and covered in gravel. She sighs. Her suitcase has a dicky wheel, and of course she's over-packed. She can't even pack a bag for a week without messing up.

'How do I get to the house?' Her voice trembles.

The driver's eyes meet hers in the rear-view mirror. 'You'll have to walk. I don't go up there, love.'

At least the rain has stopped, although the sky is black with threat.

I should make him take me all the way. I should say, drive me up. I don't want to walk. They're only words. I will ask him to continue up the driveway.

But her body refuses. *Weak*, she chastises herself as she taps her card against the machine he offers.

'Thanks so much,' she says and immediately hates herself.

He lurches out of the taxi, keeping his face averted from the driveway, and dumps her lurid pink suitcase on the ground. Desley blows on her hands. It's far colder than she'd imagined it would be. The weather forecast on her phone had displayed a little snowflake at the end of her week here. She'd shown her daughters and promised to send photos if it snowed. Queenslanders through and through, they'd squealed with delight at the idea of it. Their experience of winter was wearing tights under their school dresses for two weeks in July. Desley had bought this jacket online especially for this trip to the Blue Mountains.

'Good luck, love. Watch out for that ghost,' the driver calls as he leaps back in the car. He's U-turned and sped up the road before Desley can respond.

Once she'd given him the address, he hadn't stopped regaling Desley with ghost stories of the house. Now, her overactive imagination has got the better of her.

'The locals won't go near it,' the driver had said. 'That's why the Council of the Arts turned it into a writers house. Couldn't pay any of us to live in it. The whole family. Dead.'

Desley had smiled politely.

She doesn't believe in ghosts. She's married. She knows there are far worse things to endure than something that goes bump in the night.

Her driver had cleared his throat as his eyes held hers in the greasy rear-vision mirror. 'Not to mention all that Jackovic stuff.'

Desley hadn't been able to reply, her mouth drying unpleasantly at the mere mention of the name.

She chews her lower lip as she gazes around. The air is crisp in the way that only country air can be. Although only a twenty-minute drive from the train station, she is standing on the edge of a velvety dark forest in what feels like the middle of nowhere.

No one to hear you scream.

Silly, she scolds herself, as she peers into the gloom of the driveway.

A wind-gnarled bloodwood tree hangs low over the entrance, its branches limp like a snapped spine. The gravel snakes into the murky darkness, shadowed either side by the still trees.

One week.

She inhales and practises the technique her counsellor taught her. She can smell wood smoke in the cool air. She can feel the rough edge of her nail where she'd chewed it during the flight. She can see … a dead crow, its broken wing jutting against the gutter.

As she glances away, a familiar feeling of panic tears through her. Her hand is cold as she presses it to her forehead.

One week.

She can do it.

Only seven days. Not long enough for anyone to find out she doesn't belong.

Clutching the handle of her suitcase, she drags it towards the path. The trees stretch their long bony fingers towards her. Almost as if warning her. *Turn back*, they urge.

Her heart trips in her chest.

If only her writing was as creative as her imagination.

Fat, foolish Desley, full of fancies.

The air in the driveway is dank; the smells are fertile, lush, mossy. She turns the corner, and the house erupts from the undergrowth. The mullioned windows blink in the fading light. It's a two-storey Federation-style house. Not exactly beautiful, although it may have been once. A balcony with chipped wrought-iron railings wraps around the top floor.

It has an air about it of years of neglect and cheap repairs.

A face flashes in one of the windows, gone as quickly as it appeared. Desley sucks in a shuddering breath. Another writer, of course. Surely. Definitely not the ghost the cab driver had spoken about. That's just silly. But still her heart beats faster.

A rotten tree stump lies across the courtyard, ancient moss-stained tiles its final resting place. An iron outdoor table stoops forlornly in the corner.

It isn't the elegant property she'd imagined when she had received the email informing her she'd won a coveted spot at Australia's most prestigious writers house.

The online photos showed a lonely old building, one that looked as if it was slipping closer and closer to the trees standing between it and the cliff's edge. But seeing it now, it's as though the forest is reclaiming the house. As if the trees are creeping closer, their branches smothering the light, casting a sickly green glow over everything.

She shakes her head. Scott's right: she's always looking for problems instead of solutions.

It's winter, and this is a not-for-profit writers house, not a five-star hotel. She is here to write, not go to spa treatments and take long, leisurely breakfasts outside. Not that she's ever done those things.

A compact wooden cabin stands sentry at the top of the driveway, directly across from the house. The wood is unpainted, raw. On a sign on the door, red writing announces:

OFFICE.

And underneath in thick black text:

DO NOT KNOCK.

Desley stops and sucks in air. The image of the broken crow flashes through her mind. The front wall of the office is tinted glass, and in it she sees the reflection of a red-faced, sweaty woman. She swipes a hand along her hair. No matter what the event, how much effort she puts in, how much preparation, she always ends up looking dreadful. The chaos of her mind always seeps to the surface.

The quilted waterproof jacket that looked so stylish online makes her look like a marshmallow. She heaves a sigh.

The welcome email said meals are provided. Small portions, hopefully. The nearest shop is a ten-minute car journey away. She can't just pop out and grab a bag of chips whenever she fancies it. This week is about writing, of course, but losing weight would be a bonus. She's been promising to start a diet for months but can never seem to find the right time to begin.

A silhouette flashes in the glass and Desley shrieks.

She stares, rooted to the spot, her hand rising and falling on her chest, clutching her Saint Christopher medallion.

The shadow moves and comes into focus and Desley releases a shaky laugh. It's a person.

Of course it is, idiot.

Desley smiles, but the face doesn't smile back.

'Can I help you?'

Desley whirls to face the accusing voice at her back. A woman has stuck her head out from the door of the main house, but her body remains inside, so she appears to be nothing more than a floating head.

'I'm Desley. I'm checking in today?' Why does she frame everything as a question? *Idiot.*

The woman snaps the door shut.

Desley turns back to the glass wall of the office, but the other face is gone. Her chest heats. These are the moments that flatten her. The moments when everyone else seems to know what to do, the next move to make. Is she supposed to follow the woman inside or does she wait at the office? The sign, at least, has informed her she isn't to knock, but what next?

The prickle of tears stings her eyes.

Breathe, breathe. Don't lose it yet. One thing I can hear, one thing I can smell, one thing I can—

'Name?'

Her eyes sling open. The woman from the door stands beside her. Desley tilts her head to meet her gaze. She is not just tall, but also as broad-shouldered as a rugby player. Mostly, though, she looks unhappy. Lines bracket her mouth, and her unnervingly light grey eyes are narrowed with suspicion. A white scarf is wound around her neck like a bandage.

Desley swallows. 'I'm Desley Armstrong. I … I have a booking?'

The statement hangs in the silence between them.

Is it called a booking here? What is she? A guest? Hardly a guest. It cost her an arm and a leg to stay this week. While spots to the retreat were applied for, they were not free. A large fee was required to stay the week, not to mention the cost of travel from Queensland to New South Wales. *A resident, perhaps?* But that makes Desley think of institutions.

The woman's eyebrows pull together as she snatches the edges of her grey cardigan across her chest.

'No booking for Armstrong.'

Desley's stomach flips. *Stupid.* It's just like her to get the dates wrong. She sways, fumbling in her oversized handbag. Why did she pack so bloody much? Scott always says she's a hoarder. She'll empty this bag as soon as she gets inside and keep it clean and tidy for the rest of the week.

If she gets inside.

Her hand lands on a piece of paper and she fishes it out, sighing with relief when she sees it's her booking confirmation. The heat in her chest and cheeks is throbbing and a bead of sweat drips into her eye. She wipes it with the sleeve of her jacket as she extends the crumpled, stained paper. The woman eyes it with a curled lip.

'That's, ah, soy sauce. I had sushi on the train on the way here.' As well as two KitKats, a stale ham and cheese sandwich, a bag of chips, and a can of soft drink. Sugar-free at least.

The paper trembles between them. The woman finally pinches it with her gnarled fingers. She runs her eyes along it and looks up at Desley.

'Desley Barron.'

Oh.

'That's my, er, maiden, uh, writing name. I write as Desley Barron because I have two daughters. Kids can be cruel and you can imagine what would happen if her friends at school got hold of my books. Not that there's any sex. Just a bit of kissing.' Desley twitters. She actually twitters.

Shut up, shut up, shut up. Fat, foolish Desley.

Thankfully, the woman doesn't wait for her to finish talking, merely turns away and pulls at the sliding door of the office. It doesn't budge. Cupping her workmanlike hand onto the glass, she presses her face against it. There are shuffling sounds from inside and when the woman turns back to Desley, her eyebrows are knitted, and she's worrying at her lower lip with her teeth.

'I saw someone in there earlier, but …'

'There's no one in there. And this door is locked.' She eyes Desley fiercely. 'The office is off limits to guests.'

So, they are guests, then?

'Okay,' Desley says, when the woman doesn't break eye contact. 'No worries.'

The moment tautens like a thread pulled tight, and then suddenly the other woman smiles, like she's remembered she is supposed to be welcoming.

There's something unnerving about the way her grey skin stretches over her cheekbones. Desley looks away.

'I'm Eliza. The custodian of Rhamnusia. Have been for thirty-five years. There isn't a single thing about this house and garden that I don't know.'

Why does that sound like a threat?

Eliza strides across the cracked concrete towards the house. 'There will be an induction meeting at five pm. Be prompt because people have better things to do than wait for you.' She turns and eyeballs Desley. 'And we won't.'

Desley drags the dead weight of her suitcase across the uneven surface. Eliza stands at the front door, glaring at Desley impatiently.

'Shoes,' Eliza orders as she heels off her battered boots. 'We do not wear outside shoes inside the property. It makes a mess. That other people have to clean up.'

The cramped portico is a time warp back to the fifties. Lurid browns and oranges mix along the faded, tattered carpet. The peeling walls are covered in yellowing printouts, curling at the edges. Fire evacuation plans. Safety notices. Rules and regulations. A giant cork board takes pride of place and Desley jolts as she sees her own face staring back at her.

It's the headshot from her first book and the bio she sent when she applied for her spot here. There are three more bios, three more faces, lined up alongside hers. She steps forward to look, but Eliza holds her arm out to shield them from view.

'You can look at those later. The induction is at five pm. Not a minute later.'

If it wasn't so odd, Desley might have smiled. Instead, she feels like a naughty child sent to the principal's office. Why does everyone she meets hate her on sight? Her stomach twists unpleasantly. It's always been this way. There is something about her that just puts people off, no matter how kind and friendly she is. No matter how much she goes out of her way to please. She always compliments strangers on their hair, or dresses, but instead of them finding it endearing, they eye her like she's a badly dressed nutter.

Eliza hands her a clipboard. 'You may not enter the house until you have completed this form. It is our health and safety rules,' she adds, as if Desley has argued the point with her.

There is nowhere to sit to fill in the form, so Desley stands and juggles her bag while trying to steady the clipboard and write. A bead of sweat crawls along her spine.

She should ask for a seat, or something to lean against while she completes the form.

And she would.

Her mouth opens but when her eye catches Eliza's, the words stick in her throat like a bone.

Continuing to fumble with the clipboard feels like the lesser of two evils. When finished, she hands it back and Eliza offers her a thick chunk of wood with the number three seared into it and a flyer with a list of rules printed in comic sans.

'You are room three. Familiarise yourself with the rules on the back of the door. That,' she jerks her finger to the closed door behind Desley, 'is the dining and reception room. Where you will eat your meals and relax, if you wish to.' Her mouth twists, indicating how she feels about relaxing as a concept. 'The induction begins in there at five on the dot.'

A shadow appears around the corner and Desley shrieks. Again. What's got into her?

'Oooh, fresh meat.' The young woman drawls in that way all young people seem to do nowadays. Americanised English. Too much screen time.

Eliza scuttles away, head down, muttering something Desley can't catch.

'I'm Maia.' The young woman lifts her steaming mug in greeting.

She's beautiful. In baggy trackpants that somehow suggest fabric rather than fat stores, and a knitted crop top showing an expanse of stretch-mark-free skin. Desley's stomach never looked like that, not even pre-kids. She yanks at the hem of her jumper, making sure it isn't hugging anything it shouldn't be.

'So, what's your genre?' the young woman asks. A question as loaded as a gun.

Desley smiles against a wave of nausea. 'I write women's fiction. Um ... contemporary stories set in small Australian towns.'

Maia's lip lifts. 'Ru-ro. Cute.' Her tone suggests it's anything but.

'It's not exactly *rural romance*. More like, "romantic elements in a rural setting".' Desley flicks her fingers into air quotes and cringes. Forcing herself to leave it there, she asks, 'What about you? Are you published?'

Maia chokes out a laugh. 'You could say that. I'm the founder of *Making Herstory*.' She pauses, waiting for something. 'It's a magazine and digital space?' she prompts when Desley says nothing. '"Australia's *leading* Arts and Culture magazine," *The Guardian* recently called it.' One shoulder lifts gracefully and drops again.

Desley nods. She'll have to google it when she gets upstairs. Her chest scalds and in twenty seconds, her face will be aflame, too.

I'm going to get found out and I haven't even made it up to my room.

She nods more vigorously. 'Cool. That sounds fun.'

Maia rolls her eyes. 'Hectic. And my fourth book is due in October. That's why I'm here. Gotta finish it.' She scoffs. 'Publishers expect you to work for those big advances.'

Fourth book? She barely looks twenty-three.

There are five unpublishable manuscripts in Desley's top drawer. The one she finally got published had taken her two years to write. And she certainly hadn't received an advance that could be described as big. Minuscule was more like it. Pitiful, even.

The heat finally reaches Desley's face. She knows to wait it out, there's nothing she can do. So she nods again, like one of those idiotic bobbly head toys her daughters love. 'Great. What's your genre?'

'I don't, like, subscribe to a specific genre, as such. This one is, like, an exploration of how women have been used as farcical iconographic tools of patriarchal oppression and, like, how that's reflected in the ongoing treatment of the First Nations women on unceded sovereign lands.'

Desley expels a breath. She hadn't understood a word. 'Wow. That sounds ... powerful.'

Maia purses her lips in response. 'Anyway, better get up there. Got a Zoom interview with *The Times*.'

Hot shame tears at Desley's stomach. 'See you later. For the ...' She waves the flyer Eliza handed her.

Maia lifts her lip again. 'That's for newbies. I'm a fellow, so this is, like, week three for me. But you have fun. Enjoy the basement with Eliza.' She raises her eyebrows knowingly.

It isn't until she hears the click of Maia's door closing somewhere above her that Desley begins to drag the suitcase up the steep carpeted staircase. Her arm is burning and even though the hallway is empty, she's too embarrassed to stop. People will think she's too overweight to manage her own suitcase. And of course she is, she knows she is, but this week will be the new start she needs. She'll finish the packet of jellybeans in her stupidly oversized handbag and won't touch anything with sugar in it for the rest of the week.

She counts the doors until she reaches number three.

The bare wood is stained dark along the bottom, and two thick gashes run from the brass number to the edge. Once she unlocks the door and gets inside, she allows herself to lean against the wall and lets the tears fall.

Don't be such a baby. You'll be fine. You're all here to do the same thing. Everyone feels like a fraud sometimes.

Only she was willing to bet these people weren't frauds. Not like her. Something uneasy stirs in her chest as she gazes about the room.

It is barren. A single bed against the wall, and a threadbare rug covering a fraction of the stripped floor exposed beneath it. A battered desk sits between French doors and the bed. The chair, its paint flaking and chalky with age, is from a wrought-iron outdoor set Desley recognises from her childhood.

She swallows.

Later tonight she'll unpack her brand-new notebooks and set up the desk with all her things and hopefully, after a good night's sleep, she'll be ready to write.

With a deep inhale, she wipes the tears from her chin and moves to the doors, desperate for the touch of cool air on her skin.

It won't be as bad as she fears. It never is.

Only Desley knows sometimes it's much, much worse.

Colette

The air through the open window is sweet and cool on Colette's face. She cracks an eyelid as the car slams to a stop. Her mouth is dry, and she blinks herself back to consciousness.

Shelly raises her Celine sunglasses and peers up the driveway. 'Sorry, babe. The Maserati is not going up that.'

Colette eyes the murky driveway. 'Ugh. Do we need a safe word?'

'Hell yes. If this is a bunch of whacko cult-ers who want to take your virginity and drink your blood, text me the safe word and I'll come break you out, babe.' Shelly grips her arm tightly. 'Just wait until after my facial.'

Colette snickers. 'Okay, our safe word is virginity. Protect it at all costs.'

'Little do they know you're such a whore.'

They laugh together. Although Shelly is laughing a little louder than strictly necessary. Especially considering since Shelly's divorce she's dated a new man every month and Colette's been married for twenty years.

Not that *that* means anything.

'Seriously babe, my facial finishes at five-thirty. I can come after if you need saving.'

Colette slaps the sun visor down and peers at herself in the mirror.

Her eyes are less swollen, but the violet bruising has leached from under her concealer at the corners of her eyes.

'Who else will be there?' Shelly asks.

Colette shrugs. 'It's got an amazing rep. Should be some big hitters.'

Not that she cares. There's a reason they'd invited her to stay free of charge. *She* brought the marketing value to *them*. And she'd only accepted due to the timing. The article was due for publication Monday, and Colette having her phone turned off because she was at a writing retreat in the middle of nowhere was as good an excuse as any.

'No one as big as you, babe,' Shelly says into the mirror, running a stick of Coco gloss across her pillowy lips. It's slick, like blood, and Colette looks away, her stomach curdling. Knocking the visor back up with a knuckle, she eyes the driveway and sighs.

Hopefully, this week won't be full of earnest types who want to discuss their manuscript in minute detail. As far as she's concerned, manuscripts are like babies. No one but you gives a shit about them. The answer is always, no, she doesn't want to see *or* discuss them.

'You're the best, babe,' Colette says as she exits the car, slinging her overnighter from the backseat. She flips her Burberry trench over her shoulders and drops her Maison Michel felt hat on. Glaring at her reflection in the door window, she angles the hat to shadow her face. Oversized sunglasses hang from her collar despite the grey sky.

'I'll speak to you tomorrow.' Colette blows Shelly a kiss and strides towards the shadowy driveway, cradling her bag like a baby. There's no way she's dragging her Louis Vuitton along the gravel.

The sulky light becomes a gloom as soon as she steps into the drive and she slows her pace, as nervous as when she first brought Jasper home as a baby. The world had seemed a dangerous place and now feels the same. Every pothole a trip hazard, every low-hanging branch an outstretched hand waiting to make a grab at her. She tips her head back to see from under the hat, which she's pulled too low and is now a hindrance.

Pausing at the bend of the drive, she feels her fingers twitch for her phone. She isn't going to call him. That's ridiculous. But her legs won't restart. She places her suitcase carefully on the stones and perches on the edge of it. Silence clots the air.

How long has it been since she's simply sat in silence?

The Vipassana retreat with Shelly didn't count because they'd filled their suitcases with wine and spent the evenings giggling into their flatter-than-Shelly's-tits pillows. The car ride here had been like being chained to the speakers at a rave. Shelly was good fun but never shut up.

Between the book tour, kids and … all that other crap, she'd had no time to just *be*. She looks up. The sky is bloody above the trees. Curls of black smoke leak out of a crooked chimney stack. Colette tips her head back and draws in a deep belly breath.

Exhaling deeply, she remembers she fucking hates *being*.

She closes her eyes, struck by an overwhelming urge to turn back. To walk along the potholed ribbon of bitumen, past the ancient, mossy, dank-looking houses, until she reaches the train station. She could buy a ticket to somewhere no one knows her name, or her husband's, and lie in bed with a pillow over her head until it all passes.

Or better yet, buy a ticket back in time.

Three months back to her marble-and-glass house perched on the edge of Double Bay, filled with the latest gadgets, her luxury SUV, a housekeeper, an impossible to use coffee machine, and Pilates with other 'working inside the home' mums.

Before *that* phone call.

But she can't.

Hot tears knot behind her lids. Her shoulders shake with the effort of holding them back.

She hasn't cried. Not once, but right now she longs to give in to it. To feel it all, to stop pretending. The trees, which had seemed so unwelcoming before, now cradle her.

Let it go, they whisper, *let it go*.

No.

Crying is for weak people. And she's not weak. Squeezing her hands into fists, she releases a blood-curdling scream. She shrieks until her voice cracks.

'*Arsehole*,' she screeches into the gloom for good measure.

The forest buries the noise and within seconds, it's like nothing happened.

A manic sort of laugh bursts out and for a moment she hovers above herself, imagining what people would say if they came across her – Colette-bloody-Halifax! – screaming and crying in the middle of the bush.

Only it isn't the bush, it just feels like it. Swallowing hard, she collects herself. It's the driveway to a writers house and someone is bound to come and see what all the fuss is about. She shoots to her feet as something snaps behind her.

Slipping her sunglasses on, she squints into the trees, unable to make out anything but menacing shapes.

There's no one there. No one but Shelly knows where she is.

That thought suddenly feels less comforting than it had. Making her way up the dark driveway, she can't shake the prickly sensation of being watched.

As Colette rounds the bend of the driveway, a woman materialises like mist. Head cowed, hands throttling the edges of a drab cardigan, she stops dead when she sees Colette. They stare at each other for a long moment. Her chest is heaving, eyes wide.

'Did you hear …?'

Colette studies the woman. Everything about her is grey. Her hair, her awful cardigan, her skin, her unsettling eyes. 'Hear?'

Her arctic eyes dart about. 'A scream.'

'I didn't hear anything.' Colette is careful to add a touch of incredulity to her tone. Straight out of the gaslighter's playbook.

And I should know.

The other woman turns and stares at the upper corner of the house.

'Perhaps not. Are you staying?' She avoids Colette's gaze, her eyes fixed on the house.

'Yes. *Halifax*. Colette.'

Dragging her gaze to Colette, she nods. 'Yes. Yes. Come in and get settled. I'll show you to your room.'

They're almost at the front door before the woman turns to Colette. 'I'm Eliza, the custodian here. There isn't a thing I don't know.' Her voice is wooden, as if she's reciting lines she can't quite remember.

She stumbles over the step into the house and presses her red-knuckled hands against the wall to steady herself. Her hands are large and square and Colette thinks of her father and his carpenter's hands. All swollen joints and cracked skin. A life lived hard. Pity knifes through her and she looks away.

The hall table is crowded with lurid green clipboards, with a sheet of paper and a pen attached to each. An aged cobbler's shoe iron crouches incongruously amongst it all. The woman jerks a large wooden key ring from a hook on the wall and hands it to her.

'Room two. Be back here for induction. Five. We start at five.'

And then she's gone as quickly as she appeared. Colette pauses with a foot on the worn lower step and a hand on the newel post.

A door in the passage leans open and through it she sees sun-bleached chairs, a cracked seventies-brown fireplace and its dull, age-spotted fender. There is heritage, and then there's this. It's shabby and, she grimaces as a ball of dust in the corner trembles, grubby.

The sound of someone descending the stairs draws Colette's eyes upwards. An impossibly good-looking young woman saunters down the steep risers. There is something of a predator about her, the way she glides, hand trailing along the banister like a spectre in a ghost story. In trackpants and Nike high-tops.

Perfect teeth bared, she says, 'Colette Halifax. I've been waiting for you.'

There's a combative light in her eyes Colette recognises all too well. Resisting the urge to touch her face, she unsheathes her sunglasses from her head and lets her hair fall around her face like armour. Hopefully, the dim light will hide the bruising.

Since Trent became a household name, she'd sharpened up, had to. Knew how to tell the harmless flirts from the ones that shamelessly pressed their numbers into his hand or followed him to the bathroom in the hopes of a quick pash. Or the sneakier ones. The ones that befriended her, pretending to have no interest in their lifestyle or contacts.

Those had been harder lessons to learn.

'Well, here I am. Nice to meet a fan. You are?'

'A fan?' The girl laughs. It's not a happy sound. 'Not quite, hun. I'm Maia. We have a ...' Maia licks her bottom lip. It's full, pillowy and plump.

Real or injectables? Colette is studying them so hard she misses the rest of the sentence.

'Sorry, what?'

'You know a very good friend of mine. Lily Raiti.'

The name strikes like a slap to her cheek and silence crashes upon them. Maia is watching her closely through those dark eyes.

What does she know?

Everyone involved had signed an NDA, but those were worthless really. People always blabbed, confident in the knowledge that unless it was in writing, any attempt to prove they'd talked would be an expensive legal exercise in nothingness.

Colette taps her chin and casts a glance at the ceiling. A strip of plaster dangles, like a noose awaiting its next victim. 'Nope. Don't know a Lily Raiti, I'm afraid. But you can imagine, once your name is on *The New York Times* bestseller list, all sorts of people claim to know you.'

Maia raises both her eyebrows and opens her mouth to speak, but Colette shoves past her. Her feet hammer up the stairs and she is grateful to find room two is close to the landing. She unlocks the door, slams it closed and leans against it, her heart racing. From somewhere in the depths of the house, a clock sings out a random chime and Colette startles. Fuck.

She snatches her phone from her bag and furiously taps out a message to Shelly.

New safe word. It's now Jesus Fucking Christ get me out of here.

Haha appears on her screen and three bubbles shimmy. *That bad?*

Worse than you could imagine, babe.

I'll be there at six to break you out x

Colette closes her message and looks at the screen.
Six o'clock isn't soon enough.

Maia

'So, when can we expect book four?' The smarmy wanker on the screen asks the question in that cloying tone male journalists use with me during our interviews. *I'm your best mate,* their tone says. The words in their article often say something different. I'm too bold, too brash, too unapologetic and take up too much space for men of his age to feel comfortable with me.

I smile tightly, resisting the urge to roll my eyes. Writing is a hamster wheel I can never get off. As soon as a manuscript is finished, I am being hounded for the next one. By my worst, most relentless critic. Myself.

'Let me finish this one first.'

'You're a vital literary voice and have been since your debut – which I believe you received a six-figure advance for, before it was even finished?'

This time I don't bother smiling. It's the same old question, same old trap, same old disbelieving tone. How could a young woman be worthy of such an advance? Shouldn't that be reserved for older, white men? Men that have 'paid their dues' (usually through Daddy's connections and long boozy lunches).

Listen, asshole, I want to say. Yeah, my debut novel received a huge advance, but it went on to win the Stella, the Banjo Prize and was nominated for a Booker and earned my publishers sixty times what I made, so I'd say I've proved myself worth every penny.

I lean closer to the screen. 'Do you ask male authors to divulge their advances?'

Instant scrambling. The 'I'm no misogynist' apology activated, but I'm not listening. A flash of movement in the garden drags my attention away from the screen.

What the hell?

I lean forward further and squint through the grubby window. There's a man in the garden.

My heart bangs and the chair totters as I scramble to the window.

'Maia?' A tinny voice from the computer. *Shit.* The Zoom call.

I pop back down into view. 'Sorry. There was a …' I jerk my hand and mouth.

'You've cut out,' the interviewer says.

I remain still, dead-eyeing the screen. *One, two, three.* 'How about now?'

Smarmy wanker smiles. Old people think they get technology, but they really don't. 'A bit glitchy. How is the writing retreat going?'

'Actually, I have to go.'

Without waiting for him to wrap up his interview – I know his type, he'll insist on one more question which will turn into three, and all of it the same crap he could find out himself if he did a bit of research – I press the red phone icon and disconnect the call.

Ducking down, I squat-crawl to the French doors and peer out into the garden. Thank God for all that strength training. I can hold this position for at least three minutes twenty-nine seconds (the exact length of *'Training Season'* by Dua Lipa, my hype song) if I need to.

A colossus of a man is lurking in the garden, ducking and weaving between the shadows of the shrubs. I narrow my eyes and watch.

Down and back up, left and then right, back down.

He's dressed all in black, a black hoodie pulled over a black cap, which throws his face into shadow. A chill creeps along my spine, slow and deliberate, like frozen fingers pressing into my skin. I think about the story Lily wrote for the magazine before I'd left. Labelled by *The Daily Mail* (sensationalist crap, but still) as the 'worst serial killer Australia had ever seen', Byron Jackovic had been found living in squalor, with three other men, in the state forest that surrounds this house. It's kilometres of forest though, I reassure myself, not to mention he'd been charged and was currently in jail. He'd maintained his innocence to the last, as they do. But, as Lily had pointed out, what became of the people he'd lived with? While they were never charged, it was impossible to believe they'd had no inkling at all that the man they lived with had stalked, kidnapped, and murdered over twenty women.

I watch the man in black shamble around the garden, my breath narrowing to a thin thread. He moves furtively in a strange duck and stoop movement before stopping and turning as if listening for something. As he pivots, something glints in his hand. A gun. My stomach plunges. No. It can't be a gun, can it?

My body locks up, every muscle coiled so tight it hurts. I don't breathe. I don't blink. I just stare at the gleam of metal, the way his fingers shift around it, the way he lifts it slightly, adjusting his grip. A sharp, metallic taste floods my mouth. My pulse slams against my ribs. My brain scrambles for logic but comes up empty. What the hell is he doing?

There's a duffle bag discarded on the ground. He crouches, yanks something out and stuffs it in the garden. My vision tunnels. Do I call out? Warn the other writers, or try and scare him away? My hand trembles as I raise it, ready to bang it against the window frame.

He presses something on the gun. A thin beam of light cuts through the dark, illuminating a bright yellow rectangle.

Oh.

My laughter paints a circle of fog on the glass. It's not a gun. It's a ring light and selfie stick. He's filming himself in the garden with his book.

Adrenaline thrums through me, leaving me light-headed and giddy. Of course it's not a gun. Two weeks in this creepy-ass house has me spooked.

I thrust open the doors and step out onto the balcony. The splintered wood snatches at my socks. I prop my hip against the balcony ledge and watch the guy angle his camera and adjust the book.

'Get away from there.'

Eliza.

'That balustrade's not safe. Get away from the edge,' she calls.

I roll my eyes and wiggle my fingers at her, slowly removing my butt cheek from the iron railing even though it feels sturdy enough to me. That woman gives me the irrits. She seems to be everywhere, all at once. Eyes in the back of her head, as Mama says.

As she *used* to say. Bile burns my throat.

The man in the garden looks up and our eyes meet. A tingle shoots up my legs. He's bloody gorgeous. But why is he in the garden? How did he get here? And more importantly, who the bloody hell is he? His face wasn't on the wall of new arrivals. I know exactly who is expected today, and I don't know him.

There are never any hot guys at writing events. Usually these things are full of aging women looking to find themselves in the pages of their memoir, wearing layers of purple stretchy fabric and bangles that rattle. If there are any men, they're ancient dudes so full of themselves it's impossible to get a word in. Their advice is so amusing, so freely offered, so unwelcome. And unnecessary. The highest-earning debut author in the country and founder of Australia's newest independent, woman-owned media company (mc) doesn't need anyone's advice. About anything.

Even from here, I can tell the man in the garden is tall. Long and lean, his tight black jeans end in chunky workmanlike boots. And I'm a sucker for a guy in a hoodie.

I squint. The hoodie in question has fluoro yellow writing on the front that I can't quite make out.

I'm not here for this, but I can't help myself. I lean over the balcony's edge, popping a hip even though he can't see it. 'You should put it in the tree,' I call, pointing behind him.

He looks to the tree in question.

A huge dead beech. Its zombie arms ever-reaching for the sky. It's picturesque, I'll give it that much. But like everything else in this house, it seems to be from another century.

It's forever 1952 here. The year Evelyn Thorne's family all suffocated in their beds from a gas leak.

The bathroom is three shades of green, the taps spit rust-coloured water for two minutes when you wake them. They drip constantly, no matter how hard you turn them. The rusty water stains the basins, the walls, the back of the toilet. It was eerie, at first. It looks like blood, but there's something artistic about it that has begun to appeal to me.

It looks good on Instagram at least. And everyone knows unless you're documenting everything, it didn't happen.

'I can't reach. I need your help,' he calls back.

A flirt too? I grin. This could be fun.

'Sorry, I'm off duty,' I yell.

'No noise between seven and seven.' Eliza again.

She's standing in the shade of the house. There's something so creepy about the way the grey light camouflages her. Like she's *trying* to blend into the shadows, unseen.

I bite my lip and wag a finger at the handsome man. 'Naughty,' I mouth.

He smiles and smacks one hand with the other. 'I can't help myself,' he says loudly, disregarding Eliza and her orders.

Sexy and a rule breaker. Exactly my type.

I smirk and turn to go back inside, but a shivering curtain in the next room catches my eye.

I pause, staring at the window. That room hasn't been filled. It must've been the wind, because the curtain is as still as a grave now. The breeze gusts along the balcony, catching my hair and flipping it around my head. I shiver as it creeps along my neck. Goosebumps break out along my arms and I rub them. It's proper cold.

Today is handover day. Guests leave in the morning, their week completed, and new ones arrive in the afternoon. All the departing guests had spoken about was the predicted snowstorm. Each watching their phones frantically to ensure their scheduled trains, flights, taxis weren't cancelled. This place is great for peace and quiet when you're writing, but I wouldn't want to be stuck out here. It's literally the middle of nowhere.

The horizon is thick and silvery. Sinister-looking clouds crouch among the mountains in the distance. The storm isn't far. I don't care when it arrives, as long as it holds out until everyone is here.

Time has moved with aching slowness these last two weeks. Every day limping closer to this one. I've been waiting for him for a long time now, so another hour or two won't make any difference. I stalk inside, slam the door closed and yank off my watch, throwing it face down on the desk with a growl of frustration.

It's like I'm tripping. My senses are so heightened. Cars idling at the edge of the driveway had me charging down the stairs, twice, but both times it came to nothing. It was merely the other women booked into the retreat. The frumpy mum and that cow, Colette.

The look on her face when I dropped Lily's name. It almost made the previous two weeks worth it. *Almost.*

I drum my fingers on the desk. Everyone is here, except him. The drone of a car breaks the silence and my stomach flips. Is this it?

I'd requested this room, once the writer occupying it (a thriller writer who won a week's residency in a competition as generic as his writing) had left. Its vantage point allows me to see the driveway leading to the office and garden, which is the only way to the front entrance of the house.

I won't get up this time, I tell myself, but I'm up and at the window before I can stop myself. The man in the garden is gone, his fluoro book too. I gaze out past the driveway to the long road that leads to the house, which can be seen clearly from this window.

The street, uneven and ancient, rises and dips at various points. A flash of blue. A car. But it turns off without continuing down the hill towards us.

I huff a breath. '*Hurry up,*' I whisper into the cold air.

Like a hologram, in my mind's eye I see him strolling up the driveway. He has a duffle bag slung over a shoulder – no unfashionable backpack for him. He walks with a slow, casual gait, in tan chinos, a puffer jacket open at the neck, a smile playing on those famous lips.

A cockatoo's screech tears through the silence and the image pops like a soap bubble.

There is nothing but trees, dancing silently to music I can't hear.

Where is he? I need to see him before he sees me. That feels important. I'm not sure what I'll give away. My face always shows what I feel and think, I can't hide it. I don't know what I'll feel when I see him, but I know what I'll say.

That part is also important. That part I have practised for years.

Yes, I know exactly what I'll say when I see this man.

The man who almost killed my mother.

Eliza

The last to arrive was the worst of the lot of them. So much cologne. It clings to the back of her throat, even now. She takes a sip of water, which does nothing to dispel it.

Why do people do that? Smother themselves in overpowering chemicals. As if that might hide the stink of them. And he stank. Of greed and ego. It rolled from him in waves.

The poets were always the worst.

'Eliza?' Jane's timid voice sounds from the small room off the office they call The Cubby.

Eliza grinds her teeth, just once, as hard as she can, relishing the sound. She tries with Jane, she really does, but Jane would try the patience of a saint with her constant fussing. 'Yes?' Eliza says sharply.

'There's been a mix-up.' Jane looks watery. About to cry. Again. It doesn't take much to set Jane off.

Kind and well-meaning, but not terribly well-functioning, is Jane.

'What is it?' Eliza asks, snatching the paper from Jane's outstretched hand.

She inhales with a hiss when she sees it.

'There's two,' Jane whispers.

'Oh no.'

This is bad. Very, very bad.

Eliza frowns at the paper. How could this have happened?

The rules are clear and have been in place for years. Long before either her or Jane's arrival. She's not sure why, but she's always believed this particular rule was one of Evelyn's.

'How?' Eliza croaks.

'The young one, Tavis, changed his dates. He was supposed to come earlier in the month and I guess … I think … someone … didn't check. We weren't careful enough.' Jane's voice quivers.

Eliza sighs. 'Well, it's too late now. We can hardly send one home, can we?'

Could we?

How satisfying that would be, to knock on their doors and tell them there had been a mistake, and they all must leave.

Through the glass sliding door that makes up the front wall of the office, she sees the house. She knows it as well as her own face. An eerie orange light discolours it. Eliza has been here long enough to know the predictions of a violent storm will prove correct, and soon.

'Oh, Eliza, we can't. Can we?' Jane asks unsteadily.

Another sigh.

No, they can't send one home now.

'It doesn't matter. A simple mistake. We will put measures in place to ensure it doesn't happen again.' She places a hand over Jane's trembling one. Her bones are delicate, like new twigs on a sapling, and Eliza resists the urge to squeeze. 'Don't you worry. I'll sort it out. Now, you get yourself sorted. If you don't escape before this storm hits you'll be stuck here with us all week.'

Unlike Eliza, Jane doesn't live onsite, and cycles the short trip from her house near the town centre to the writers house daily.

While Jane bustles about, tidying her desk and collecting her belongings, Eliza studies the application forms.

A sick kind of dread hovers, then lands in her lap with a thud. They'd gone and broken one of the ten rules of the house. The Rhamnusia Commandments, they called them. Important rules, unbreakable rules, that underpin the very meaning of the house and its use by writers.

They'd booked two poets in at the same time.

Worse still.

It's two male poets.

Desley

The doors to the balcony are jammed.

Desley jiggles the handle but nothing happens. A small barrel lock holds the doors closed and is caked with pitted, yellowed paint. So much for fresh air. It's too cold, anyway. She can't tell where is colder, inside or out. Her room is colder than a grave.

A radiator hangs on the wall but when she presses her hand to it, it's freezing. The heat dial on the side points to zero. Desley tries to force it but it doesn't budge. It might prove to be a good thing she over-packed. She can wear all her clothes at once.

It will be okay. Her heart flutters in her chest like a caged bird. *It will be okay*, she repeats over and over until the sound of her phone beeping shocks her thoughts into silence.

Three texts. Scott. Her heart lurches.

He must be texting to see how she's going, that she managed to find the place okay. She's terrible with directions, always gets muddled up, even in their area and she's lived there for ten years. Scott always drives when they go out together – her driving drives him mad, he says. He's joking, but he's right; she always chooses the wrong way, or the long way.

She pulls her phone out of her bag with shaking hands. Maybe he's texting to apologise about the argument he'd picked this morning before she'd left.

Flicking open the message app, she scans the texts.

You put the wrong lunches in the wrong bags!
Where are swimming bags? Not in laundry.
Hannah can't find her ballet shoes. Bloody hell. Work is crazy. What a time for you to take a week off!

Desley chews her lip. So much for an apology.
She texts back quickly.

Togs in mud room. Red bags. On hooks.

Which was outlined on the schedule she'd printed and pinned to the kitchen wall before leaving. Along with fourteen dinners, each carefully measured and packed into glass containers and labelled, clearly, with each girl's name and the day of the week on which to reheat it. The girls won't eat the same meals, and it's too much to expect Scott to cook his dinner as well as the girls'.

Never mind that's exactly what she does every day of the week.

Sorry re lunches …

Her thumb hovers, at war with her mind. She shouldn't have to apologise for taking this week. And she wouldn't. This week is so important for her career, and she'd certainly given up enough for his. He could parent his own children before and after school for five measly days. Desley had arranged playdates after hockey on Saturday and asked his mum to come over on Sunday so he could golf. Desley will be home Monday.

To restart the endless, mindless drift of it all.

She presses send on the apology text and leans against the wall, clutching the phone to her chest. Her bottom lip trembles. She can't do this. The room is too cold, too unfamiliar, too far away from her warm and comfortable home.

And her girls.

Her breath shrinks. This week will be the longest she's ever spent away from them. Even when her mum had her operation and needed Desley to collect her from the hospital, she'd waited until both girls were asleep before leaving. Even though she hates driving in the dark.

Her counsellor has assured her they'd all cope for one week without her.

Of course they would. Scott is their father, and it's important to let Scott do things his way. She complains too much, Scott's right about that.

Desley's a glass-almost-empty kind of girl, he often declares when they're in group settings. (*It's a joke, Des. Jesus, this is exactly what I'm talking about.* His tried and true response when she asks him to stop.)

The face of her watch glowers at her. It's almost five. She doesn't want to be the first downstairs, waiting earnestly like a complete nerd, but she hates being late.

The expression of the custodian, Eliza, as she warned Desley not to be tardy shoots through her mind and she shudders. She has a hunch Eliza would find five o'clock on the dot 'late'.

And she can't be the last to arrive, because she'll look huge lumbering down the stairs while everyone stares up at her.

She pinches her bottom lip between her fingers as she considers what to do.

A bang sounds somewhere below and she twitches as if stung. Another guest closing their door, leaving for the induction already?

Jerking into motion, she grabs a notebook and pen. Is that too pathetic? Will she need to take notes? Gnawing her bottom lip, she tries to decide on the notebook. Why are even the simplest decisions so difficult for her?

No. She puts it back down. No notebook. She'll pay extra special attention to what Eliza has to say and write it down when she gets back.

After smoothing her jumper across her hips, she pauses at the door. Prickles of heat bloom on her chest and begin the slow creep to her neck.

Not now, not now.

One thing she can see … She breathes in deeply until her heart slows to its normal (already quite frantic) pace. Tries to think of anything except the panic rising.

She thinks of the images of the other writers on the wall in the entry. Why had Eliza stopped her looking at them? Of course, she probably wouldn't even recognise any of them, but she didn't want a repeat of what happened with Maia. It would have been helpful to look up their books, here in her room, where no one can see she's a complete loser. Her cheeks tingle when she thinks back to Maia's explanation of her writing.

And the look on her face when Desley told her about hers.

Ru-ro, she'd said with such a derisive curl to her lip.

It wouldn't set the world on fire but being a published author was a tightly held dream that Desley had worked towards for years and had been proud of.

If only the deadline for her next book didn't loom quite so threateningly. The buzzing sound starts up in her ears again. She presses the pressure point on her thumb, the way her therapist had shown her.

Time to go downstairs. She places a trembling hand on the doorhandle and pauses.

A brown stain scars the bottom of the door. Desley studies it with a shiver. It's rust coloured, like blood.

It can't be.

The house has been a dedicated writers space for decades, but Desley can't help thinking about its previous life, as the home of the Thorne family.

Who had all died in tragic circumstances.

Here. In this very house.

No, that isn't right. All but one died.

Evelyn.

Evelyn, who lived here, alone, until her own death, running painting, poetry and writing workshops.

A shiver scatters along her spine. One of the family members might have died in this very room. The taxi driver said Evelyn's ghost had been seen regularly since her passing.

How regular is regularly? Once a year? Nightly?

Keeping an eye on the house, he'd said Evelyn had loved like it was a person.

Perhaps because it was the last remaining thread to her family. Memories of better times stitched within its seams.

At any rate, the ghost of Evelyn isn't half as terrifying as the custodian, Eliza. Her unfriendly face pitches through Desley's mind. Time to go, she cannot be late.

Pressing her ear to the crack at the door, she listens. Silence.

Desley mentally prepares the speech she'll make when she reaches the bottom of the stairs. Light and breezy, easy-going Desley.

Nothing to see, nothing to hide.

She edges into the dimly lit hallway and makes her way to the landing.

At the edge of the balcony, she pauses and peers over the banister. It's loose under her hand. The stairs are steep, the carpet is bunched and uneven, the lighting dim.

How easy it would be to fall.

She inches closer and presses her hip against the loose railing, testing how much it will yield. It could collapse at any moment, send her hurtling towards the floor. She sees her head smashing open on the floor like a watermelon.

A clock chimes and she is thrust back to herself. Forcing herself away from the age-smoothed banister, she takes a tremulous breath and averts her eyes from the drop.

She will stay present and calm, she vows, as she makes her way down the stairs.

As part of their application to Rhamnusia, everyone was required to provide samples of their work. Desley had been chosen, the same as the rest of them.

Only ... she isn't the same, and she knows it. Her stomach wrenches.

Fat, foolish Desley.

Fraud, fake Desley.

Eliza stands at the bottom of the stairs. Her cloud-grey eyes meet Desley's, then stab to her wristwatch. Desley skips down the remaining steps. She's the first one here so why does she feel late?

The hall is foggy with smoke. It seeps from the open door at the right of the portico. Desley searches for the smoke detector. It's mandatory to have alarms, particularly in old houses like this.

She ducks her head into the room, looking about anxiously. It's a long room, with one end set up as a dining room, the other as a lounge, sagging aged chairs arranged around a fireplace. The fireplace is an old-fashioned type, not a wood burner like everyone uses nowadays, but a gaping space in the wall. With no guard.

Surely that isn't safe? Someone could fall onto it, or a spark could jump. That ancient polyester carpet would go up like tinder.

Heat prickles on her chest as her heart rate increases. Places like this are subject to workplace health and safety regulations like hotels, aren't they? She'll ask Eliza when they'd last had an inspector out.

But one look at Eliza's pinched lips tells Desley that Eliza will not be open to a discussion about inspectors and current safety standards.

Desley coughs and waves a hand in front of her face, unable to help herself. She has to ask; she won't be able to think of anything else if she doesn't. 'Is this amount of smoke normal?'

'Don't mind that. The chimney smokes during rain or snow. It will stop when it stops.' Eliza's tone is dismissive, her gaze trained on the staircase.

A prick of excitement. 'It's snowing?'

Eliza stares at her with disdain, as if she's said something enormously stupid. 'It's raining.'

Desley's cheeks heat. 'Snow this week. They say.'

Whoever *they* are, it's clear by Eliza's raised brow she doesn't hold much truck with them.

They stand in a silence that swells and billows like the smoke crowding the hall.

Desley studies the bios pinned to the wall.

Maia stares back boldly. Her hair, full and curly, is lit from behind in a way that creates a glowing halo. She's all cheekbones, lips and youthful confidence. Desley never had that kind of confidence, had been born worrying about doing the wrong thing.

Although, perhaps if she'd looked like Maia, she wouldn't have cared so much. She pulls her jumper lower over her hips. The waistband of her jeans pinches.

'Oh.' A thump of recognition as she spots Colette Halifax's face on the board. She's married to that funny guy on *Good Morning*.

Desley smiles. She used to love watching that show. Before kids, when she'd had time. Now her mornings are spent screaming about missing socks and hats.

His name appears in her mind.

Trent.

He did whacky segments. So funny, and so very handsome. A pang of jealousy knifes through her. She'd bet her life savings that Colette and Trent lead a glamorous life and have a marriage full of laughter and fun. Not to mention money.

Colette's headshot screams expensive. The designer dress, the pose, the clearly professionally applied make-up, the immaculate hair. Probably taken by some famous photographer like the Beckhams' son. Although hadn't he given up his photography to focus on his Instagram chef career? Desley had watched a few of his videos, puzzled by the fuss he'd made over sausages in bread. She assumed he was being ironic and retro in a way too hip for Desley to understand. Colette probably gets it.

Something black and ugly unfurls in Desley. She moves to the next photo.

Alan 'Laurie' Lawrence. Poet.

Desley leans closer. There's something of another era about his photo. It's black and white, artistic. Eyes narrowed, while a coil of smoke, not unlike a discarded silk stocking, obscures the lower half of his face. A phallic-shaped cigar held suggestively between full lips. Nothing screams bad boy of poetry – if there's such a thing – like this photo. It seems as if he belongs to the world of James Dean and Frank Sinatra. When men smoked, drank, openly shagged anything that moved, and hit their wives and girlfriends with gay abandon. Her eyebrows lift as she reads his extensive list of achievements. Poet Laureate. Twice.

What the hell is she doing here? Not for the first time, she wonders if there was a mistake in the booking and she received someone else's spot. Perhaps there were two Desleys applying at the same time and they offered the wrong Desley the place.

The front door crashes open with the unmistakable scent of marijuana and the damp smell of the forest. The man she had been staring at on the wall now stands in front of her – a number of years older, based on the lines that now bisect his face.

He clearly still thinks he cuts a figure though. Pausing for effect, he leans against the doorjamb, a raffish eyebrow raised. The posture causes his jacket to part, showing a white t-shirt hugging a pot belly. She thinks of the rock stars her mother favoured during Desley's childhood. Their sexual energy and snake-hipped dance moves sliding into a predatory desperation as they aged. Desley's teeth ached every time another gossip column mentioned their young wives or printed their eighth baby announcement although they were already grandfathers.

Laurie stamps his bright orange trainers, the same pair that her fourteen-year-old nephew had recently demanded for his birthday, and lets out a low whistle. 'It's colder than a nun's proverbial out there.'

Waves of disapproval flow from Eliza, who spears him with a glare that makes Desley's skin crawl. She fights the urge to fill the silence by digging her nails into her palm.

'Alright, darling? I'm Laurie.' He flips his fingers into guns and pretends to shoot her, making a smacking noise with his lips.

Desley strangles out a smile. 'Desley.'

'Desley, eh? I knew a Desley once. Or was it Debbie? Either way, she was a tiger in the sack.' He holds her gaze with a wolfish smile.

Desley blinks rapidly, grasping for something to say. But thankfully she doesn't need to, as he's already turned his attention to Eliza.

'Alright, Lisa? Will we open the wine now, take a shifty glass with us on your magical mystery tour?'

Eliza busies herself adjusting the already orderly clipboards. 'I will discuss alcohol and its consumption during the induction.'

The stairs whine. They all turn and watch as a towering man, dressed all in black, appears. He's handsome, in that way young men all seem to be nowadays. Desley doesn't recall a single boy looking like him when she was his age. They were all scrawny, spotty and utterly charmless.

He smiles and Desley almost sighs. He's not handsome: he's drop dead bloody gorgeous. Right on cue, heat crawls along her neck.

'Hi, I'm Tavis.' He extends his hand and holds her gaze in a way that makes her want to giggle. What's wrong with her? This boy, while certainly not young enough to be her child, is definitely too young for her. She places her hand in his and gazes up at him, swallowing loudly. There is something about his breadth, his height, that makes her feel delicate. Perhaps for the first time in her life.

'I'm ...' *Christ. Those lips! What's her name again?* 'Desley.'

'Desley.' He murmurs it softly, like a prayer, and she's suddenly breathless.

He turns to Laurie, extending a hand. 'Hey, mate. Tavis.'

Laurie lifts a lip and the energy shifts suddenly, like a spinning top crashing to an abrupt stop. He grips Tavis's hand and pumps hard. A common enough blokey gesture but there's a shimmering tension between the men.

'Travis, is it? Laurie Lawrence.' Desley almost expects Laurie to hold his arms wide and yell *ta-da*, like he's presenting them with a gift. He's standing too close to Tavis, stealing his space, but Tavis doesn't step back.

'It's Tavis. No R.'

Laurie snorts. 'Yeah right. What kind of woman looks at a baby and thinks, I'll name this little walnut *Tavis*.'

Tavis ignores him and focuses that blue, blue gaze on Eliza who, judging by the cheerless stare levelled back at him, is impervious to his charms. 'Hello again, Eliza.'

'It is five o'clock and regardless of some people's disrespect for other people's time, we shall begin,' she announces by way of reply.

She spins on her heel and stomps into the smoky room off the hallway.

Is all this smoke an indication the chimney is blocked? Desley grabs her thumb. A woman had recently died when her blocked chimney exploded. Exploded! Right as she'd sat down for *A Current Affair* and a cuppa. Desley can picture it – the dust, the bricks, the carnage. Her stomach swoops and her thumb tap, tap, taps.

Tavis touches her on the arm gently, bringing her back to herself, and the cheerless, smoky room. He raises his eyebrows and gestures for her to enter the room first. A gentleman. If it wasn't for the looming death by fireplace, she might've swooned.

But Laurie beats her to the doorway, swaggering through without a backward glance. A waft of cologne throttles her and she coughs.

The room is somehow ten degrees colder than the smoky hall. As in the rest of the house, stepping into the reception room is like stepping back in time. Bay windows dominate both ends of the narrow room, hemmed by drooping wooden shutters whose warped frames press inwards, as if the room itself is being squeezed. Two dusty, sun-stained chairs sit in front of the heatless fire. The mantlepiece is covered in trinkets that bear no connection to each other: a cuckoo clock, gnarled pieces of wood polished to a high shine, and, bizarrely, rocks of all shapes and sizes.

One wall is floor-to-ceiling shelving, filled entirely with books.

An ugly dining table imposes on the room. A bleached stain marks the middle of the dark wood. It makes Desley think of slabs of marble and morgues.

'Right …' Eliza lifts her cardigan sleeve and checks her watch. 'Sit.' A pause. 'Please.' The word sounds odd, as if it's been wrenched from Eliza's lips. She gestures to the chairs with her claw-like hand.

Sucking in her belly, Desley lowers herself into one of the hard-backed chairs around the table. Ankles crossed, knees clutched tightly, hands in her lap, she tries to meet Eliza's frigid gaze with an interested (but not too earnest) expression but Eliza is studying her clipboard.

'You look like you're about to be sentenced,' Laurie says as he pitches himself into the chair beside her.

Instinctively Desley lowers her shoulders, mimicking his languid pose. 'Just being respectful.'

'I bet you were a good girl at school. Did what you were told. Are you like that in bed?'

Desley jerks at his words, as if she's jammed a fork into a socket, her back ramrod straight again. His crassness steals the breath from her lungs.

'Excuse me. I am about to start.' Eliza directs to Desley.

How unfair, Desley wants to exclaim, *it wasn't me talking – it was him!*

But this isn't school and Eliza isn't listening. She is reading from her clipboard, her voice as staccato as a machine gun.

Desley tunes out as Eliza lists the many rules of the house. She studies Tavis's boots, stretched out beneath the table. They're chunky, manly, and give her a strange sort of thrill.

She presses her fingers to her cheeks which are suddenly aflame. *Desperate Desley*. Dragging her gaze from Tavis, she stares at Eliza and shapes her face into a mask of polite listening, smiling and nodding. Like a normal person.

Not like the real Desley at all.

Colette

'Give me a break.' Colette grinds the gum hard between her teeth as the error message appears again.

She taps the trackpad of her laptop harder.

You are not connected. Please check your router.

'Stuff it,' she mutters, switching her phone onto hotspot and connecting the laptop.

The red bubble flashes on her phone, adding another number to the ever-increasing notifications.

Nope. Colette throws the phone face down on the bed, ignoring the brambly anxiety pulling at her. She won't look. Whatever messages – from whomever – are on that phone will wait.

The little dinosaur that tells her the search engine isn't working appears again, and she clicks refresh. Her body has been hijacked. She is merely a puppet at the whim of its master. It's a compulsion. One she'd given in to, too many times to count. She's almost surprised the keys on the keyboard haven't begun to wear off.

Her stomach churns. This is making her sick. She knows it.

The sleeping pills help her switch off enough to get to sleep but at three every morning she jolts awake, alone with her thoughts in the darkness.

How had this become her life? Where had she gone wrong?

Not one for self-inspection usually, it is all she can do now; turn the shards of her life over in her palms, trying to find what broke them.

That's not true. She knows what broke them.

She thinks of that girl on the stairs. Maia. Her comment about Lily.

Recalling their brief conversation causes a syrupy, sordid feeling to pulse through her.

When the search engine finally appears she surprises herself by typing Maia's name into the box instead of Trent's, as she usually does.

The internet is frustratingly slow, like the dial-up of the old days. How is this a place of business? She can't be expected to work in conditions like this.

Although maybe they run slow wi-fi to encourage the writers to get off their socials and get words on the page. After all, that is why they're here. But everyone knows a big part of being a writer is checking up on other writers and jealously analysing their social media posts. Are they doing better than me? Got a bigger marketing budget? Getting more free things?

For some anyway. Colette hasn't given a shit about those kinds of things for a while. She has bigger problems to worry about.

Her shellacs tap a tune against the keyboard while the webpage loads. But when it does, she wishes it hadn't. Page after glowing page appears about Maia.

Articles, newspapers, reviews, opinion pieces, a magazine she started and runs, a website she pretentiously calls a 'digital space'. What the hell is a digital space? A blog? Blogs are almost as naff as podcasts. *Almost*, because in Colette's opinion there is very little to like about podcast tryhards, with their faces for audio, trussing up their 'vying for viral' nonsense as facts.

Hyperbolic articles shadow each other.

A vital literary voice for Australia's youth culture. A voice of a generation. Masterfully pushes against genre conventions.

Colette mimes a gag and clicks the link to Maia's website. She refuses to even think the words *digital space*. There, on the front page, is a list of regular contributors.

Lily Raiti.

Her heart beats hard and heavy beneath her ribs. Colette had researched Lily thoroughly, back then. There isn't much more to learn here. A double degree in Creative Arts and Journalism from The University of Melbourne. Various short story collections. Academic publications. No agent.

Colette clicks through to Maia's bio page. No agent for her, either.

Usually, not having an agent is a sign you aren't good enough – yet another yardstick by which writers judge each other. The bigger the agent, the hotter you're considered, but Colette has the sense that with Maia, it's all that arrogant youthful I-know-it-all stuff.

What a load of rubbish. How old is she anyway? Colette can't find anything that gives a definitive answer, but she thinks of all that fresh, plump collagen. Early to mid-twenties. Colette clicks her tongue.

Maia's list of achievements would be impressive for someone twice her age.

Although Colette remembers thinking she too could, and would, take on the world in her twenties.

'Just you wait,' she mutters to Maia's photo.

Colette has an agent – Lucinda. The best agent in Australia. Impossible to find contact details for online. But Colette has Lucinda's *personal* phone number and has been to her house more times than she can count. Lucinda will have details on Maia. She had something on everyone in the literary scene. What Lucinda didn't have to tell wasn't worth knowing.

Colette spits her gum into the small desk bin as she pulls up Lucinda's number. The phone purrs in her ear, three times, before switching to voicemail. Dread pulses through her.

Lucinda always picks up her calls. *Always.* They'd had conversations in the back of cabs, in airports and while Lucinda dined with other authors. No matter what she's doing, she takes Colette's calls.

Something is wrong.

When did she last speak with Lucinda? She sifts through her memories. It's been a while.

She'd been so distracted with … everything.

A cold sweat erupts along her skin.

'Hi, Lulu,' she says, when the beep of the voicemail sounds, 'it's me. Babe, I've arrived at Rhamnusia and it's …' She gives an incredulous laugh. '… basic, in more ways than one. A super quick one for you, babe. What can you tell me about Maia McKenzie? She's here and …' What can Colette say over voicemail?

She's threatened me with Lily's name and if that little bitch has told anyone, then not only is my life over, but my career too, and you can't help me with my life, that's in the toilet, but you damn well better make sure they don't stuff the rest of it up for me or I will seriously go postal and more than one person will die.

Hardly.

'Call me back, okay? Love!' She jabs the red button like it's responsible for her feelings.

She and Shelly had stopped for lunch – wine mostly – at the swanky hotel Shelly is staying at in the centre of town. All blocky, Mexican-inspired architecture and blush and tan colours, it's far more Colette's vibe. Perhaps she'll book a room there and just come back here during the day for the writing stuff. Maybe there's a wellness centre in town; a magnesium float wouldn't go astray. Some kind of detox massage, and some sound healing to reduce her stress.

She'll charge her phone and have a nap while she waits for Shelly to finish her facial. Once she's comfy between crisp hotel sheets, she'll send that ghastly grey woman an email and ask for the schedule for the week. She'll attend the sessions that appeal and leave the rest.

She collects the clothes already strewn around the room – how has she made such a mess already? – and jams them into her suitcase.

Her phone pings.

Sorry babe, change of plans. Gerald has come to surprise me. Chat tomorrow.

Colette slaps her hand onto the desk.
No. No. No.
This is typical bloody Shelly. She's a flake. The ultimate fair-weather friend. Good fun if you never actually need anything from her, but if you did, forget about it.

Come pick me up anyway, I'm booking into the hotel tonight.

She waits for the bubbles to show Shelly is typing a reply. Nothing.
She jabs the call button and paces the tiny room as it rings out.
Voicemail.
Twice in two calls?
She's Colette-bloody-Halifax! No one sends her to voicemail.
Shelly's probably busy shagging Gerald already. Not that it will keep him. Shelly's man-friends tend to lose interest after five dates. And who can blame them?

Colette presses her fingertips to her eyebrows and massages them. The urge to be out of here strikes her like a hammer. This whole trip was ill advised. This shitty old building, the cold, the damp, all that nature, it's not her thing. What was she thinking?

She thinks of that receipt. The penthouse of The Park Hyatt. Thousands of dollars spent on one evening. While she was reeling from appointment to appointment, a brave face presented for the kids. While he ... Bugger it. She'll book the best hotel room the town has to offer.

Opening a new tab, she enters the details for the one hotel in town. It chugs slowly, the images unfurling like a ribbon as the page loads. A navy button flashes at the top of the page. *Book Now.* She doesn't wait for the remainder of the page to load, just clicks the button. Once, twice.

Stupid bloody piece of ... Breathe, Colette. Just breathe. Full inhale in, relaxed exhale, let go. No pauses, like a fountain as her transcendental meditation teacher – who also worked with Hugh Jackman in New York – had shown her.

She leans back in her chair and presses her fingers to the bridge of her nose.

Her heart slams to a stop as pain shears through her face.

There's a cloudy mirror the size of an A4 sheet of paper screwed to the wall, and she rushes to it, studies herself in its haze. It's fine. She's fine. She needs to get a grip. Pressing exploratory fingers around her cheeks, she feels for any bumps or sponginess as she'd been taught. Finds nothing but the dull ache that has dogged her for days.

Tears sting behind her eyes. Again?

Along with being sent to voicemail, she's now a crier. *Wonderful.*

No, she tells herself. She isn't. She is Colette-bloody-Halifax, and she doesn't cry. She gets shit done.

Popping another blister of gum into her mouth, she grinds it hard and waits for the nicotine hit. When it comes, she forces herself to walk slowly to the computer.

Book a room, then call Shelly again. If she can't get hold of Shelly she'll book a taxi. Anxiety buzzes in her ears.

Why is she acting like this? She is perfectly capable of getting to a hotel on her own.

But ever since Shelly had met her at the entrance to the Central Sydney Private Hospital, she'd felt raw, as if a layer of skin had been peeled back. More likely it was the effects of all the drugs wearing off.

That's it. She needs another painkiller.

Only they make her so drowsy and she needs to get to the hotel. She's been so careful with that prescription. Her life has become such a shitshow that the temptation to leave reality by relying on the buzz of the painkillers is a temptation that is far too real.

She would take one once she got there. The thought of the hotel's starched bone-white sheets and silent room is a balm that both soothes and energises her. A good night's sleep and a phone call from Lucinda and she would know what she was dealing with here. Then she would call her lawyer and hit both Lily and Maia with a cease-and-desist letter so terse it'll make their eyes water.

No one messes with her.

Trent found that out the hard way.

The hotel webpage finally loads. She chooses the most luxurious room and clicks the dates on the electronic calendar.

A draught of air hisses through her lips when the website shoots back: *Nothing available for your chosen dates. Next available date ...* She squints and leans forward in her chair.

But that's two months away!

That has to be some kind of error. She searches the site for a contact number. She'll call and speak to the manager. They'll find her a room. There is always a room or two held back for special visitors. Countless times she's called fully booked restaurants and dropped Trent's name only for a table to magically become available.

She locates the phone number, stabs it in, kicking her Celine boot along the worn floorboards as she waits for an answer.

A number of small black pellets are evenly spaced along the skirting boards. She bows to inspect them, recoiling once her brain kicks in. Mouse droppings. She gags.

Can this place get any worse?

Her gaze lands on a spider's web crowding the corner of the window, as thick as cotton. A fly buzzes frenetically, throwing itself against the glass.

Colette blinks. The room is caving in on her. The ceiling feels low. The air is glacial but stifling. Again and again that fly throws itself against the glass.

The roof continues to press down on Colette. Her breath is pinched sharp in her chest.

Jamming the still ringing phone between her ear and shoulder, she slides the screen open and lifts the window latch.

The window doesn't budge.

She shoves at it harder, using her spare shoulder. Without warning the window flings open and Colette stumbles, cracking her shoulder hard against the jamb.

Placing her hand against the frame to steady herself, she watches with dismay as her phone slides from her shoulder and sails out the window, landing with an ominous crack on the concrete below.

Maia

My spine cracks as I elevate into a headstand. I love it when it does that. Reminds me I'm alive, strong.

The blood rushes to my head and spots dance in my vision. My whole body tenses as I work to hold myself upright.

I can hear them talking downstairs; this house echoes strangely. It carries voices along its nooks and crannies, sometimes as loud as if the people are in the next room, and other times the merest hint of a whisper. The other night I could've sworn I heard someone speaking, but when I got up to use the bathroom, the house was completely silent.

It can keep this conversation to itself. The induction was one of the most mind-numbing things I'd ever participated in. The seriousness of Eliza and her love of rules would be laughable if it weren't so pathetic.

The sound of male laughter shatters the still evening air like the splintering of a tree. My feet thump to the floor so heavily the ancient paintings on the wall rattle in their frames.

Gooseflesh scuttles across my skin.

He's here.

I know it deep within my body.

Outside the wind gathers, like a drum roll. My moment is nearing.

He's finally here and although I have been waiting for him, a longing for him to leave stabs through me. Suddenly, I want him to remain a ghost, nothing more than a spectre, a story I tell myself.

Because him *actually* being here changes everything.

I will never be the same again.

And neither will he.

I lie on my back, staring at a water stain stealing across the ceiling. The bare floorboards are cold against my back. After standing sentry all day, he shows up the moment I relinquish my post.

That feels meaningful.

It's not, I tell myself. Humans need to create meaning because it lulls us into a false sense of control. I haul myself upright. No, not false.

I am in control. I know exactly who, and what, he is, and he has no idea who I am.

Or what I'm planning.

'Alright, Mama,' I whisper. 'It's show time.'

Rolling to my side, I plank for a full minute before dropping into five slow push-ups. I love feeling strong. There's pleasure in the deep ache of a well-worked muscle. My party trick is arm-wrestling likely looking lads in the pub. The loser gets the next round.

I haven't bought a round in three years.

The induction is supposed to last an hour, but by the time Eliza finishes lecturing the writers on the myriad things They Must Not Do while they're here, it's more like an hour and a half. Dinner is usually served straight after.

I flow through my yoga poses and rise to standing.

An unsettling sort of energy thrashes through me, a mis-tuning, like a radio signal as you drive beneath a thicket of trees.

Fear?

No, I'm not scared of him.

I'm strong, unbreakable. I've been through the worst thing that could have ever happened and I'm still standing.

'*Unbreakable*,' I whisper.

Anger thrums inside me, with its familiar thorny heat.

There's time to kill. Maybe I should call Lily and tell her that Colette-bloody-Halifax has turned up. Shake the details from her, what she can share without getting sued, anyway.

This feels like an opportunity too good to pass up. I'll ask Lily to write an article on the ill-effects of privilege and how women like Colette perpetuate and participate in patriarchal oppression.

Colette and her ilk seem to believe it's their birthright to gatekeep, as if they get to decide who is allowed inside the hallowed hall of financial security. Friends and family, people that look like them, that went to school with them. The same circle of privilege moving in ever-decreasing circles excluding everyone else. They only ever hire their friends' sons and daughters, or arrange loans for those sons and daughters to open their bougie boutiques and hedge fund firms. Daddy taking care of River and Roxy and any other stupidly named relative that might appear. That's why I'd started *Making Herstory,* as my way of pushing back, creating space for creatives without the backing of large platforms, or family money.

I roar an exhaled breath.

It had just been me and Mama growing up. We'd grown up together, Mama used to say. She'd barely been older than I am now when I thrashed my way out into the world.

You changed me on a molecular level, Darling Girl, Mama used to say. She'd been young enough to embrace motherhood with a type of abandon my friends' mothers were missing. We'd moved often, always just the two of us, to wherever Mama's art called her.

Six months in a remote community on the tip of the country. Two years in a wind-blown cottage perched on the edge of a cliff in Tasmania. My days filled with raw salt air, rain, my school the long stretch of sand on the beach below, or the kitchen table, head bent over Mama's neat writing while she painted at the window.

I gasp for breath, momentarily floored. I miss her like a missing limb. Will it ever ease?

That's what fuels me. What burns deep and hot, like a furnace, stoked livid by years of lean winters, donated school uniforms, boxes of non-perishables collected from kind-eyed ladies in church basements.

The last time I'd asked Mama about him, her hand had tightened on her handmade mug. Fleeting, but I'd still caught the white knuckles, the tremor in her steady artist's hand. *That man deserves nothing from us,* she'd said fiercely. *Not. A. Thing. Not even our thoughts.*

She'd reached out and stroked my hair. Her hands were rough from working clay, cleaning brushes, using her nails as tools, and caught in my hair. I'd yanked my head away, irritated. *Who cares when we have each other, Darling Girl?* she'd said.

I'd never asked again.

She was right. We never needed anyone else.

But Mama is gone, and I'm left here alone.

Abandoned.

Angry.

Looking for vengeance.

And I know exactly who is going to provide it.

Colette

The front door betrays her – slamming closed with a groan and a bang. When she looks up from her shattered phone, four pairs of eyes are watching her from the window she's standing in front of.

Shit. The induction.

She shakes her phone. A cobweb of cracks smother the screen.

It's not a bad thing, considering. The phone has been on 'do not disturb' for days. The red number of notifications twitching higher and higher, and with it, her anxiety. She'd wanted an excuse not to look, not to call or text. And now she has it.

Her shellacs click against the screen. One last check.

A horizontal line flickers along the screen beneath the shattered glass. It's impossible to use.

Movement at the window catches her eye. The hulking shape of Eliza lurches towards the glass, her face pinched.

She'll have to attend the stupid induction meeting now. Colette sighs. Annoying, but not life or death. What can go wrong in an hour?

As a crow shrieks overhead, that traitorous front door creaks open and Eliza's disapproving face appears. 'The induction started at five.'

Colette holds her phone in the air between them, showing Eliza the cracked screen.

That unnerving grey gaze of hers doesn't shift from Colette's eyes.

'My phone,' Colette says, as if dropping her phone is an excuse for being tardy.

Eliza's silent disapproval tells Colette she doesn't agree.

'Well, I'm here now. I'm sure one of the other writers will be happy to catch me up on what I missed. After the induction has finished, of course.' Colette smiles.

Eliza takes a step backward; Colette's tone has not placated her. Colette sulks into the house like a rebuked teenager. Eliza doesn't shift as she enters and Colette is forced to brush against her. The woman smells like mothballs and something darker, danker. Almost like the forest itself.

The lock clangs like a cell door closing as Eliza turns it behind her. They are in the middle of nowhere, so why lock the door? Is she locking them in, or locking someone out? A shiver creeps along Colette's arms and she thinks suddenly of Byron Jackovic. Her mouth dries as she walks into the room.

She perches on the edge of the closest chair, which wobbles dangerously, so she clamps her thighs together, ready to spring should it collapse underneath her. Meeting the gaze of the only other woman in the room, she smiles. But the other woman dips her gaze to the hands clasped tightly in her lap without returning it.

The older of the two men turns towards her and recognition thumps through her. On the older edge of middle-aged, he has one of those craggy faces that while roughly hewn, is still attractive. Isn't that just the way for men? Wrinkles and greying hair and they're distinguished, while the same features on a woman earn her the title of hag.

There's something overconfident about him, despite the too-young clothes and the ridiculously bright trainers.

Where does she know him from?

His gaze lingers uncomfortably, and she shifts her focus to the other man. Long and rangy, he's sprawled in the uncomfortable-looking dining chair, long legs crossed over thick chunky boots. A pang of nostalgia hits her. Something about his posture reminds her of Jasper, in the way all young men do now.

She'd spent the early days of motherhood wishing the kids would hurry up and grow up – become independent and allow her back into what she saw as her *real* life. Guilt and regret about that had circled in her head while she was in the hospital, like a giant spiralling black hole that consumed everything in its wake, leaving her wrung out and empty. She'd give anything to have those days back. Nowadays they never called unless it was to ask for money.

Suddenly everyone is standing and moving towards a doorway. Colette lurches from the chair and follows suit. The older man waits for her.

'Laurie,' he says, extending his hand. As she grasps it, the name pings in the recesses of her memory. The famous Alan 'Laurie' Lawrence. In his day he'd been the Liam Gallagher of poetry. Colette had interviewed him once, back in the early days when she'd had an equitable marriage. Before kids and Trent's rising star had fooled her into believing it 'made sense' for her to give it all up.

She'd also interviewed three of his ex-wives for the article. 'Selfish bastard' was the consensus.

She eyes him. Age has, in fact, wearied him. Too many years of hard living takes its toll on the most immortal, and immoral, of us.

'Colette.' She places her hand in his. Instead of shaking it, he presses it to his lips, holding her gaze with an affected air that might have been sexy when he was younger, but is pure sleaze now.

'While you were trembling on the brink, was I out yonder somewhere blinking at a star,' he says, quoting a line from *Gigi*, the play that had skyrocketed Audrey Hepburn to fame.

She doesn't bother to hide the roll of her eyes. He's overblown, too full of himself to take seriously.

'I did a piece on you back in your first round as Poet Laureate,' she says, yanking her hand from his grip and wiping it along her jeans. 'You said the same thing then.'

He laughs, a loud *ha-ha* pronounced as if he's only ever read the words.

It's unnerving.

'What can I say, every writer knows you must practise to perfect. I've been waiting all these years to perfect our meeting again.'

A hiss sounds from the doorway. Eliza is staring at them darkly.

'Oops.' He leans so close that she can smell his breath – something woody and the lingering scent of alcohol that the mint can't hide. 'I think we're in trouble.'

She jerks her head away as a memory bites.

He'd grabbed her during their interview, and she, too young and green, and yes, too awed by his star power, had done and said nothing. Even worse, she'd smiled and simpered and followed up the interview with a gushing note telling him how wonderful he was.

Things are different now, she thinks, as she gives him a thorny look. *She's* different.

'You are holding up the induction. I must show you the switchboard,' Eliza snaps.

They follow her through the portico into a narrow, dim hallway that twists and winds beneath the staircase. It feels as if they're walking between the walls of the house, a sensation that only increases when Eliza unseals a door hidden in a panel of the wall. The door yawns open to reveal a staircase that drops steeply into the bowels of the house. Cool air, musty and thick, snakes up the risers.

'In a house this age, you can't expect things to be the same as modern ones,' Eliza says as if one of them has complained. 'Sometimes the switchboard will short, particularly,' she glares at each of them in turn, 'if you are using a lot of electrical items. Hair dryers, phone chargers and the like.'

She gestures down the stairs.

'Down here you will find the switchboard. If it does blow, you need to take the torch from the wall,' she points to the yellow-handled torch hooked on the wall, 'come down here and reset it. Follow me and I will show you how.'

She descends the stairs carefully, throttling the handrail as she goes. Each tread screams like a dying animal under her weight.

Dumpy woman turns to them with a look of horror. 'I'm not going down there.'

Tall boy coughs a laugh. 'What's scarier, the basement or Eliza?'

They all laugh uneasily at that. Echoes of Eliza's footsteps sound above them. Colette bites her lip. How strange, it sounds so much like someone is walking overhead. She peers down into the gloom. Eliza has disappeared from the circle of light at the bottom of the stairs.

'You're young and fit, why don't you go ahead and learn how to reset the switchboard? You can be the captain of the switches. I'll buy you a bottle of ...' Colette considers the young man. He probably favours obscurely flavoured gin. Like Rosemary and Bog Water exclusively sourced from the back of Bourke. 'Whatever you drink, if you do it.'

He grins at her. 'You're on.'

Laurie scoffs. 'You wouldn't know a switchboard from your arse.'

The group stills.

'What's that?' Tall boy cocks his ear towards Laurie. Generous, offering Laurie the chance to redeem himself. But he doesn't take it.

'You're barely out of nappies, kid. Don't think you've changed many fuses in your life. Probably don't even know what one is.'

The 'kid' holds Laurie's gaze with a coolness that gives Colette a little thrill. He's not going to take Laurie's shit. The atmosphere pulses between them for a moment. Then, tall boy turns and gives Colette a jaunty salute. 'Captain Fusebox to the rescue. Payment of any full-bodied red accepted.'

He ducks his head under the sagging ceiling and makes his way down the stairs.

'I'm Desley.' Dumpy smiles.

'Colette,' she says coolly, still smarting from Desley's earlier non-response to her welcoming smile.

Desley wraps her arms around her body. 'The switchboard won't really need attending to, will it? They must have it regularly maintained by a professional? There are rules about this stuff.' She peers fretfully into the gloom.

'Captain Fusebox will sort it for us if it does,' Colette says with certainty. There isn't much you can't bribe a young man into doing.

'Tavis,' Desley says. 'His name is Tavis.'

Her tone is soft but there is reproach in it. As if Colette has been remiss in not asking his name. Colette rolls her eyes. She's only been here five minutes, there's barely been an opportunity, not to mention she just doesn't care.

Eliza's face suddenly appears at the bottom of the stairs. The light throws her face into shadow, creating a horrifying mask. Desley shrieks, which makes Colette jump.

'Jesus,' Colette says, clutching her chest.

'Come down. Now,' Eliza barks. 'You are holding us up.'

Desley grips Colette's arm. Colette shakes her off.

Laurie steps forward. 'If you don't mind, Lisa, we are going to sit this one out. Travis has kindly offered to take care of the switchboard if it blows. Only one of us needs to know how to fix it. We'll head back to the lounge, open a bottle and meet you back there.'

Colette can't help her smirk. No one has the balls of a middle-aged white man who has experienced a modicum of success in his life.

Eliza takes a step forward, resting her workmanlike boot on the bottom rung of the steps.

Her voice is curdled with barely repressed rage. 'You will do no such thing. Workplace health and safety demands we demonstrate how to operate both the switchboard and the boiler. If I cannot tick off your induction process, you cannot stay. That is the *rule*.'

'Okay, don't get your knickers in a knot.' Laurie shoots Colette a colluding look which she ignores. Eliza is irritating, but he makes her skin crawl. She will not align herself with him, and not against another woman.

Colette starts down the stairs with a huff. What does it matter if she stands in here for two minutes and listens to Eliza explain the bloody switchboard. The stairs shudder under her feet and damp air crawls around her ankles. She tries not to shiver. When Colette reaches the bottom, Eliza stands aside.

'It's a matter of health and safety,' Eliza mutters to Colette as she walks into the gloom. A wave of fatigue overcomes her and suddenly she couldn't care less about any of this.

I'm leaving as soon as I get back to my room. And not coming back.

Writing be damned. One night in the swanky hotel and then ... she draws a blank. There is nowhere for her to go. Nowhere is safe for her right now. Maybe she could leave the country. Hell, didn't Agatha Christie take herself off to a hotel with a fake name and hide out? Perhaps that's what she'll do.

All she knows is whatever it is she chooses to do, she won't be doing it here.

A circle of light encircles Tavis. He's standing beneath an ancient-looking switchboard, the torch pointed at his feet. It isn't until she stands right next to him that she realises how big he is. He could snap her like a twig if he decided to. Discomfort throbs through her. She is standing in the pitch dark with a large stranger.

Silly, she tells herself, just some kind of primal fear. A throwback to every fear women have ever had about men. There are people right here. He wouldn't do anything.

But she can't shake the fear that grips her and she steps away from him.

'Would you like to hold the torch?' He sweeps its beam along her feet.

'I'm not sure I can handle the responsibility.'

'It's a big job, but someone has to do it,' he quips.

Her good cheer has faded. 'It will have to be you I'm afraid. Electrical repairs are not in my job description.'

He gestures to the ancient box. The corner has been eaten away by something. Termites? Rats? It hangs drunkenly. 'I'm not keen on touching this to be honest, it looks like it could explode at any moment. No wonder it keeps tripping. We'll be lucky to make it out of here alive.'

Frosty fingers stroke her neck. She bats at it, the hasty movement sending something scuttling into the darkness.

And then it hits her. Without warning, like a truck rounding a blind corner.

The blackness swells until it is a live thing. It presses upon her, crawls up her legs, into her lungs. A buzzing takes up in her ears and she presses her fingers to the bones under her eyes; spongy, far less sturdy than they were. Bruised, aching.

Just like the rest of her.

The ground rocks and rolls beneath her feet. She can't breathe.

Her chest is full of bees, their buzzing increasing louder and louder until it is all she can hear, all she can feel.

Tavis's concerned face appears in the torchlight, his mouth moving but she can't hear a word. His hand is strong beneath her elbow. It's the only thing holding her up.

'I can't breathe,' she gasps. 'It's ... I can't ...'

From outside herself she hears him. 'I think she's having a panic attack.'

He's steering her past a gawping Desley and a disapproving Eliza, his hand tight, too tight, on her elbow. His fingers dig into the soft skin of her arm but she's grateful for something to think about other than the fear crushing her.

Her bum is on the bottom step, his hand on the back of her head, pressing it between her knees.

'Big breaths. Breathe. You can do this. I believe in you.' He sucks in a breath in demonstration. 'As Gandalf said, this too shall pass.'

His words snap her out of the panic fugue. 'What? No, he didn't.'

'Sure he did.'

'He said *you shall not pass*.'

'Oh.' He shrugs, unconcerned. 'Maybe it was Gandhi then.'

It's not clear if he's joking, but she laughs anyway.

Tavis is stroking her hair and as suddenly as it came on, it's gone. She's back in her body and irritated at him messing up her hair. She flicks his hand off.

'Thank you. I need ... I just need ...' *To be anywhere but here.* 'A glass of water.'

And her pills.

'Can you stand?' Shame chafes at his tone. Like she's an old duck having a senior's moment. He's so young, she probably seems ancient to him. The thought makes her angry. Fucking youth.

'Of course I can,' she snaps.

He helps her stand anyway and hovers close to her elbow as she climbs the stairs.

When she reaches the top, she hears Laurie.

'If I'd known all it took was a bit of heavy breathing to get out of this, I would have faked a panic attack too.'

Maia

I inch open the bedroom door, my breath heavy in my chest. The hallway is clear. Voices drift along it. The house has revealed some of its secrets to me over the last two weeks. If you stand in the corner of the hallway you can hear what's happening below almost as if you were there yourself.

A man and a woman in the dining room, or *the reception room* as Eliza calls it. One of her many affectations. I creep past the other doors, closed as tightly as fists, towards the voices. My skin prickles.

Laurie Lawrence. The man I've been waiting for. Australia's most famous poet, admittedly more famous for his bad language and even worse behaviour than his poems. Widely believed to have started the fire at Montségur that almost burned down the entire artist's colony back in the nineties. Although no charges were ever laid, of course. Men like him manage to slip out of every net cast to catch them.

As I pass room three, a ringtone shreds the silence. Eliza will be most displeased. Rule six hundred and fifty-four: no phone calls in the bedrooms. The walls are paper thin. There is a telephone room tucked into the wall at the bottom of the stairs, complete with built-in bench seat and table and an old, dead phone. The type that needs to be plugged in. The room is so small your knees almost touch the wall as you sit, but it's quaint. Wild to imagine people used to have to make an event out of every phone call.

Pausing at the top of the stairs, I lean over the banister. Thick black boots beneath long lean legs appear. Hoodie guy – who *is* he? The earlier disquiet from when I'd first seen him in the garden returns. Their conversation is too muted to make out, so I slip down the stairs in my thick socks, trying to avoid the parts of the stairs that shriek and moan like they've had enough of carrying the weight of other people.

Well, haven't we all.

I march through the doorway, shattering the room's stillness. He is standing David-like in front of the now raging fire, and Colette huddles over an open bottle of red. Colette's eyes meet mine and our earlier conversation echoes in the tightness of her jaw, the wary glint in her eye. I smile.

Good.

A gash of darkness splits the curtains. Rain finger-taps at the windows, increasing in ferocity like the wind, which is now hissing through the windows. Despite the fire, the room has a damp feel to it.

'If it isn't my friend from the garden.' I lay claim to him early. 'I'm Maia.'

Tongue between teeth as I reach for his hand, chest thrust forward. I know what I have and how to work it. His pupils dilate and his gaze slides to my lips. One corner of his mouth lifts, slowly, showing a row of straight, white teeth. Thank God. I have a *thing* about teeth. I'd once ghosted a guy because I'd noticed he was missing a tooth during the date. It wasn't noticeable until he'd laughed. It had given me the ick, so I'd excused myself, taken my bag to the toilet and left the restaurant out the back door.

'Tavis.'

Even his voice is sexy.

'Has the induction finished already?' I make a show of gazing about the room. 'Usually Eliza holds everyone captive for as long as possible.'

His gaze snakes to Colette, who glowers at her wine glass. 'It's finished for us. I think the others are still going.'

I humph. 'How did you manage that? She's pretty passionate about *The Induction*.'

Probably used his charm; surely even that dried-up stick Eliza isn't immune to this tall glass of water. *And* in a hoodie. He's close enough now that I can read the fluoro writing. *BadKarma*.

'You like this page?' I ask boldly, jabbing him in the chest with my finger. It is pleasantly firm.

'Yeah, it's alright.' He grins. 'It's my Instagram page.'

I let out a hoot of delighted surprise. 'You're BadKarma? No way. I follow you! Share your poems all the time.'

'Thanks.'

'That one about all the things you thought you wanted but didn't get.'

'Yeah.' He nods, looking uncomfortable.

'And then you'll find, I'm it.'

'Huh? What's that?'

'Your poem? Isn't that its last line? *And then you'll find, I'm it.*'

His eyes shift to the left. 'Yeah, yeah. Of course.'

I poke him in the chest and flutter my lashes. 'I'd expect you to remember the last line of your poem that went viral.'

He rocks on his heels, gaze flicking around the room. 'Yeah. It's just once the poem is out there, I tend to forget about it. Always on to the next thing y'know?'

Are we still talking about poems or something else? Not that I care if he's warning me anything with him will be short-lived.

None of my relationships make it past five weeks. I get bored, turned off easily. One eye on the door, my best friend has accused me more than once and she's not wrong.

Anyway, I'm here for one reason and one reason only and it has nothing to do with finding a man.

Actually, it has everything to do with a man. Just not this man. Although I definitely wouldn't *mind* a bit of fun with this one. The thought that's been tapping at the back of my mind like a branch at the window appears again.

'Are you a last-minute booking? I didn't see your headshot on the wall.'

Tavis squats to the hearth and pokes at the burning logs, sending a sneeze of smoke into the room. He stands, waving his hand in front of his face.

'Huh?' he says in response to the questioning look I'm giving him.

'Are you a last-minute ring-in? We weren't expecting you?'

A slow smile spreads along his delicious lips. 'We? I didn't realise you worked here.'

I smile back. 'I don't, but you might as well find out now, I know everything.'

We stare at each other too long for it to be comfortable. Finally he says, 'A last-minute thing. They messed up my booking. Drink?'

My eyebrows pull together as I consider his words. Messed up his booking? That surprises me. Eliza is anally organised.

'I'll get it,' I say. 'You keep watch on that fire.'

On cue, it spits a vivid ember onto Tavis's shoe.

After collecting a dusty goblet from the buffet, I stride over to Colette and pour myself a big slug of red. I hold her gaze as the wine gurgles into my glass. Then I lean forward and refill her almost empty glass. Colette twitches a brow, and the movement pulls at the soft skin under her eyes, showing lines of shadowed skin. I study her with a narrowed gaze. I've watched enough medical TikToks to know that there's only one thing that blackens both eyes like that ... a broken nose. But her nose is small and straight. Perfectly straight. Just like it would be if she'd had a nose job. Everywhere else, she has clear, unblemished skin. Tiny creases stretch from her eyes towards her ears. She looks good, in the way all rich women do. Money can't buy you happiness, but it can make sure you look good while you complain.

There's only one decent chair in this room, the one which requires you to sit with your back to the door, a position I find deeply uncomfortable. So I throw myself sideways across it, with my legs over the arm, crossing a thigh high over the other.

It wouldn't hurt for Tavis to get a glimpse of my toned ass. Why waste all that hard work?

'I spoke with Lily earlier,' I announce over the rim of my glass.

Colette's spine straightens, just briefly, before she relaxes against the back of the chair. Her face remains blank. She'd make a good card shark. Women like her always do.

'Thrilling,' she responds blackly.

'Who's Lily?' Tavis tugs a chair from the table, spins it around and straddles it. His knee presses against my leg and I'm surprised by how much I enjoy the soft touch of his denim.

I take a swill of wine. It's cheap, acidic. But I've drunk plenty of cheap wine in my life; it doesn't bother me. Colette, however, looks like she hasn't drunk anything that costs less than two hundred dollars in a long time.

That thought ignites the smouldering resentment inside me.

'Lily is a mutual friend of ours,' I tell Tavis.

'Sweet.' Tavis nods.

'Not *sweet*,' Colette says sharply. 'I told you earlier, I don't know any Lily.'

I drag my finger along the side table, through the thick layer of dust that smothers everything in this house. An idea glitters in my mind. What would a woman like Colette be willing to pay to keep her secrets safe? I take a sip and swirl the cheap red wine around my mouth as I consider. Enough to keep me in good wine for quite some time, I'm willing to bet. Not that I need her money – I don't – but the satisfaction of making her pay gives me a macabre thrill.

'My *friend* …' I emphasise the word, 'is a writer too. A bloody good one. Knows a lot about community.'

'Communities? She's a town planner?' Tavis's joke collapses into the space like a felled tree.

'Like, an exquisite writer who could write an entire 'how to' book about rebuilding authentic connections in a fractured world. *Community*. And she'd write it so beautifully you'd realise you had never truly understood the word until then.'

'Right.' Tavis nods and stares about the room, attention waning.

Outside the storm picks up, and the rain begins to demand our attention, tapping loudly against the glass. A bang reverberates through the house. Silence knots around us.

'Where is everyone else?' I ask.

'Last I saw them they were in the dungeon with the switchboard.' Tavis holds my gaze. His eyes are as blue as a summer sky.

I run the tip of my tongue around the sharp edges of my teeth and watch his eyes track the movement. 'The dungeon. That's perfect. Did you find any corpses down there?'

'Only my own.'

'Oh good, been looking for it long?'

'An eternity.'

We smile at each other and something begins to unfurl in me. Another beat of silence. 'So, who else is here?'

My voice is strained, overly casual. But he doesn't know me, can't determine whether the tremor of my voice is higher than usual, or see my finger tremble as it traces the rim of the glass.

'Who did we have, Colette? Desley, she seems nice, Eliza and that …' He pauses. '… fella. What's his name?'

There is the merest roll of Colette's eyes. She clears her throat. 'Laurie Lawrence.'

Hearing his name is like being slapped awake.

The storm increases in violence outside. A cool draught is carried through the window. The fire splutters and spits another burning ember onto the threadbare carpet at the hearth. Tavis springs from his chair and stamps it out and suddenly Mama's spirit is all around.

I blink.

It isn't that he withheld anything from us, Darling Girl, it's us that withheld everything from him. Everything that man touches turns to rust beneath his fingers. My beautiful, effervescent mother had been little more than a skeleton by that stage. Her hair gone but regrowing, so cruelly similar to the downy tufts of a newborn. She had been lucid one minute and swimming in memories the next.

Not swimming.

Drowning.

And I never wanted to share you. I only ever wanted you all to myself. She'd cupped my face with a hand that had once been so strong and nimble, but was now little more than a claw. *I never told you, I couldn't … it wasn't right … what he did …*

She'd drifted back along the morphine river, her words forgotten. But not by me.

The words buzzed like a fly against the window. As I made arrangements for the funeral, packed away her clothes. Crying on the floor of her wardrobe, a dress pressed against my face, I would find myself thinking, *What, Mama? What did he do?*

A crack of thunder jolts me back to the present. Tavis snatches back a frayed curtain and peers into the gloom. There is no twilight this evening, only darkness as black as pitch and the rain's patterns on the glass.

'Lucky we're here for the week,' he says, as the curtain falls back in place with a puff of dust. 'Looks like this has really set in.'

'It's supposed to snow,' I say. 'The last lot were disappointed to have missed it.'

Tavis shrugs. 'Surely not with rain like this?'

I take a sip of wine, trace my tongue around the acidic residue on my lips. 'Probably a blizzard, followed by a heatwave, the way the mining companies are destroying the climate.'

'People underestimate angry kids.'

'What?'

'Greta Thunberg said something like that. Kids are angry about being left to clean up the mess the older generation has left.'

It's not until I notice the wine rippling in the glass that I realise my hand is shaking. I take a sip to avoid replying.

'So, where are you from?' he asks me.

A pause. *Where indeed?* I used to have an answer, as inane as the question is, but now ... Now, alone like this, no family to speak of, the question lands like a fist to the stomach. I settle on, 'I live in Melbourne.'

'Really? I wouldn't have picked that.' He runs his gaze along my body. A fiery tingle takes up in my crotch, which is confusing. Since Mama died, I've felt nothing. Too tired, too raw, too goddamn angry for sex. I'd ended things with my friend with benefits and taken to bed early with my laptop and housewives from various counties.

'I'd have picked you for a Sydney girl. You're not wearing enough black,' he offers to my silence.

I raise a pointed eyebrow at his all-black ensemble.

'You?'

His eyes slide away from mine. 'All over the place. But I love Melbourne,' he says. 'Although I better watch myself saying that around you.' He directs that to Colette, at the table.

I jolt. I'd forgotten all about her. She is sitting in the exact pose she was in before, hunched over her wine.

'What?' she asks crossly, as if he's interrupted her during an important task. Her hands move to her nose and hover. She blinks at them and twists them together before resting them on the table.

'Because you're from Sydney.' He gestures with his head to me. 'All that rivalry.'

Our eyes catch. Colette looks away first and a tiny thrill of victory threads through me. Colette lifts and drops a shoulder lightly and I'm struck by how suddenly fragile, and young, she looks.

'I don't care about all that nonsense. Anyway, I grew up in New Zealand.'

I'm surprised. Not a shred of accent remains. She is all cut glass and standard English.

'Oh no! Hide the silverware,' Tavis shrieks, clutching his chest, and despite the charged atmosphere in the room, both me and Colette laugh.

Humour. My currency. I love it when a man can make me laugh, genuinely laugh. They're rare. I sneak another glance at him. Broad shoulders narrow into loose-hipped legs that seem to go on forever. Another lick of desire flames through me.

A door slams somewhere in the house and the overhead light flickers as if in warning. Voices drift along the hall. Cold sweat springs along my skin.

Outside the storm sharpens, stirring louder, increasing in violence.

This is it.

The moment I've been waiting for.

But suddenly I'm overcome with the desire to flee. *Leave*, I think, before all of this becomes what it is destined to become.

I feel as if I'm trapped inside one of those grimy escape rooms, full of aging furniture, strangers and nasty surprises. If only I could pick up the phone, call time and have someone switch on the lights and unlock the door.

But there's no easy escape from this mess. Just hidden clues and signposts declaring *this way to disaster.*

A hot wave of dread swirls through me, boiling over and over.

Run, go, leave.

I'm in the doorway before I even realise I'm moving.

The voices close in; they will be coming from under the staircase. Eliza likes to show newbies some – not all – of the hidden nooks and crannies of the house.

Taking the stairs two at a time, I run to my bedroom where I lock the door with trembling fingers. My heart is banging so loudly that, for a moment, I think someone is knocking on the door. My breath saws through the stillness of the room.

I'm okay, I'm okay, I reassure myself.

But as the storm outside gathers strength, I wonder.

I might be okay now, but at the end of this week, will I still be?

Will any of us?

Desley

The hallway is narrow and Laurie's hip bumps against hers.

'Sorry,' he says.

'I'm okay, I mean, that's okay.' Desley rubs the Saint Christopher medallion between her fingers, imagining the warm friction as strength.

Actually, she feels off, drained, as if the induction had involved a walk for miles through the forest, rather than just around the house. The strange energy of Eliza, the anger that emanated from her, the clipped words, narrowed eyes, particularly after Tavis and Colette left, have worn on Desley. She takes on other people's energy and often feels emptied after social interactions. Her psychic always performed a *qi* clearing before she started Desley's quarterly readings.

She spins at a puff of cold air across her nape.

There is no one there.

She blinks into the gloom.

'Has Eliza gone?'

Laurie turns. 'Looks like it.'

Desley peers along the shadowed hallway. 'I didn't see her go.'

'This place has entrances and exits all over the shop,' Laurie says. 'I've been coming here since the nineties and, oh boy, the stories if walls could talk.'

He's standing too close to her. She steps back until she is pressed against the wall.

He goes on. 'I think they've closed them in now, but a couple of the rooms were joined by a secret passageway.'

'Really?' Desley looks to the ceiling as if she will be able to see the secret passageway through the plasterboard.

Stupid.

'Back before all this woke crap, you know? When art was art and nothing else mattered. We didn't have to hand out prizes just for the colour of your skin or because you identify as some letter of the bloody alphabet.'

Desley presses her lips together. Conversations that include the words *woke crap* only went one way. She's exhausted and doesn't have the energy to listen to a tirade of racist, homophobic or misogynistic nonsense that she's expected to smile politely and nod through.

'I expect you all had a great time,' she says as they duck beneath a low doorway. 'Oh.' She lets out a gasp.

They have popped out under the staircase. She turns in a slow circle and gazes about. 'This is not where I expected we were.'

Laurie taps the side of his nose. 'I told you. The whole house is full of secrets.'

He grins in a way that makes her stomach clench. A flash of motion draws Desley's attention to the top of the stairs, but it's little more than a spark of colour, footsteps and a slamming door.

'There you are. We were worried you'd got lost.' Tavis has silently appeared in the doorway of the reception room. For such a big man, he moves as silently as a cat.

The portico is still shrouded in wood smoke but some heat has seeped from the dining room. Desley hadn't realised how cold she is until the cloud of warmth envelops her. She shivers.

'Where's that wine?' Laurie booms as he brushes past Tavis roughly. 'Pour me a drink, old man, what?'

Desley walks to the sparking fire and rubs her hands in front of the livid flames. Movement flashes in between the slash of the curtains. She blinks, trying to make sense of it. Her mouth is dry. There can't be anyone out there. Rain hammers at the windows and roof. A vengeful sounding wind is pressing against the house.

But.

She could have sworn she saw someone outside.

Should she tell someone? No, they'll think her foolish. She tucks her trembling hands into her armpits. Aside from the fact they're in the middle of nowhere, there's no way anyone would be out in that weather.

Tavis is stoking the fire. Laurie stands over him, barking directions.

Colette is lounging in front of a half full glass of wine.

There's something so put together about her. Her hair is sleek, and soft looking. It falls effortlessly in a way that Desley could never hope to recreate. How does she do it? The sleeves of her jumper are pushed up – cashmere? Looks like it. All three colours of Cartier Love bracelets encircle her wrist. Desley fingers the fake version she bought from Target on a shopping trip with her eldest daughter, Chloe.

She'd fancied one so badly. Had promised herself she would buy one with the advance from her first book, only ... she can't remember now why she didn't. It just seemed so frivolous when it came down to it. Scott had been right. He'd said that money would be better off on their mortgage. Especially as she hadn't been contributing financially to the family for so many years.

He always emphasised the word *financially* when talking about her contribution, as if he recognised the rest of her efforts. But then, she couldn't help but wonder, if he did appreciate her work at home with the kids, why did he bring up her *lack of financial contribution* constantly?

She'd thought when she'd finally (finally!) received a book deal it would be bells and whistles. A trip overseas, emails from her publicity team, author events, invites to lunch – but all she'd received was a generic, and disappointingly small, offer via email. And her publisher still spelled her name wrong in their communications.

Desley's stomach churns. That last email. She presses her fist against her mouth.

'Wine?' Colette stands before Desley, a greasy-looking glass and an open bottle of red in her hands.

'No, thank you.'

Colette smiles, her gaze shifting to Desley's belly. 'Congratulations. How far along are you?'

Desley screws her eyes shut. *Don't cry, don't cry.* 'I'm not …' A wave of humiliating heat stings her chest.

'Oh, fuck. Sorry. It's not—' Colette waves a hand at Desley's midsection. 'I just assume anyone not drinking is pregnant. God …' She swills her drink. 'Maybe I should just assume everyone is a recovering alcoholic. That's probably safer isn't it? Less offensive anyway.'

Is it less embarrassing to have a stranger assume you're pregnant or to tell her you avoid drinking because you invariably end up locked in a bathroom crying your eyes out after two glasses?

'Maybe I will have one after all. One's fine,' Desley says.

Only it's never just one. And it's never fine.

Colette looks gratified and Desley hates herself. Why does she sacrifice herself to make other people happy? She shouldn't care less what a stranger thinks of her, but women like Colette, with their toned bodies, shiny hair and easy confidence, bring out the worst in her.

Colette sloshes some wine into the glass and shoves it at Desley. They stand in silence, Colette's clanger hanging between them like a ripe fruit, ready to plummet to the ground, explode its insides all over their feet. Desley takes a gulp of wine, grateful for the acidic heat as it travels along her chest. She imagines she can feel the alcohol fizzing in her veins.

Hurry up and work, she wills it.

Laurie and Tavis are talking, or rather Laurie is talking *at* Tavis. Tavis is staring intently at Laurie with a look Desley can't decipher. It almost looks like … disgust, or hatred. Laurie is what Desley's mum would have kindly called a 'larger than life' character. They're not the words Desley would choose. His voice echoes around the cavernous room and pierces Desley's head. She feels a headache coming on.

'It's cold, isn't it,' Desley says.

Colette murmurs a response to her wine glass.

'Supposed to snow apparently.' Desley cringes at her desperate tone.

'Mmm.'

'That would be exciting, wouldn't it?'

Colette isn't listening, her gaze trained on the partially open door.

Bored already, obviously, and Desley doesn't blame her. The weather? She calls herself a writer, and all she has to talk about is the weather?

Fat, foolish Desley.

The wind roils outside the window. A sharp gust lifts the curtains as if someone has been playing hide and seek behind them and impatiently wishes to be found.

Desley catches Tavis's eye.

'The ghost of Evelyn?' he asks with wide eyes.

'Can't be. She's downstairs with the switchboard.'

They share a smile and Desley's back unlocks at the safety of their communal joke.

The induction through the house had been equal parts fascinating and terrifying. Desley loves old houses. For her, there's nothing better than rummaging through a second-hand store, turning worn items over in her hands, imagining their previous lives.

But this house is like a stopped clock, and instead of filling Desley with intrigue and wonder, it's made her nervy, jumpy. Fanciful. It was probably more to do with the atmosphere created by the dim lighting, Eliza's frigid resentment, and Colette's panic attack.

Memory jogged, she turns to Colette. 'Feeling better now?'

Colette startles as if woken from a trance. 'Yes. Alcohol fixes everything.'

In Desley's experience it usually made things worse. 'I meant after your … in the … with the switchboard.'

'Oh, that.' Colette purses her lips, although the rest of her face doesn't move.

Botox? Of course. A woman like her probably held Botox parties with her friends. Desley remembers seeing pictures of her online with that once-famous pop singer who'd had so much plastic surgery that the media had nicknamed her Barbie. Shelly Stackhouse. She'd had a hit song about kissing in the rain back in the eighties. Desley had loved it. Her stomach twists. What a glamorous woman like Colette must think of Desley. She hunches her shoulders, trying to disappear into herself. Any clever or amusing conversational tool Desley might've used is buried deep beneath layers of self-consciousness and awkwardness.

'I just needed to eat,' Colette says dismissively.

A prickle along the back of Desley's neck alerts her to movement in the doorway and Eliza appears like a ghost. Gone one minute, there the next. Eliza glares around the room with those accusatory grey eyes. 'This is a writers house,' she states.

Her words land in the room with the grace of a bomb. Laurie opens his mouth as if to make a smartarse remark, but wisely shuts it again.

'As such, you are required to participate in a number of writing activities. When Evelyn imagined transforming this beautiful, peaceful space into a writers house, she envisioned a venue where writing took centre stage. Where writers were offered the time and space to *retreat*,' she stresses the word, 'to their imaginations. We don't ask much of you during your time here, aside from the dinner dishes.' She narrows her eyes. 'You are adults after all.'

She sounds as though she harbours doubts.

'There are no chores here. Your days are to be spent in flow. Thus, between the hours of seven and seven the house is to be as still and as silent as possible. This means no mobile phone usage in the bedrooms.' She glares at Tavis. 'Never interrupt another writer – no knocking on their door uninvited.' Her glare shifts to Laurie.

Desley could imagine Laurie drifting aimlessly about the house, knocking on door after door, wine bottle in hand. Mid-morning.

Laurie wanders over to the bureau and rustles open the bag of chips lying next to the wine, crunching loudly as Eliza continues.

'And every night at six pm before dinner is served, we ask that you take turns sharing your work and offering feedback.'

Desley feels as if the floor has opened up beneath her. Share their work? She taps her thumb against her palm. It doesn't help. Her breath comes in gasps, her vision swimming.

She is going to get found out. She is going to get found out.

Her gaze flutters about the room, finding no one else looks even slightly perturbed by this news. Laurie has been here before so he must have already known about the readings, but both Colette and Tavis seem utterly unbothered.

She's alone. Of course she is. The other guests are professional writers, winners of accolades and awards, titles and bestselling lists and she's …

Desley.

She shakes her head. Eliza is looking at her curiously, as if she has been addressing her for some time and she hasn't registered it. 'Sorry?'

'You go first. Tomorrow night. Desley *Armstrong*. It's fairest to work our way through it alphabetically.'

A sharp stab of fear spikes through her but Desley strangles out a smile and nods. 'Lovely. No problem.'

How the hell am I going to get out of this?

I told you so, the nasty little voice in her head sings. *You're going to get found out. Almost immediately.*

Desley takes a gulp of wine, and then another, enjoying the heat of the alcohol as it weaves through her chest.

Maybe she can fake an illness, a sudden bout of gastro would still any questions. Yes, the idea swells inside her, gastro would keep her trapped in her room, avoiding the obligatory shared dinner experience Eliza informed her (no less than four times) was non-negotiable. Desley gazes at her and wonders if anyone ever tries to negotiate with Eliza. Almost as tall as Tavis, she is as broad as any man Desley has ever known, and fiercer. There is something deeply frustrated about her, as if she is a stretched-thin mother, and they her incessant charges.

'Everyone will get their turn,' Eliza announces in a hard voice, as if they'd all begun to clamour for their go. 'You may distribute your work beforehand electronically, or,' —she gestures to the curling paper on the wall— 'it is ten cents per page to print. But most of our writers prefer to orate and receive immediate feedback.'

Desley slugs the wine again and chokes as it hits the back of her throat. Tears stream from her eyes as she struggles for breath. She is vaguely aware of someone – Colette? – banging her too hard on the back, which only brings another round of coughing.

Finally the coughing ebbs, and she straightens, cheeks flaming, eyes streaming. She grabs the nearly empty bottle of wine from the mantle and slops the remainder of it into her glass, sending it spinning greasily up the sides.

Black chunks of tannin drip from the neck.

There's no getting out of this.

She's well and truly trapped.

Colette

'So, who got the haunted room?' Tavis digs his hand into the bag of chips Laurie traps protectively against his chest. He's hoarded the chips since opening the bag like he owns them. Not that Colette cares; she's not eaten chips since the Spice Girls were trendy. Although, sometimes for a treat, she'd open one of the kids' fun-sized bags and lick all the flavour from them, dropping the soggy chip into the sink waste disposal. But the constant rustling and crunching from the men is doing something strange to her, like Pavlov's dogs her mouth is watering and she can almost taste the salt on her tongue.

She'll have sashimi delivered to her room when she gets to the hotel and will eat it in bed. Her hands fish in her pocket for her phone, stilling when the sharp glass of the cracked screen slices across her thumb. Yanking it out of her pocket, she stares as a violently red bead of blood forms along the crease of it. She shoves it in her mouth. The metallic taste mingles unpleasantly with the wine.

Her head's still jumbled from the panic attack in the basement, the wine and her medication. How many glasses has she had? She will just turn up to the hotel. As she learned in her early days as a rookie journalist, it's harder to refuse someone face to face than it is over the phone.

And once they see who she is, they're certain to find a room for her. But then they'll know who she is and when the story breaks it wouldn't take more than a phone call to have the hotel swarming with paparazzi. Her mouth waters unpleasantly. At least here no one cares who she is.

'I did,' Laurie says around a mouthful of masticated trans-fats and processed potato.

Colette looks away, her stomach twisting.

'Haunted room?' Desley squeaks beside her.

Tavis rounds on her with a devilish grin. 'The ghost of Evelyn lives on in her old bedroom.'

A small charge of fear flashes through the room.

'Haunting the house to check the writers are complying with all the rules?' Colette quips.

Tavis takes the bag of chips from Laurie and offers it around. Desley glances at Colette guiltily before taking a fistful.

Colette shakes her head and glances around. The curtains at the back of the room are open and she experiences that same brambly, stalked feeling she'd had along the driveway.

No one could be outside. The wind sounds almost squall-like and the rain has only increased since it began and shows no sign of easing. She strides over and snatches the curtains closed all the same.

'I've seen her. The ghost.' Laurie licks his fingers with a disturbing smacking noise.

Of course you have, Colette wants to say. After smacking him around the head with the bag of chips.

Or something heavier.

Desley's eyes are wide and her cheeks are flushed red.

'She walks the hallway all night. You'll hear it. Bangs the pipes, moves the curtains. She's a frisky minx is our Evelyn.'

'Didn't her parents die here?' Tavis asks.

'And brother,' Colette chips in. Journalist tendencies are hard to relinquish. Her interest had been piqued when she'd read that. She'd fallen down a rabbit hole, spending hours searching for articles about it on the internet. Instead of quoting recovery percentages, her surgeon should've just promised Colette so much lying around that she'd have time to actually read all the open tabs on her phone.

'Evelyn came home from visiting a friend to find them all dead in their beds. Gas leak,' Colette says.

Desley's mouth is a little moue of fear.

'Or maybe Evelyn went to visit the friend, snuck back and cut the gas line, and killed her entire family,' Tavis says darkly.

Colette scoffs. 'We have more to fear from Jackovic's friends still living in the forest than we do a ghost.'

Desley turns her round eyes to Colette. 'The serial killer?'

Colette nods, enjoying the tension in Desley's shoulders. 'He lived, and killed, in the forest behind us.'

A squeak escapes Desley's lips. 'B ... b ... but ... friends? I thought he was a loner?'

Tavis stares at Colette, his jaw set. There is a strange energy pulsing from him. As if he's angry and trying to hide it. 'Not just behind the house. The state forest is huge. It stretches for kilometres.' He steps toward Desley and places a hand on her shoulder. 'And he's in jail for life. His friends and family shouldn't be held accountable for anything he may, or may not, have done.'

Colette *tsks*. 'May not have done? The bodies of twenty women were found buried in the forest behind us, and some of their belongings were found in his house. If he didn't do it, he's the world's unluckiest man.'

'They say he worked with at least one accomplice, but they've never been able to prove it.' Maia leans against the doorjamb, a smirk on her full lips. 'For all we know, they all could've been in on it.'

A shiver shuffles along Colette's spine, not of fear, but foreboding. As she had on the driveway, she feels watched, hemmed in. Trapped. Panic begins to rise again. From the depths of her pocket the chirp of a notification sounds. Her heart kicks, before a hot wave of relief as she remembers: her phone, once her lifeline, is shattered. Unusable.

She has a legitimate excuse not to reply or respond or read, read, read.

Seeing Maia in the doorway reminds her of her phone call to Lucinda. Maybe that notification was her, with news that Colette can use to stop this little upstart.

Before things go too far.

Because Colette has to do something to shut Maia up. This is one thing she can control. She's not going to let this kid take the last thing she has.

Maia struts into the room. She is the model on the runway, and they the covetous gaze of the audience. The energy changes as soon as she enters. Desley begins to edge towards the corner of the room, looking as if she wants to hide amongst the furniture. It's both Tavis and Laurie's turn to become Pavlov's dogs now, their bodies turned eagerly towards Maia, mouths hanging open, and if they had tails, they would be wagging.

It's pathetic to watch.

And painful.

It had once been her that held men's gazes. Now she is invisible, an aging lady that needs her elbow held instead of a lingering hand on her lower back.

Colette unscrews the lid on a fresh bottle and refills her wine glass with a gurgling sound, anger simmering in her chest.

Laurie's shoulders are thrust back, chest out (and thus belly), and he's on Maia like she's the last delicacy in the box and he's a starving man.

'Laurie Lawrence. Two-time Poet Laureate.' He reaches for Maia's hand. She hesitates.

There's something fragile about her confidence that wasn't there before. Her eyelids flutter, and as she reaches for his hand, her fingers tremble like leaves on the breeze. His large hand envelops hers and Maia shudders. As he pulls her hand towards his mouth – obviously his regular party trick – Maia snaps it away. The look she gives him is as dark as the forest outside the window.

'Do not put your mouth on my body without my permission,' she snarls.

Colette returns Desley's wide-eyed gaze with a smile. She might hate the girl but Colette would've loved to have been as self-possessed as that at Maia's age.

'Got a little feminist on our hands here, do we?' Laurie's tone makes Colette's jaw hurt.

A flash of movement snags her attention. Desley has upended her glass into her mouth. For someone who said she didn't want a drink, she's sure polished off her glass quick enough. Colette gestures to her with the wine bottle and she nods gratefully.

The tension inside the room rises with the battering of the rain against the window, and the wind in the trees sounds like the ocean roaring through the room. Colette thinks of tsunamis and how the power of water can cause utter destruction if all the elements are just right.

She dumps wine into Desley's glass, waiting for Maia's response. 'This should be good,' she mutters.

'Got a little misogynist on our hands, do we?' Maia's hands are on her hips, that overfull mouth a twist of belligerence.

'Come on, darling,' Laurie says with that strange laugh. *Ha-ha.* 'Let's not fall out straight away. Unless you want to kiss and make up.'

It's as if he's slapped her. Two pink spots appear on her cheeks and all the feline languidness leaves her body. She's as stiff as a stick.

Turning to Tavis, she smiles rigidly. 'Where's the wine? This weather.' As if the two remarks are related.

It's shameful to admit, but Colette's grateful she isn't the only one in the sight of Maia's shotgun tongue. Laurie's old-fashioned bullishness should take the heat off her until she can get out of here. She grimaces. The storm has thwarted her plan to walk to the hotel. One more glass of wine and she'll order a cab and go.

Colette considers Desley. With her wide, dark eyes and skittish energy, she reminds Colette of a bilby, rummaging quietly in the dense undergrowth, secretly, watchfully. She radiates something unsettling, as if she knows something terrible is going to happen and is waiting for it.

She has her wine glass pressed to her mouth, as if it will protect her from the energy that crackles through the room.

No chance. This is going to be a shit show. Colette is almost sorry she's going to miss it.

'What do you write?' Colette asks Desley.

Twisted psychological thrillers where a serial killer stalks the female protagonist throughout the series? Or is she one of those deceptive types that surprise you when they announce they write erotica? Colette eyes her. She looks the type to write fantasy novels involving group sex, aliens and time travel.

Desley turns to Colette with glazed eyes. 'Nothing. I mean, romance. It's just fluff, really.'

She waves a hand, and the wine sloshes in her glass. She hiccups and does something weird with her thumb and finger. *Tap, tap, tap.*

Is she drunk already? Medicated?

'Ru-ro is what *she* called it.'

There's a hard emphasis on the word *she*, and Colette smiles.

'Easy to read is hard to write, as they say,' Colette offers generously.

Desley manages a trembling smile.

'Anyone who manages to write an entire book should be proud of themselves.' Colette feels magnanimous. What does it cost to be kind to this anxious, self-deprecating woman?

Colette runs her gaze over her, cataloguing the oversized knit in a cheap-looking poly-blend, poorly fitting jeans that almost certainly have an elastic waistband, and the orange tint to her blond highlights. She reads an existence of school runs and tuck shop volunteer shifts, ferrying the kids from after-school activities, milk bottles and egg cartons saved for crafts and a complete lack of self care or knowledge even of what makes her happy anymore.

If she ever knew.

Overweight in a manner that screams of leftover chicken nuggets snatched from kids' plates, drenched in tomato sauce, and pasta dinners in front of the latest binge-worthy show, hubby mindlessly scrolling on his phone beside her. Like a neglected cupboard that sits in the corner of the room, never noticed until someone requires something from inside its depths. Handy, but unappreciated.

Deep. Colette laughs at herself as she sips the sharp wine. Perhaps her next book could be an exploration of finding oneself after motherhood. The low-level hum of guilt that chased mothers everywhere they went, one foot in motherhood and the other on the corporate ladder, feeling as if they're failing at both.

Her hand on her phone again. That twist in her stomach.

No, it wouldn't be about motherhood.

Anything but that.

Tavis and Maia are laughing together, heads bent over another bottle of wine as they work to dislodge a broken cork.

Laurie leans insouciantly against the edge of the table, arms crossed. His shirt hugs his belly and a splash of red wine blooms like a blood stain on his chest.

'This place is like a portal into the fifties,' Colette says as she really looks at the room for the first time. It's warm but cloudy with smoke. Faded floral sofa crowded with dusty, threadbare cushions at one end, a rustic dining table at the other.

The wall with the door has been converted to a floor-to-ceiling bookcase, and coloured spines march along the sagging shelves. Reminder after reminder that Colette is stranded miles from her state-of-the-art house, friends and children. No phone, recalcitrant wi-fi, and this motley bunch of strangers.

And the looming announcement.

Her heart tap, tap, taps, like Desley's thumb. No phone and crappy wi-fi is probably a blessing.

She pats her pockets before remembering with a slap that she no longer smokes and has left her gum upstairs. The idea of rising from the couch and returning to her room to collect it is exhausting.

Laurie saunters over. 'What's happening over here, ladies?'

'When's dinner?' Desley asks, peering around the room as if Laurie hasn't said a word. 'Eliza said we don't have to cook?'

She sounds incredulous, like a lottery winner who cannot believe their luck.

'A local woman cooks it offsite and Eliza dishes it up,' Laurie says. 'Her chicken curry is good enough to make you believe in the institution of marriage. Almost.'

Desley looks panicked. 'In this weather?'

Laurie shrugs, unconcerned. 'I'll eat chicken curry in any weather.'

'I meant—' Desley shakes her head, as if trying to clear her thoughts. 'How will Eliza get the food here? The weather is awful.'

As if to prove her point, a crack of thunder snaps overhead and the lights flicker, plunging the room into absolute blackness for a brief moment.

'Who cares? They can't leave us here to starve,' Laurie states.

'Can't or won't?' Colette suspects if Eliza had her way, she would do precisely that.

As if they conjured her, there is a rattling sound at the doorway and Eliza appears, pushing an unwieldy metal cart. Her hair is wet and hangs in ratty ringlets on her face. She hasn't bothered to remove her rain jacket, and it leaves a trail of dark stains along the carpet behind her.

She crashes the jug of cutlery onto the centre of the table and eyes them accusingly.

'Dinner,' she announces like a threat. 'Beef stroganoff with couscous. Non-meat eaters' —given her tone, it's clear Eliza doesn't hold much truck with that concept— 'have a vegetable couscous below.' She jabs a finger towards the second tier of the cart. 'If you do eat meat, please eat the meat meal, *not* the vegetarian one.' Said in the long-suffering voice of someone who has listened to more vegetarians complain than she cares to count.

'You are required to attend to the dishes. Tonight. Make a roster. You are all adults. I should not have to explain to you that after someone has made you a meal, it is polite, and *respectful*, to tidy up afterwards. For those that missed the induction,' she glares at Colette, 'you will find the cupboards and drawers are all labelled. There are photos that show where every item belongs.'

'Is there really?' Colette murmurs out the corner of her mouth.

'Laminated,' Desley whispers behind her wine glass.

'There is no excuse for items to be left on the bench or misplaced. This makes it very difficult for people to find the items they are looking for.'

'Thanks, Lisa.' Laurie slaps his stomach. 'Smells delicious. Barb outdid herself again. Give her my love, won't you?'

'I am not here to pass messages on for you, even if Barb*ara* was interested in receiving them from you, which I highly doubt.' Eliza throws them all one last reproachful look and storms out.

It does smell delicious. The air is rich with the wonderful fragrant scent of the stroganoff. The room has warmed, the seat is comfortable and the wine is dulling the edges of her anxiety.

Hunger takes her by surprise.

She hasn't been hungry for months.

Her stomach, sick with betrayal, has done nothing but roil and roll. She's buttoned up so tight against all feelings that she's shut off any feeling at all.

Her clothes hang from her like she's a little girl playing dress-ups in her mother's wardrobe. Years spent counting calories and working out like a demon only to lose weight now without even trying.

And the irony was, she would swap it all in a heartbeat.

She'd take a tight waistband over the dull ache that chases her like a bounty hunter. Everywhere she looks – a relaxing bath, her once comfortable bed, the family dinner table, women in activewear walking, running. All of it makes her want to vomit.

Everything that has been taken from her.

Desley releases a small sound. 'She terrifies me.'

'Eliza?' Laurie scoffs.

So he does know her name, clearly uses the wrong one to niggle her.

'She's a pussy cat, really. I've been here four times and every time she gets crankier but that's what happens as women get to a certain age.' He taps the side of his nose.

Colette rolls her eyes. *Dickhead*.

'Does she live here?' Desley asks, her gaze trained on the doorway.

A crack of thunder shakes the house again and they all jump. The lights dim but don't go out. Desley jolts from the sofa and Colette finds herself standing too.

Her question goes unanswered as Tavis sings, 'Kids, diiiiiiinner.'

'You look like my mum too,' Laurie says. ''Cept she was a bit manlier.' He elbows Desley, trying to pull her into his joke. He knocks her so hard she stumbles.

There's a ruffle of disquiet as they wait for Tavis to respond. He stacks the dishes on the table wordlessly.

'She has my sympathies. Having you as a son,' Tavis says, when the last dish is on the table. His gaze is black. His silence had been one of restraint, not of acceptance.

Laurie takes a step. 'Don't you talk about my mother.'

'Cut it out,' Colette says, channelling the idea of the type of mother she dreamed of but had never been: firm but patient. *Gentle parenting* they call it now. As if mothers don't have enough to deal with, they now need to be gentle while they do it all. 'Dinner smells amazing and I'm famished.'

Her hand rests upon the rigid spine of the chair, but before she can sit in it, Maia throws herself on it, as if Colette has offered it to her.

'Thank you,' Maia says, all fake niceties.

She's goading her. Trying to press her into a confrontation, but she won't get it. Not until she's spoken to Lucinda and has all her ammunition locked and loaded. Revenge is a dish best served at a time that suits the server.

Clenching her jaw, Colette moves to the opposite end of the table. There's no getting away from Maia at this six-seater table but she'll be damned if she will sit beside her. Choosing the seat on the long edge of the table, farthest away, she'll at least have the choice to look at her or not.

Thankfully it's Desley who sits next to her. Laurie and his roving hands would be too much for her tonight. She's already wound as tight as a spring.

And just when she thinks the night can't get any worse, Tavis speaks.

'Let's play a game.'

Day Two

Desley

One thing she can see ...

Desley looks around. She can't do it. She can't stay a minute longer in this cramped, airless room. She's told herself all morning she will write, but it's a lie. She won't. She can't.

It feels as if the walls are growing closer around her. Even the desk is threatening.

Everyone else will be writing, of course they will. This *is* a writing retreat.

But Desley can't summon the energy to even pull her laptop out of her suitcase. The thought of the blank white space of the writing software is too much for her.

The house is on the edge of a national forest. A walk might clear her head, get the blood flowing. All the writing podcasts she listens to suggest walking in nature to help with writer's block. After lugging her suitcase onto the bed with a grunt, she flicks the combination lock and pulls out her leggings. A walk through the forest will be good and start her weight loss journey off right too. There might be a café she could stop at along the way and get a hot chocolate or a chai. Maybe a slice of cake.

One wouldn't hurt.

Yes, she tells herself as she pulls a second pair of leggings over her first, she will start strong tomorrow. She deserves a break. Last night's wine has left her feeling dehydrated and lethargic. A walk will clear her head.

Then, *then*, she will get started.

The house is silent, almost as if she's completely alone. She's not, she tells herself as goosebumps prickle. Everyone's working, as she should be. Desley flinches. She should be writing. All she wants, all she's ever wanted, is to be a writer. She had convinced herself that having a book published would prove something.

Look, she could say to her imaginary enemies (why do they all have Scott's face?) *I'm not useless, I'm worth something.*

Once she'd even believed it. She'd dreamed of being a travel writer. Had believed herself capable of anything, powerful even.

Such delusional youth.

Travelling the world with little more than a backpack, she'd spent her time scribbling furiously in her notebooks, fuelled by the belief that recording it all, labouring over the most compelling words, constructing a punchy sentence would change her life. She'd pored over travel guides, studied other authors' writing styles, mimicked them. Planned submissions like an ambush.

But then she'd met Scott and things changed.

She'd changed.

Scott was passionate about getting on the mortgage ladder young, and without meaning to, she'd let her roots grow in the city he'd grown up in. They'd moved to a dull and brutalist suburb that offered nothing but cheap housing filled with other young people looking to maximise their mortgage years.

Her dreams of flights, beaches, and foreign languages had been smothered by repayments, children, endless chores, until it was all nothing more than a petrified memory.

A coil of guilt. The girls. Her babies.

They'd changed her, and she wouldn't do it differently, if only for them.

It had been easy in the beginning to leave behind the boring, go-nowhere office job to spend the days with her new baby. The wonder of watching Chloe sprout. Marvelling as she learned to grasp, to sit, to toddle on those deliciously chunky legs.

It had crystallised Desley. Made her feel as though she was worthy, essential, needed. Important to someone in a way she'd never been.

But, she muses, as she tightens the laces on her dusty trainers, as her babies had floated into childhood and the playdates became drop and go, and parents were discouraged from sitting in the gymnastics and ballet classes, Desley found herself unravelling. And now, in the tweenie years, she's little more than an embarrassing Uber driver, leaving her with too much time to think, waiting for hours, alone in her car. So much waiting.

That's how her writing had restarted. At first it was merely a way to pass the time, but quickly her passion had reignited.

She'd been good once. At writing. Hadn't she? She'd begun to wonder if that was just one of the many stories she told herself.

She shrugs on her coat and locks her door behind her, carefully placing the key in her pocket. A walk will clear her head and she can start tomorrow. There is no need to feel guilty.

The air is colder than expected when she steps outside. Pausing for a moment, she closes her eyes and sucks in a breath. Concentrating on the smells, the sounds.

How lucky I am, Desley tells herself fiercely. Lucky to be here. A place where hundreds of people applied every year, and only a selected few were accepted.

Shaking her hands, she visualises the hangover, the bad energy, the fear and depression leaving her body.

She sets off towards the back of the property where a sign, mouldy and rotten, hangs forlornly off its perch.

Forest path this way.

She peers at the flayed lettering beneath.

Beware of …

Whatever she was to beware of was gone, peeled away. It has been some time since the forest path has seen feet. The edges encroach the track, and it's now a tangle of leaf litter and vines. The impression she'd had upon arriving threads along her spine again. That the forest is inching closer and closer to the house, like children in a game of red light/green light. When you turn to look, it freezes, as still and silent as an oak, but once your back is turned, it creeps ever nearer.

Silly.

She blows on her hands and sets off along the path. The air is sharply cold, her breath perfect white cones around her face.

Suddenly, a hand grasps her ankle, tugging violently.

She shrieks, kicking out, but the hand doesn't relent, instead tightening its grip and pulling her to the ground.

Landing heavily on her hands and knees in mud, she turns to face her attacker.

A rope-like vine is snarled around her shoe.

She's tripped on a vine. There is no attacker. Hot shame flushes through her.

Only she could go for a walk and make a mess of it. Tears gather as she struggles to her feet. A gash has cut the knee out of her leggings, exposing skin as white as bone. Both pairs of leggings are ruined.

'You drunk already?'

Desley whirls around at the voice.

Laurie.

The shock of seeing him steals her breath. He is standing off the track, amongst the copse, half hidden in the shadows.

How long has he been standing there? And why is he in the foliage, rather than on the track?

She looks down at the vine wound around her ankle.

Thick and pliable, it's been sliced sharply at either end. The trees above show no sign of the other parts of the vine. Had it been wound around the tree trunks either side of the path with the intention to trip someone?

Desley takes a halting step backwards, and then another. Laurie steps forward. He is blocking the path back to the house.

Suddenly the dimness of the tree canopy feels too close, too dense.

Laurie advances. 'Have a nice trip?' He laughs. 'You really went flying.'

'Yes. I did,' Desley says, voice wobbling.

Her heart kicks in her chest, her palms slicken. She feels stupid that he saw her fall, but another feeling overrides it all. Something primal.

Fear.

She's left her phone inside the room.

They are completely alone.

Gazing past Laurie, she sees the house isn't visible, but surely she's still close enough for someone to hear her if she yells?

'Actually, I might go back to my room.' She steps forward, but he doesn't move.

'I was just taking a piss,' he says, gesturing to the forest. 'Heard you crash pretty hard.' He steps forward again. Desley takes another step back. 'Are you hurt?'

'No. No, I'm fine.' Desley can hear she doesn't sound fine.

'You were off on a walk?'

She nods, unable to trust herself to speak.

'Have you made it out to Lovers Leap yet?'

She swallows and shakes her head.

'Well.' He bears down on her. 'You're halfway there, and already wet and muddy, so you might as well make it all the way.'

No, her mind screams. *Absolutely not. No way.*

No chance is she going to walk deeper into a dim forest in the middle of nowhere with a man she has just met. A man who is looking at her with the same intensity she imagines a fox might have when stalking a hen house.

'Um.' She licks her lips. 'I might, um, just head back?'

'Nonsense.' He grasps her arm and whirls her around.

They take off along the path in the opposite direction to where she wants to go.

Just say no. Shake his hand off. Tell him no.

But her mother's voice is too strong. *You don't want people to think you're rude, Desley. Smile for goodness sake. With looks like yours, you're going to need to rely on your personality. Keep quiet and smile.*

So, she falls into step beside him, her traitorous feet keeping in time with his.

How can she get away from him?

I will just tell him I no longer want to walk and am heading back to my room. She licks her lips. *I'll just say it.*

'Bunking off too?'

Desley's mind scatters at the sound of his voice. 'Sorry?'

'Not writing today?' He rummages in his pocket and pulls out a hand-rolled cigarette.

Only it's not.

Even she, Desley Armstrong, mother of two, knower of Taylor Swift lyrics and all the moves to the Nutbush, knows that is a joint.

He doesn't break stride as he pulls a lighter from his other pocket and ignites it. A fragrant cloud of smoke envelops him.

'Waiting for the muse to strike?'

She huffs a breath. She is ridiculous. Worse than ridiculous. He is Laurie Lawrence, twice crowned Poet Laureate, and her heart is banging so hard he must wonder what the sound is.

Fat, foolish Desley. Scared of a fellow writer.

'The muse has well and truly departed I'm afraid,' she replies.

'Ahhh.' He exhales a long plume of smoke and gestures to her with a questioning look. She shakes her head, *no*.

'Like that, is it?'

She nods unhappily.

'In my experience, the muse is a fickle and faithless slut. One you are best to chase off through sheer determination to put pen to paper. Or fingers to keyboard as the case may be.'

She'd heard it all before. All the old adages. Just keep writing, bums on seat, word counts and sprints. Timers, phones in lockboxes. Old-fashioned work ethic. None of it has worked.

Suddenly, it occurs to her that she has an incredible advantage here. An uninterrupted audience with Australia's best poet. She could ask him for advice – he must have something he could share with her. Some kind of tip, or trick, a secret he uses to switch his thinking mind off and his creative mind on?

Before she can ask, he's gesturing to an overgrown fork in the path.

'Come with me.'

He's high-stepping over tufts of knotty ferns, decaying logs lying like dead bodies. He ducks under a low-hanging branch. The canopy of trees locks tight behind him, and he's gone.

Desley stares at the trees, anxiety feathering through her. She doesn't want to go deeper into the forest, alone, with a man she's only just met. She thinks back to how he'd popped up in the forest before.

Fearless, she tells herself. Not like her.

'Come on.' His disembodied voice calls from the depths.

She picks her way through the debris of the forest floor with care, although what does it matter now? Her leggings are torn and muddy, the palms of her hands grazed and caked with dirt. After cautiously poking her head through a narrow gap of branches she releases a startled breath.

The forest gives way to a steep cliff's edge. Laurie is standing on a strip of smooth rock that protrudes from the cliff wall like a surfboard.

Beyond him is a seemingly endless canyon of craggy rock and rambling blue-green trees.

A river glitters along the bottom.

'This is incredible,' she exclaims, clambering down to join him.

He holds a hand towards her. Desley hesitates before her fear overtakes her distrust of him and she grasps it, dropping it the second she reaches the rock.

They stand in silence for a moment, each of them taking in the vista beyond. The air is crisp and cool.

Suddenly, the feeling she experienced at the balcony overlooking the stairs returns.

The soles of her feet tingle with the perverse urge to inch closer to the edge. To dangle her toes over and feel the wind whipping around her, urging her closer.

She would never jump, of course she wouldn't, but …

As if sensing her thoughts, the wind snaps through her hair.

Desley leans against the cliff face, her hands scrabbling for purchase on a tough tussock of grass, as if holding on will stop this uncontrollable feeling.

'Scared of heights?' Laurie glances at her hands, white-knuckled around the grass.

Quite the opposite. She longs to throw herself to the mercy of the wind that tunnels through their jackets. Sees herself leaping into the abyss, her body smashing against the rocks, can almost taste blood.

Telling him that would be weird, she knows that. Normal people don't clutch banisters, rails, grass, just in case their body betrays them and flings itself off a great height.

'Lovers Leap, it's called,' Laurie says, shooting her a sideways glance. 'Care to take a guess why?'

'A pair of star-crossed lovers who couldn't be together threw themselves off, preferring death over separation? Together for eternity?'

An unpleasant smile plays at the edges of his mouth. 'Of sorts. The age-old tale. He loved her, she didn't love him. So he dragged her out here and threw them both off the cliff.'

Desley blinks into the wintry air. There is a Dickinson quality to Laurie's expression. A thrill in the obscene nature of his story.

He likes to shock, she tells herself. He doesn't mean it.

'Lovely,' she says weakly.

Laurie stomps his feet against the chill, making Desley jump.

Suddenly, he lunges for her, hands closing around her wrists like irons.

Cold air floods her throat as she screams. Her feet scramble uselessly against the jagged face of the cliff. His hands clamp tighter the more she struggles.

It's like being trapped in a nightmare: nothing makes sense.

Her knees buckle, and her feet, scrabbling against the shifting rock, suddenly meet air.

She's flying.

Laurie's eyes, wide with panic, hold hers. 'Jesus Christ. Hold on,' he pants.

Something is tearing at her clothes. Her brain, already in fight or flight (isn't it always?), has completely betrayed her. Something is happening but she can't work out what.

'Stop bloody moving,' Laurie grunts.

The ground has opened up beneath her and slipped down the cliffside, nearly taking her with it.

She is lying on her stomach, legs over the ledge.

The only thing holding her to the side of the cliff is Laurie's sweaty hands around her wrists.

'Help me. Please.' A sob cracks her voice.

'I'm going to pull, and when I do, I need you to shift towards me. Dig your knees in, push. Ready?'

She nods mutely.

'One, two, three.' He grunts as he pulls.

Her knees scrabble against the rocks. The sharp edges of the ledge tear her flesh.

And then, just like that, she's on her back, staring at the grey sky. Eyes and mouth wide.

Astonishingly, the world continues on. A hawk wheels above, poised to dive bomb at any moment. Clouds shift quickly, smothering the grey sky with dense, black shapes.

There's no air, at least she can't get any. It's too thin, her lungs can't get any purchase on it.

Laurie's hand is on her shoulder, shoving her up into a sitting position.

'Up you get,' he says. 'Let's get off this ledge before we both fall in the drink, eh?'

How is he so calm? Desley nods, she'll burst into tears if she speaks. Fear has her by the throat.

She almost died.

Lurching on trembling legs, she leans hard on Laurie just as the sky cracks open.

Boom.

A slash of lightning splits the sky, forking into the mountains that crowd the horizon. Seconds later, another, and then another. The air is filled with a greenish-yellow light, the sky violently purple.

A dank, mossy smell sweeps along the wind, which is now surging towards them. Hands clasped, they half climb, half fall back to the walking path. Once they reach it, Desley places her elbows on her knees, gasping for breath.

The temperature has dropped dramatically and thunder grumbles its displeasure in the distance. They won't be able to outrun the rain.

Fog creeps along the forest floor, as thick as smoke, soaking her trainers and the bottom of her tights.

Heart racing, mouth dry, Desley punches her hands into her pockets and thumps towards the house.

I almost died. I almost died. I almost died.

As she'd hung on to Laurie, a single thought had circled her mind like that hawk.

What if I just let go of his hand?

Colette

The pipes thump as the water trickles to a stop.

Colette isn't sure what's causing the banging, and the water pressure had barely been enough to get her hair wet. She runs the threadbare towel along her body and cringes. It's soaked already. It's a long way from the 100% organic cotton Sheridan towels her housekeeper rolls and displays artfully in the under-lit marble shelves of her ensuite.

The dim light bounces off the mirror and she circles her fist around it, clearing the mist. A jolt of surprise at the colourless ghost mirrored back to her. Dabbing thick eye cream along the soft skin under her eyes, she studies herself.

Sans make-up it's easier to see how much the bruising has faded. Light stripes of custard yellow and lilac spread beneath her eyes toward her ears.

Better than the black and violet it had been.

Pumping the brush in her concealer tube, she turns her head this way and that. Will she ever get used to this new version of herself? She smooths four thin layers of flesh-coloured paint until she's camera-ready, just as the tube promises.

After running the toothbrush around her mouth, she spits into the rust-stained sink.

She needs to get her shit together.

Yesterday's travel, panic attack and too much wine had distracted her. After boldly promising to take care of the dishes at the latter end of the week – Ha! Not likely, she'd be well gone by then – she'd fallen into the stiff bed with its passionless pillow and slept like a corpse.

The room, although cold, remained dark until after seven and she was surprised to find herself awake hours later than she'd woken since … well … next topic.

Colette flips her head upside down and scrubs uselessly at her hair with the sodden towel.

Hopefully by the time she's done her face and hair, Shelly will be up and will finally respond to her emails for help.

Irritation spikes at the thought of Shelly. She's really let Colette down. Although, Colette has always known Shelly is who you call for a good time, but when the going gets tough, Shelly up and disappears, only resurfacing once certain trouble is over and everyone is ready for a good time again. Lately Colette has appreciated Shelly's lack of curiosity for anyone but herself but her abandonment now has irked her. Her own fault for relying on someone other than herself, she muses, as if she hasn't had that reinforced enough lately.

Maybe a couple of days here will prove interesting in a way that remains invisible to the naked eye but shows itself with hindsight, as clues and signposts are wont to do.

Although, she thinks as she eyes the grubby bathroom, she doubts it. The house is old and creaky, the people alternately irritating and dull. It's more likely to be a lesson learned about attending nonsense like this. Next time she needs to disappear for a bit, she'll book a first-class flight to a tropical island.

She rubs her fist on the mirror again. The bathroom window is nailed open – or closed, whichever way you look at it – allowing only an inch of fresh air. The fog that's filled the room has nowhere to go. She'll need to blow-dry her hair in her bedroom.

Stacking her products back into her make-up bag, she then tucks the pathetic towel around her armpits and unlocks the door.

'Oh.'

Eliza is standing at the door.

Her gaze runs slowly over Colette, as if cataloguing everything.

'Excuse me.' Colette takes a step to her left but Eliza doesn't move, refusing, or unable, to take the hint.

'Colette. I'm glad I caught you.'

Colette gestures with her make-up bag. 'This isn't the best time, Eliza. Can it wait?'

'It cannot, I'm afraid.'

Colette sighs. 'Not even until I'm not naked?'

Eliza stares at her towel, unshakable.

'There has been a complaint.'

Colette's heart hammers, her stomach wheeling. 'Oh?'

That little bitch, Maia.

She's gone and said something. About Lily. Shit, they won't ask her to leave, will they?

A loaded, shameful, silence presses on Colette. She can sense what's coming. Closing her eyes, she clutches her hairdryer to her chest like it's a weapon. She's been waiting for the other shoe to drop since her book hit the NYT list. Her heart in her mouth the whole time, waiting for someone to ring a clanging bell and shout. *Shame. Fraud. Liar.*

But Eliza's words when they come are not the bullets she expected.

'Someone has been spending too much time in the shower.' She lifts the saggy arm of that dreadful cardigan and spears her watch with a sharp glance. 'There is a timer in the shower. If you'd attended the induction—'

'Yes, sorry about that,' Colette says dismissively. 'I felt unwell.'

Eliza blinks once, with a reptilian speed. 'Yes, well. As I was saying, there is a timer in the shower. If you had attended the induction, you would have heard me explain that the optimum length of time for a shower is four minutes. With the number of people this house supports, we simply cannot sustain longer showers. We run on tank water.'

Colette hitches up the towel. Maybe she should let it fall, see how keen Eliza is to chat then.

'I think we'll be all right for water.' The rumble of thunder was an ominous soundtrack to her shower. 'Sounds like a lot of it is on its way.'

'The tanks,' Eliza says cryptically.

'Okay, four-minute showers. Received loud and clear.'

Colette steps forward, uncomfortably close to Eliza, who doesn't budge.

'Is there anything else?' Colette asks.

'Yes, actually there is.' Those strange grey eyes of Eliza's bore into Colette's.

Colette takes a step back.

'We are a not-for-profit organisation. Evelyn kindly donated this house, and her worldly possessions, into the custodianship of the trust, but as you can imagine, it takes a lot to ensure things run as smoothly as they do here.'

Colette thinks of the tripping fuse board, how it hung precariously on a rotting shelf, the wind that gusts through the crooked windows, the smoke curling into the room from the fireplace.

She grits her teeth. Eliza is going to ask her for money. As everyone does.

Since Trent's first appearance on *Good Morning*, money became a constant problem. How much they had vastly differed from how much everyone – family members, postman, waiters – believed they had. Of course, as Trent's popularity rose, so did his salary, but between private school fees, their yearly holiday – which could only be taken at Christmas when filming wasn't on, which meant everything was ten times more expensive and crowded than it should be – kids' extra-curricular activities, hair appointments, Pilates, eating out, the cost of merely living in Sydney, they weren't left with as much as everyone seemed to assume.

Mortgage repayments in Double Bay didn't come cheap.

But everyone had their hand out.

'Oh?' Colette isn't going to make it easy for her.

After sidestepping Eliza, she treads the shabby floorboards to her door. The heat from her shower – yup, longer than four minutes – has dissipated in the chill of the hallway and gooseflesh puckers her skin. The keratin treatment will protect most of her hair but if she doesn't get the hairdryer to her head immediately, it will dry frizzy and the curls she's battled her entire life will spring back.

'The fees paid by the writers cover meals, the use of electricity, and internet should they need it while *working*.' Eliza swallows, her Adam's apple bobbing. 'The internet is for professional use only. Small work-related tasks, or communications.'

Thunder rolls above them, sending the house into spasms.

Colette opens the door to her bedroom, done with the conversation. She isn't a patient person at the best of times, let alone in a towel, shivering in the hallway of a draughty house in the middle of winter.

'I have had the privilege of being the custodian of Rhamnusia for over twenty-five years. I know how much five writers need.'

Eliza pauses, as if for dramatic effect.

It makes Colette want to scream. Why won't she just get to the point and bugger off?

'Someone is using too much wi-fi.' Her voice is low and angry.

'Sorry?' It's so ludicrous that Colette explodes into laughter. 'Too much wi-fi?'

'The internet.'

'Yes, I understand what wi-fi is. But how can we use too much? Isn't everyone on a bundle or something nowadays?'

'Usage is already halfway to the allocated amount.' Her eyebrow lifts as if to underscore her point. 'I know what is going on.'

Somewhere below a door slams. Eliza pauses, head cocked, gaze trained on the wall behind Colette's now freezing shoulder.

Colette's stomach drops. She'd spent quite some time searching for information on Maia. Surely Eliza couldn't tell what she'd been looking at? Are there hidden cameras in the house? That's her worst fear. Every smoke alarm in every Airbnb was closely examined on holidays. Every time she and Trent left the house they were surrounded by people pretending to take selfies but secretly filming them. *Watching* them. Paparazzi had been hiding along her street since the news had leaked. She snatches the towel tighter.

'I can tell,' Eliza lowers her voice as if imparting a secret, 'that *someone* is watching videos online. Streaming.'

Colette studies Eliza's face. Is she serious? It appears she is.

Jesus wept. This place just keeps getting more bizarre.

'It isn't me.'

'No, no. I'm not accusing you.' Eliza darts a glance either side of Colette along the hallway. 'I just wondered if you had any idea who it is?'

Colette shrugs, and the towel sinks lower. 'I have no idea, Eliza. Now if you will excuse me, I really need to put some clothes on.'

Eliza's foot snaps out and stalls the door as Colette tries to close it. Colette eyeballs her foot pointedly but she doesn't move it.

Colette has always despised the way humans act when grouped together, the way they fall upon irrelevant issues like starving dogs on a bone. A draining weight has taken root inside her and nothing feels important.

Or even interesting.

Life is short, and they are all one wrong step away from oblivion.

All the to-do lists, the petty jealousies, the ambitions, the needs, the wants, the would-be-nices will one day turn to dust, along with their bones.

And there isn't a damn thing you can do about it. The good die young while the downright evil rot in cells for far longer than they ought. Like the young women who had their lives senselessly snuffed out by Jackovic. While young mothers, and teenagers who should've been planning schoolies, or which uni to choose, were instead in the waiting room of surgeons, red eyed and white knuckled. Once you'd stared down the barrel of your own mortality it was difficult to summon a single shit about fitting in. Something she'd been obsessed with her whole life.

What a waste.

Colette heaves a sigh. 'If people want to spend their time watching a video, instead of writing, then what is it to do with us? They have paid to be here, after all.'

Eliza straightens and leans away, but still doesn't move that foot. 'The nominal fee covers the—'

'I understand all that.' Colette waves her away.

'They should be writing.'

Colette nods, absurdly tired of this conversation. 'They should.' She abandons the door and places her toiletries on the bed.

Eliza hovers in the doorway. 'No one is accusing you.'

Colette raises her eyebrows.

'You understand how these places work. No, I was wondering if you could keep an ear out for us, as it were.'

Colette's eyebrows pull together. Who is this 'us' she speaks of?

'Let me know if you hear anything. These shows, movies, apps, click-clock or whatever it's called, it disrupts the peace.'

Eliza wants her to dob on her fellow writers? The cheek of it.

Although she understands there's a difference, slight as it is, between her and the others as paying guests. Her stay didn't cost her anything, but Colette knows, more than anyone, nothing is ever really free. She'll be damned before she runs around telling tales on her fellow writers.

Although.

Maia's smug face slips into her mind.

This might be the perfect opportunity to get rid of Maia before she can spill her secret.

Colette digs in her bag for her comb. Her hair has begun to dry, a fine halo of frizz forming around her head. As she tugs the comb through the damp knots her eyes snag Eliza's in the mirror.

'I'll let you know if I hear anything.'

'Good.' Eliza sweeps an assessing gaze around the room, pausing on the discarded knickers crumpled on the floor, the bra hanging over the back of the chair. The intimacy of it all is suddenly too much for Colette. She bends, the blood rushing to her head, and plugs her hair dryer in with a snap. Her thumb against the switch blasts hot air and noise into the room. Colette waves it over her chest, as it's as cold as a morgue in here. The radiator hadn't worked last night, the dial stuck permanently at zero, no matter how hard she'd tugged at it.

Eliza is still in the doorway, and an air of anticipation emanates from her. She makes a gesture with her hand to indicate she wants Colette to turn the dryer off.

Colette flicks it off, and the room falls into silence.

'I'll leave you to it.'

Finally, blessed relief, she turns to go.

'Oh, and Colette?'

Colette rolls her eyes at the wall before turning. 'Yes?'

'You should really keep your door locked.' Eliza fists those large, workman's hands. 'While you're inside *and* when you're not.'

Maia

The sky cracks open with more lightning. Rain hammers down in silver sheets that batter at the roof, and rages at the trees, their branches bending under the weight of it.

I shift. My left butt cheek is numb. I've been leaning against the table in my room, watching the courtyard for ages now. My toes tingle as they reawaken.

I'm not used to so much sitting around. Maybe I need a run.

During my first week here, when this was still nothing more than a plan, I'd run through the forest. Lungs burning, hair flying, gaze trained on the path. As in life, always on the lookout for anything that might trip me.

I'd felt unstoppable, drunk on the exhilaration of everything falling into place. The audacity it had taken to dream of it, let alone enact it.

Audacious. Tenacious. Relentless.

I am all of those words.

All the time.

From the moment I'd sent the opening eight thousand words of my first manuscript and received a deal that most only fantasised about, my hands had not stilled.

I'd gone on to write more manuscripts, won prizes, done press junket after press junket and used my eye-watering royalties to start my media company.

What started as a vehicle to amplify LGBTQIA, non-white, and disabled folx own voices is now generating advertising revenue that is four hundred and eight times what I had anticipated.

It's not about the money – although it helps – my digital space gives outliers a space to be heard, and I am proud of it.

No one would have believed it of me. Sometimes I barely believe it of myself. Onwards I push, and push, always running full speed towards the next thing. The next book is always planned and plotted before the current one is complete. But by the time I receive the edits back on my manuscript, I feel nothing towards it. After labouring over it like a difficult birth, once it's swaddled and plump, I hand it over and move on to the next thing.

Like my relationships. Not that I *do* relationships. I don't need anyone. My work fulfils me in a way no man or woman ever could.

But I have enough self-awareness to know that nothing will ever be enough. There will never be a point at which I look around and don't feel like everything could be snatched away without warning. Like a game of snakes and ladders, one wrong move and I'll be thrown back to where I'd started.

The new kid. The poor kid. Wearing someone else's clothes, living in someone else's home. So different to everyone else: no dad, a young mum dressed in handmade clothes and always covered in paint.

The image of Mama in her paint-covered dungarees at the school gate is a blade twisting in my ribs. What I wouldn't give to see her one more time.

This is the closest I can get to atonement for all those times I'd dropped her hand as we'd neared school, or laughed along with the other kids as they'd mocked our lifestyle, or when, as a teenager, I'd demanded boarding school and a 'normal life'.

Clouds glower, sinking closer and closer to the tips of the trees. Shot through with threads of black and violent green, they bring a rolling mist that shrouds everything in an otherworldly hue.

A flash of colour, and Desley appears, tension evident in the hunch of her shoulders, the bowed head. It could just be a response to the rain but something tells me it's not.

Something's happened.

I watch. There's something about Desley that makes me feel sad. She's fragile, nervous, jumpy like a kicked dog.

Her face when we'd met.

I cringe. I'd been brittle with her, unkind. Wound to a breaking point, I'd heard Eliza open the door and rushed down to the kitchen under the guise of making (another) cup of tea. Disappointment hurtled through me when I saw it wasn't him and I snapped like a dry branch.

I might feel guilty, if I had the bandwidth, but I don't. All I can think of is *him* and my plan to make him pay.

He appears, a couple of steps behind Desley. My gaze spirals between them like a sycamore seed on the breeze. Desley's shoulders, hunched, the mud caked into her tights at the knee, up her side. Laurie's rumpled clothing. His jacket is skewed, as if he's put it on in a hurry.

Rain pelts the ground around them but neither seems to notice, as if they are too caught up in their own thoughts to pay it any mind.

I press my fingers to my temples.

This morning I woke with an ache in my chest and a throbbing head that hasn't eased.

Who am I kidding? The banging in my head started when Mama died and I don't think it'll ever leave me.

The invisible thread that connected us has snapped and I'm like a shopping trolley with a dicky wheel. Round and round my thoughts go, getting murkier, more vengeful, with every loop.

Lily's article about Jackovic and his crimes sparked something in me. An obsession I can't shake. What makes a person do those things, so many times over? It's a sickness, and one I've started to understand.

I glance out the window again. The mist has thickened and covers everything as if a blanket has been rolled out. Suddenly I'm claustrophobic. There's no escape, nowhere to run.

The enormity of what I'm about to do makes me dizzy. The months of plotting and planning are all coming to their conclusion.

I can't breathe.

My hands shake as I fumble with the catch on the door.

I slink out of my room. My heart has moved up into my throat, is beating so hard I can barely swallow. The door sighs closed behind me. I tiptoe along the hallway, hugging the shadow of the wall. The air in the hallway sucks like the pull of a wave as the front door opens.

Rustling, stamping of feet. The murmur of voices. I pause, ear cocked, the flock of the wallpaper tickling my damp palm as I press against it.

'Listen—'

The crinkle of polyester, the smell of rain.

'Don't touch me.'

'I didn't mean for that ...'

'Why on earth ...'

The rain beats against the roof like a drum. I strain to hear the conversation but can only grab snippets.

'I would have never—'

'You did.'

What are they arguing about? Desley's voice is raised, trembling. What did he do?

A door opens behind me and I jump. There's nowhere to hide.

'God.' My hand against my chest.

He starts too.

It's sexy Tavis. He must be heading to the shower, his feet are bare, his long legs encased in trackpants that fit him in the most absurd way. Low on those narrow hips. A crisp white V-neck T-shirt that looks so soft that I want to stroke it. A leather bag dangles from long fingers.

'Sorry, did I scare you?'

'Yes, I nearly jumped out of my skin.' My tone is defensive, accusatory, like it's his fault I got caught sneaking and spying.

He's too gracious to say anything, though he must be thinking it. Has to be.

'Were you planning to use the bathroom?' He gestures with the wash bag.

'What? N ... no,' I stutter, scrambling for an excuse for loitering outside his door.

This is ridiculous. I don't stutter. I gave a TED Talk to over three thousand people about digital publishing and how diligent, innovative inclusion in the digital era will change the face of humanity and didn't even break a sweat.

'Cool. Do you mind if I ...' He nods toward the bathroom.

'All good. I was just ...' I move my head in a way that hopefully indicates something other than mental incapacity, but probably implies exactly that, and jog to my door.

Back in my room, I flop onto the bed and let out a frustrated sigh.

I missed my chance.

The rain hammers the roof, strikes against the windows.

The storm has arrived.

I shudder at the same time as the house at the roll of thunder, biblically loud. A harbinger of doom, bringing death and destruction.

That's not right though, because whatever bad is going to happen is already here, in this house.

I should know, because I'm the one who's set it in motion.

Nothing good will come of this.

And yet …

I can't stop.

Desley

Desley dresses carefully in the one good outfit she's packed.

A plain navy dress that skims all the right places and doesn't make her look like she's trying too hard. As if she always dresses smartly. Like Colette. Or the way Maia makes even a tracksuit look effortlessly sexy.

Desley is one of them tonight. At least, she'll give the impression of it.

She lifts the papers, with their scent of fresh ink, and looks them over again. It's been a good distraction, having to read her work to the others tonight. She hasn't been able to write a thing, how could she when she almost died? It's not her fault, no one could be expected to write after that.

She'd practically run up the stairs once she and Laurie had returned to the house and has barely left her room since. Her hands are still trembling. It wasn't Laurie's fault, but she can't shake the feeling that he had been lying in wait for her, hiding in the bushes. And it had been his suggestion to go out onto the ledge. Desley shakes her head. All the stories about Byron Jackovic and the ghost have her spooked. There is no way Laurie could have known the ledge was going to collapse beneath them. And as for him hiding in the bushes, another one of her fancies, surely.

So, to keep herself busy, she tidied up the first five pages of her current manuscript. Pointless really, but it's something to take her mind off ... all of it.

The cursor blinks at her, like a warning, on the blank page of her document.

No. She clicks it closed.

Her palms are sweaty. It's not a big deal. It's just some feedback on her work. From strangers. All much more experienced and professional than her. Poet Laureates and award winners.

That's okay. She deserves to be here too.

Her bottom lip trembles.

Not now.

Desley catches sight of her fragmented reflection in the oil-dark window. It's distorted, misshapen. Again, her exterior reflects the interior.

The storm has not let up today. Although it is only late afternoon, it is as pitch-dark as midnight. The rain hammers at the roof relentlessly. Usually she doesn't mind the rain. There's something delicious about staying inside, warm, safe and dry, during a storm but the atmosphere in this house is uncomfortable. Cold and draughty. And the house rattles like it might not withstand the barrage of rain.

She throws a glance to the stain blooming on the ceiling. Is it growing or is that her imagination? Visions of the ceiling collapsing on her as she sleeps crash into her mind.

Stop. A deep breath, another glance at her watch. She doesn't care if she's tragically early tonight, she needs to be prepared. No stumbling about, rushing, spilling things or generally making a fool of herself, as she usually does.

She presses her palm against the glacial radiator and shivers. Hopefully the lounge is warmer than her room, which is still as cold as a fridge.

Even so, sweat pools beneath her breasts and behind her knees.

Clutching the precious papers to her chest, she stumbles into the dim hallway, down the squealing stairs, and into the smoke-choked lounge. She is grateful to find it is, marginally, warmer.

Will she stand and read her opening pages, or will they sit, read silently and discuss afterwards?

She places the papers on the edge of the coffee table and stands in front of the fire, her numbed feet prickling back to life. Her gaze flicks along the spines of the books that line the wall. It seems endless, the number of writers who'd been here before her. She'd heard of the tradition of leaving a signed book behind, had even packed one of her own, but saw now how foolish that was.

The names of the other authors ... There is no way she can put her silly little book amongst these giants.

Her hand reaches into her dress pocket for her phone, feeling only air. Her heart gives a little skip. Should she go and get it? What if Scott, the kids, need something?

They had ballet lessons today, Scott might have forgotten Chloe's inhaler? Hannah doesn't love her new teacher and has been anxious and dysregulated before class. Scott goes straight to yelling, but Hannah needs a softer approach. Or something might have happened on the way to ballet. Desley pictures their car (specifically chosen due to its high safety rating) spinning out of control, hears the tinkle of glass as it shatters, sending glittering shards across her daughters' faces.

Images of her babies hooked up to wires in a sterile hospital flash through her mind.

Fat, foolish Desley.

She has time to go upstairs and give Scott a quick call. Just to check.

'Wine o'clock?' Laurie's voice, coming down the stairs.

Desley lurches into movement, not wanting to be alone with him.

Like one of those images on loop on social media, the way he'd grabbed at her, how he'd appeared out of nowhere in the forest, replays over and over in her mind.

He had saved her though, hadn't he? Without him she would've been over the side of the cliff. He's not that bad, it's all in her head. Fanciful, overactive, as usual, but she can't help the urge that overcomes her to be out of the room and away from him.

She's timed it wrong, and instead of getting out of the room before he appears, they collide in the doorway. He reaches for her, his large meaty hands gripping her forearms. It's so much like the ledge that she cries out.

'Woah there. Saved your life again.' His voice is too loud, his eyes wide and wild. She thinks of Jack Nicholson in *The Shining*.

'Where are you running off to?' Thankfully his attention span is short and his hands are off her and onto the wine bottle quickly. 'I think we deserve a drink, after our day, eh?'

He twists the cap with a violent snap.

'I was just …' Desley gestures to the door weakly. 'I have to …'

'Don't leave me down here drinking on my own.'

She doubts that's ever been an issue for him but hovers awkwardly in the doorway regardless, unable to voice her needs. He swills wine into a glass and holds it between them. He makes no attempt to come nearer. She thinks of a trapper, luring animals to their death with the promise of food.

Foolish.

She takes a halting step towards him, hand reaching for the wine. It's only when the sting of the cheap acidic wine hits her throat that she remembers she's reading her opening pages and shouldn't be drinking.

Just the one, she promises as she takes another sip. On second thoughts, she'll put it down and have a glass of water. Until after the reading.

To her horror, Laurie is riffling through the papers she's left on the table.

'What's this?' His eyebrows pull together, marking a perfect 11 between his brows.

Desley longs to snatch the paper from his hands. Not him. Not like this. Her precious words, so laboured over, and him, Poet Laureate. Twice!

Watching his eyes dart back and forth across the page is like driving past a car crash; the ambulance door is wide open, the paramedics are working and you tell yourself to keep driving, keep moving, don't look, but as you pass, your head turns and you look.

You always look.

His lip lifts and his jaw moves like he has a seed stuck in his teeth.

Finally he grunts and the paper wilts from his hand. The draught catches it and it slips to the floor.

'I'm starving,' he says. 'Must be all this healthy country air.'

There's a bag of chips next to the wine bottle and suddenly it's open, and his hand is in it, rummaging.

Desley's gaze rests on her precious words, discarded on the floor.

Should she pick it up? Would that seem rude? Passive aggressive? She doesn't want to cause offence but … her heart is a tight knot in her chest.

Maybe he simply didn't notice it had fallen to the floor.

It's as if the chips and wine being opened has rung a silent bell and summoned the rest of the household. There are footsteps and laughter along the stairs. Tavis and Colette walk in together. He's said something that makes her explode with sudden, beautiful laughter.

Desley studies her. She moves with a silent grace that makes Desley think of the ballet and her skin and hair (how on earth does she get it so glossy and swishy?) shimmer, as though she is lit from within. *How easy life must be for someone like her*, Desley thinks as a thorny feeling begins to bite at her.

'Wine?' Colette asks Laurie.

'You betcha,' he replies, sounding happy to have someone other than Desley, someone more attractive, more interesting, to talk to.

Desley takes a slug of wine. It stings like vinegar on her tongue.

Colette takes the glass from Laurie and joins Desley at the fire, the heel of her boot on Desley's discarded page. She catches Desley staring. 'Successful day?'

'Sorry?' Desley asks.

'Did you have a successful day? Word count, et cetera.'

'I ... I ...' Desley goes to take another sip of her wine but, weirdly, her glass is empty. 'I didn't write a single word,' she says, shame heating her face.

Colette shrugs. 'Some days are like that. You'll get into it tomorrow.'

How can Colette be so casual? She probably sits in her glamorous study overlooking the Sydney Harbour and writes perfect first drafts that don't need any editing. Desley read an article about a famous writer who wrote her *New York Times* bestseller in three evenings, while in a flu fog. Desley had taken three cold and flu tablets the following day but they'd only made her drowsy and she'd slept the day away instead of writing.

Laurie appears in her vision (what is it with him and popping up everywhere?) brandishing the wine bottle. She smiles gratefully as he refills her glass without asking. Saves her having to make a decision. She'll sip this one, she thinks, as she raises the glass to her mouth, drinking deeply.

'Eliza isn't coming tonight.'

Heads swivel towards Laurie. He smiles widely, loving the limelight. 'She left a note.' He nods his head towards the bureau where the chips and wine had been.

Tavis strides over and picks up a note that Desley doesn't remember seeing when she arrived in the room.

He reads it silently and nods. 'The storm is supposed to hit tonight. She's left the dinner on a low heat in the oven.'

He clutches the note to his chest. 'She's coming around. Trusting us to serve ourselves. Like adults.'

They all laugh and the heaviness in the atmosphere lifts.

'We don't have to do the reading thing, do we?' Colette groans. 'Can't we skip that crap?'

Desley's warm feeling vanishes.

'Someone's phone's ringing up there. Non-stop.'

Desley and Tavis look to the doorway.

Maia stands there, and how long she's been there is anyone's guess.

Usually the stairs betray themselves, they're so noisy, but she's arrived as quiet as a cat. The atmosphere instantly changes, becomes charged. Tavis and Laurie fall over themselves to begin waiting on her. Would she like a drink, something to eat, a warm seat?

Desley watches Colette watch the performance, resentment – jealousy? – simmering.

'Do-dum-de-dooo,' Maia sings in her husky voice.

Desley's stomach drops. That's her special ringtone for Scott.

But instead of rushing to call him back, she finds she can't summon the energy to leave. The wine is buzzing pleasantly through her veins. She's comfortable here, warm finally, and wants to read her work now. Decent feedback is difficult to get. She'll never be in a room with such talented, skilful, successful people and maybe some of that will rub off on her. Something bright and positive blooms in her chest.

Yes, yes, yes, she thinks. This will be life changing for her. An unparalleled opportunity to improve her writing, really make something of it, find out what's holding her back from success. One of the spiritual gurus she follows on Instagram did a video recently about how negative feelings block your manifestations. That must be Desley's problem. She'll need to make notes of all their feedback. Her notebook! She's left it upstairs. With her phone. Should she go up and get it?

Heat pools in her cheeks.

Her wine glass is half empty. Instead of getting her notebook or phone, it makes more sense to just sit on the couch. Just for a moment.

If she goes upstairs she won't be able to help herself. Desley knows how this goes. She'll answer or call him back and then get sucked into the vortex of parenthood and miss her opportunity here.

'How was your day?' Tavis asks, as he sits next to her.

Desley slumps into him as the sagging couch bows under the weight of two people. He's warm. She doesn't move away. It's snuggly here on the sofa. 'Not ideal. I thought …' What had she thought? A humming noise starts up in her head, like the buzzing of insects.

Enough wine.

She places the glass on the coffee table, misjudging it slightly. It slams down with a crack. She needs to eat. 'Should we do the reading and then have dinner?'

'I'm starving,' Colette declares.

Laurie winks at her. 'What big teeth you have, Grandmama. Travis isn't the only *new man* around here. I'll don my apron and help you serve, eh?'

Desley watches as her chance to read slithers away.

Maia begins to move things from the table, piling them haphazardly onto the coffee table on top of Desley's pages.

Tavis catches her eye.

'Wait, we're supposed to be doing your reading, aren't we?'

'It's fine. It doesn't matter. It's not important. We're all hungry.'

Fucking tears! She's pathetic.

'It does matter. It's only five minutes.' He rises from the couch, shooting Desley sideways. 'Come on, everyone. We'll do Desley's reading first.'

There's a pause. A lull in activity, but it's more than that. It's a hesitation as everyone considers how to get out of it without offending her.

But there is no getting out of it.

She's sitting right here. There is nowhere to hide. She wishes the ground would open up and swallow her.

'It's fine, really. I'm hungry.' To her shame her voice breaks. She's so weak. No wonder no one wants to listen to her stupid pages.

Tavis stares at her and she shifts her gaze to her nails.

'Right, everyone. Sit down. Desley is going to do her reading and then we can all pitch in and get dinner served.'

A silent groan fills the room, Desley can hear it. The groan her kids give when she asks for a kiss goodbye at the school gate, the sound of frustration, of irritation, whenever she begins to speak to Scott.

Fat, foolish Desley.

She bites down hard on her bottom lip to still its quivering. Tavis shuffles her papers and hands them out. 'Come on, sit down, sit down.'

She's piteously grateful for him. A wave of warmth strikes for his boldness, his protective energy. 'Thank you,' she whispers as he throws himself back onto the couch.

He shoots her a wink and something fizzes low in her belly. Her face flames again. What's she doing? She's too old to have feelings like that for a stranger. He's so young. And tall. Sexy. There's no denying that. That's just an objective fact. Her wine glass is empty again. Another objective fact. She blinks at it. She doesn't even remember picking it up.

'Come on then, let's get this over with.' Laurie ambles over, wine bottle in hand. He refills all their glasses before collapsing onto the other sofa, the bottle clamped phallically between his legs.

Maia hesitates at the edge of the room.

'Come on, Maia. I won't bite.' Laurie pats the cushion next to him, sending a puff of dust into the air. 'Unless you want me to.'

A strike of lightning flashes X-ray bright and then plunges it into absolute darkness. Thunder shakes the walls. The lights flicker on and they look at each other, eyes wide.

Colette springs across the room and almost throws herself onto the sofa next to Laurie. Maia places one perfectly round butt cheek on the edge of the couch arm, next to Desley. She looks away from it, wishing it wasn't quite so close. And round and perky.

'How would you like to start?' Tavis asks.

Desley's never done anything like this. Ever. These people have all been here before and probably have attended hundreds of these types of things.

How is she supposed to start?

'W – what do you think?' Scott's voice is in her head (*make a bloody decision for once*) and she cringes.

'Do you want to read out what you have and we can discuss?' Tavis's voice is melodic, gentle. Like the girls' piano teacher. Except she's a woman. And about thirty years older than Tavis.

Focus.

She nods, then downs the rest of her drink. It splashes along her chin and lands on her chest.

'Whoops.' She giggles. But the alcohol has taken the edge off any shame she'd usually feel. The giggle continues. She's having fun, that's a good start.

Fuck it.

She sucks in a breath and begins to read aloud.

She's not been able to eat today, her stomach was fluttery with nerves, a sweaty too much coffee feeling. Lifting her wrist to her upper lip, she dabs at the dampness on it.

Why is it so hot in here?

As she reads, her voice wavers. Not a lot. No one here would notice, anyway. Perhaps she's lisping – slurring – a little but that's okay. The wine has gone straight to her head, but she's holding it together and she finds herself thinking, with a surprised kind of wonder, that her writing isn't bad.

It's a strong start. Her protagonist wakes to find herself in hospital, collapsed from overwork, and is told to move home to the country to recover. She's devastated to hear her boss order her to take some time off, she loves her job, but her ex, the love of her life, still lives in that small town—

A burst of laughter cuts through her thoughts and she fumbles to a stop.

'Sorry, sorry.' Laurie smacks his hand. 'I can't help being naughty.'

Heat prickles along Desley's chest, her warm glow extinguished.

'Go on,' Tavis says kindly.

Two livid spots of colour burst high on Colette's cheeks. Her jaw is set, gaze glazed, unfocused but fixed at some point across the room. 'We're listening,' she says unconvincingly.

Desley can't remember where she was up to. The words swim on the page. 'I … uh…'

Maia is muttering. Colette hisses something in response. The room is suddenly too close, overheated.

Desley's cheeks burn and her fingers tremble as she holds the paper aloft, at arm's length so she can read it. She should have printed it in a larger font but had got so caught up in how many pages she needed to print and how she really wanted to end on a part that showed her characters' goals and motivation.

They just wander about doing nothing for most of the book.

Out of the corner of her eye she sees Colette lean over Laurie's knee towards Maia. He leans back, laughing. Her finger is aimed like a gun at Maia's face, her own contorted as she spits spiteful words.

Maia fires something back in return. They can't even be bothered to pretend to listen to Desley. Their lack of respect for her (Maia's face when she'd spat the words *ru-ro*) is like a blade in Desley's stomach. No, it's in her chest because she's finding it impossible to breathe.

The words swim on the page and suddenly Colette explodes out of her seat.

She storms to the bureau and opens another bottle of wine. Maia leans back against the couch, a satisfied expression on her face. She lifts an eyebrow as if to say – *what?*

Laurie shoots his machine gun laugh. *Ha-ha.* 'Should I get my camera out? You ladies can fight it out on film? Take your tops off if it helps. Ha-ha.'

Desley lowers the page, the useless, pointless words that she has laboured over all day. Not just today, for months. The paper shakes as she discards it on the table. The fireplace coughs a spark onto the hearth and hisses as rain falls through the chimney.

The storm is still raging outside, much like the storm raging inside.

Desley watches Maia take another sip of her wine. Not even a hint of apology about her. It's as if Desley is invisible. And she supposes she is to someone like Maia — glittering literary darling, lauded by critics and journalists. Desley is insignificant. A nobody who means nothing.

Another crash of thunder and Desley jumps, her heart banging in her chest, suddenly angry. The arrogance of her, of all of them. She is so tired of the competitiveness, the snobbery. She'd been on top of the world when she'd received her two-book deal, it had felt like a dream come true, but it quickly twisted into a nightmare. Poor reviews, low sales, and finally, the email from her publisher rejecting her second manuscript.

Why? She wants to scream at the other writers. *Why isn't it the same for you?* Desley has spent thousands of dollars on craft books, online workshops, courses but is still missing something.

Give it up, it's never going to happen for you. We need you here, with your family, taking care of the girls. I earn enough. Forget about it and stop wasting your time. Scott's familiar refrain.

But she can't. To give up on her dream of writing really would break her heart. She could never walk into a bookshop again. As it is, she has to avert her gaze from the stacks of books calling like a siren's song from the department stores. She used to spend hours in bookshops, caressing the covers of new releases and bestsellers, telling herself fiercely that one day, one day, her book will be amongst them all.

She knows better now. Whatever magic it takes — because it is magic, creating a vivid world that transports people somewhere else, with words strung together from your imagination — she just doesn't have it.

Writing had been her safe place, her only friend, no matter where she was, alone, watching other people her age drink, flirt, sunbathe topless shamelessly, she was never truly alone because she had her notebook, her words, her writing. It was her portal into another world. A world where she didn't always say the wrong thing, flush so furiously.

Writing was a lifeboat.

But she saw now the lifeboat had a leak and all the bailing out in the world wasn't going to stop her sinking.

Her dream was nothing but a silly childish fancy. Things like bestseller lists, six-figure publishing deals, author speaking events, they didn't happen to people like her. They happened to shiny, beautiful, already-rich-and-don't-need-more-money people, like this lot. They happened to people like this who were spiteful, petty and – Desley runs her gluey tongue around her lips as she stares at them – awful.

Her heart is an anvil in her chest. Packing her thoughts away in that metaphorical trunk – so full – she stands.

The storm rumbles overhead, the lights flicker again, and this time they are plunged into darkness for longer.

One, two, three.

Just when Desley thinks maybe the lights won't come back on, they stutter back to life.

'Should we get the torch? Just in case we need to go downstairs and switch the generator on?' Maia asks, but she doesn't get up.

It was obviously the royal use of the word 'we', Desley thinks caustically. Used to men falling over themselves to do things for her.

A sudden burning hatred shatters through Desley.

Her glass is empty, and her mouth tastes sharp, metallic. She presses her fingertips to her lip. Has she bitten her tongue? Is it blood or just bad wine?

The room dips and sways as she reaches for the bottle. It topples as her fingers clash against it, and it spins to the floor with a clatter.

She laughs, unembarrassed. Why should she feel embarrassed? No one notices her anyway. Fat, foolish Desley is one of the little people in a room full of giants.

'Let's eat. And I need more wine.' The room spins as she lurches from the couch and she stumbles, banging her hip hard into the arm of a chair. 'Whoopsie.' She digs her nails into the fabric of the chair to steady herself.

Tavis unfolds himself from the cushions in that way tall, lanky men do. She cranes her neck to gaze up at him.

'Are you okay?' His brow is furrowed, eyes concerned.

He's lovely. And so attractive. His eyes are a clear blue, like the sky. The unlined skin of youth. What would it be like to be with a man so attractive? She'd never been with anyone but Scott, who, back in the day, had been handsome enough, in an earnest, pale way.

Life for people like him must be so easy.

She suddenly longs to hit something, hard.

'You're very tall,' Desley says on a hiccup.

He laughs, showing a perfect straight row of gleaming white teeth.

Like the rows of bleached bone-coloured gravestones in the war cemetery.

'Come on. Come sit down and we'll get some food into you and discuss your work.'

He crooks his arm at her, like he's helping an elderly lady across the street. She can't find it in herself to be offended, she just tucks her arm through his and enjoys the feeling of his warm, firm body pressed against hers.

And why not? She's not hurting anyone if she allows these warm feelings to bloom inside her.

No matter what happens, no one could blame her. Never her.

Eliza

Eliza loves Thorne House as though it is a living, breathing thing.

Because, for her, it is. Such wonder in how the buds of plants and flowers planted by Evelyn continue to bloom and thrive under her care.

Evelyn lives on in them. The thought never fails to please Eliza.

It's painful to watch guest after guest arrive only to ignore its beauty, its uniqueness. So focused on themselves, their *precious* words, like writing a book is as worthy as curing cancer. She used to leave enough wine out for the week, but they'd drink it dry the first night, play music into the early hours, smoke cigarettes or marijuana in the bedrooms, without a thought to how long it took to air the rooms, to get the stench of their dirty secrets out of the hundred-year-old upholstery.

They're high on the freedom Rhamnusia offers. Instead of behaving like adults who've left all their responsibilities behind for a week (although, one wonders quite what responsibilities writers have. Making up imaginary characters and waffling on about them isn't real work, is it? Not like the back-breaking work of caring for a guest house) they are like unruly teenagers without parental supervision.

So they installed smoke detectors in the bedrooms, which doesn't always stop them. She turns the wi-fi router off at random intervals, has adjusted the internet speed so it crawls, creeps around tidying up after them all day so all they need to do is write.

Their ingratitude bites. Bites isn't the right word, perhaps. It grinds away at her, rubbing the same spot until she is raw. And angry.

No one notices Eliza. She's not surprised. She's invisible to the writers. So drunk on their self-importance, Eliza is merely a robot that provides them with food, wine, and a sounding board for their endless complaints. Rooms too cold in winter, too hot in summer. Airless in the spring.

Writers, it seems, are an unpleasable bunch.

As soon as they have unloaded their complaints onto Eliza, making them her problem, she is invisible again.

So, she hears it all, the secrets, the confidences, the gossip. It's amazing how small the world is. So often a writer will arrive and she'll discover this one is the one that another mentioned. This man is the lovingly devoted husband of that one, but he's in another's bed.

And that's the thing about being the custodian of a place like Rhamnusia. She can show them how to restart the switchboard, fix the boiler, make them dinner, provide them with a peaceful place to practise their craft.

But she can't make them better people.

All they have to do is follow a few small rules and offer common human decency and respect each other.

But they never do.

They just can't help themselves.

Colette

I hate her.

Maia and her obsessive carry-on about bloody Lily. As soon as they sat down to listen to Desley's story, she'd rounded on Colette. Going on and on about privilege and oppression, threatening to 'out' her.

That was the last straw. She's out of here tomorrow morning. Fuck the paparazzi. She's going home. To her expensive, clean, silent house that smells like Jo Malone candles. If it wasn't for this stupid storm she'd be out of here tonight. But there's no way she's getting out tonight. The rain is relentless, it fair thunders against the roof and hasn't eased since it started.

She sinks another glass of wine and watches as Desley stumbles into a dining chair. Her eyes are glittering stones in her flushed face. Her voice is too loud, slurred. At least the reading is over.

The room is warm and filling with smoke from the fire which is now hissing away like an angry snake. It's hard to breathe in here.

Suddenly, Colette needs to get out, to move, to be far away from this dirty, dank room.

Not just to be away from this room.

To be the Colette of a year ago.

'I'll get dinner.' Her throat is scratchy. The room is now cloudy with smoke haze. With any luck they'll all asphyxiate like the Thorne family before she returns with dinner.

Laurie drains his drink and stands. 'I'll come with you.'

She'd rather he didn't. He unsettles her. His gaze lingers a little too long, his attempts at jokes irritate her.

'Okay,' she says, because although she would never admit it, Maia's attack has rattled her and the last thing she wants is to be alone in this cold noisy house. She lets Laurie lead the way through the inky hallway into the cavernous kitchen.

It's obviously a late addition to the house; it feels separate, tacked on sloppily. They step down into it and the air cools by at least ten degrees. Like everything else in this place it's an homage to the past. A curved Formica bench top edged with stainless steel snakes around the edges of the wall, a window – black with night – takes centre stage, flanked by ancient-looking cabinets. Every door has a peeling sticker on it: GLASSES: DRINKING. PLATES: DINNER AND SIDE. POTS: COOKING. PANS: FRYING, LARGE AND SMALL.

Eliza either thinks the people that stay here are complete idiots or she has some control issues. Colette suspects it's a bit of both.

There's a note on the bench, and as Colette skims it – *dinner is in the oven on low. Ensure you turn the oven off* – Laurie opens the back door, allowing frigid air to press into the kitchen. He lights a cigarette and leans against the doorjamb.

So much for help.

Her fingers, still trembly and angry, leave greasy fingerprints on the glasses as she stacks them onto the dinner cart. How badly she wants to take the cigarette from Laurie. She can almost taste it.

Just another thing she can no longer have, can no longer do. She'd given up smoking on the day of the first CAT scan. The one that had shifted the mild uneasiness (it'll be nothing) into full blown fear and panic. A mass found in her nasal cavity, an extension of a primary intracranial mass. A tumour. For years she'd ignored the symptoms: restricted breathing, dizziness, blurred vision. All easily explained away by stress, Botox, too many wines the night before. Until it wasn't.

The tumour had turned out to be invasive and aggressive, and benign, but she'd never restarted smoking.

Fuck it, life is short. Something has to kill her.

She's about to ask Laurie for a drag when he speaks.

'So, what's all that about?' Laurie jerks his head towards the lounge.

Colette fills a glass of water from the tap and throws it back. She grimaces. It tastes like the forest, of moss and decay.

'Jealousy?'

'Hmm.' Laurie expels a plume of blue smoke into the doorway. A gust of wind blows it straight inside. It's not a cigarette. It's a joint.

'Plenty of that to go around,' he says.

'What?'

'Jealousy.'

Isn't there just?

He stares at her with a look like a search light. It's uncomfortable, she feels the light of it exposing all her secrets. She busies herself searching for tea towels to wrap around her hands before she takes the dishes from the oven.

'Art isn't easy,' he says. 'And as soon as you monetise it, the joy disappears. It becomes a competition, individual success, however you define that, becomes king, the rest of it paupers. A beautiful phrase, the feeling of finding the exact string of words that can explain the agonies of the world, the beauty of pain, the hellishness of love becomes writing to market, career trajectories, advances, bestseller lists. Envy, rage, hate, vanity, ego, backstabbing.'

He's such a parody of himself that she's forgotten he was – is – a well-respected poet. A man who, once at least, saw the world with an artist's eye. The beauty and pain of it all.

Colette nods, peeling back the layers of tinfoil, allowing the scent of the pasta to mingle with the stench of Laurie's joint and the mustiness of the kitchen, the forest, the rain.

She's taken aback by his insight. He's right. And she's participated in all of it herself.

Why is she surprised? He's probably fought his own shadowy group of haters, pitchforks raised, moving silently through social media sites, Goodreads – *This only got published because her husband is on TV! Absolute shit, not worth the paper it's printed on, used it for toilet paper!*

The silent slipping away of her old journo friends once she'd abandoned them for motherhood, only to receive slyly worded emails once *Kindred* hit *The New York Times* bestseller list (*What a surprise – didn't realise you were still writing?*).

But she hadn't been. Writing.

Over a boozy lunch Lucinda had convinced her it was time to write a book. That the post-covid world wanted something light, and she assured her that with Trent's platform and contacts she was guaranteed a bestseller. So they'd settled on *Kindred*, a 'how to' find and rebuild real connections in a fractured world. How to turn our attention to the connections that sustain us, and guide us forward, rebuilding our sense of belonging and rediscovering the strength of community after the darkest of times. Cheesy, cliché and ridiculous but the Australian public ate it up.

She reeled from event to event; bookshops, fashion nights, champagne, oysters, ignoring the constant exhaustion, and paid someone to take care of those mundane tasks that kept her from that glamorous adoration. All those pesky chores. Housework, children.

And her husband.

Someone else had been taking care of him too.

The smell of the food is suddenly stale, sickening. Colette is hurled back into the present. She dumps the last dish on the trolley.

'And then you stick us in a deserted house, nothing to do but obsess and watch each other.' He flicks the joint out into the wet night and when he turns back to her, his eyes glitter like stars in puddles of water. 'No one can claim to be surprised when it all turns to shit.' He smiles, a jerk of the lips, flash of teeth.

Colette turns back to the trolley.

'You can push that,' she orders and stalks from the room.

She is many things, but not a dinner trolley pusher.

Never that.

As soon as Colette re-enters the lounge and sees Maia's expression – so menacing – it's clear Maia knows her secret. The knowing flutters in her chest like a trapped bird. She clutches the edge of the door while the floor dissolves beneath her. Maia smiles and Colette's heart is in her mouth. Her gaze flicks to the phone in Maia's hand, and then back to the savage expression on her face.

Fuck.

Like watching a movie, Colette sees herself racing up the stairs to that bare, pathetic room, yanking her suitcase down and skipping down the steps towards a waiting car.

She would close the front door and never think of this awful place again.

But now is not a time for running away. She's done enough of that. While earlier than expected, the media announcement was due any day. This will be the first time of many, she might as well take the hits and get used to it.

'Dinner,' Laurie sings falsetto. How enjoyable the role of submissive housewife is when you can leave it behind at will.

Colette presses against the door, her eyes never leaving Maia's.

Anxiety sharpens her senses like a tool. She notices the fire burning low in the grate, twists of thick smoke uncoiling into the room, wine as red as spilled blood soaking into the tablecloth, the relentless hammering of the rain on the roof.

Maia is watching her, eyes narrowed, poised, waiting. The guillotine tremors above Colette's neck. There's nothing to do but hold her breath and wait. Laurie has managed to find another two bottles of wine somewhere and is brandishing them like a winner with a trophy.

The others cheer.

Colette walks towards the table, appetite abandoned. There is nothing to do but sit and drink, brace for the blow that's coming.

Glasses are filled, plates handed around. They've left the lasagne in the oven too long. The edges are charred, blackened, dead. As sharp and hard as a rock.

Colette grips the fork like a weapon and attacks the pasta. It's thick and sticks to her fork like glue.

The mood is jovial, as if they're a happily dysfunctional family sitting down to Sunday dinner. When they're finally silent, save for the clinking of cutlery on china, Maia speaks.

'You will never believe what my friend just sent me.'

She'd waited until she had their undivided attention. How Colette hates her. Imagines, for one thrilling moment, slapping her face, or bringing the pan of lasagne down on her head.

The mood pivots sharply. Maia's tone is gleeful, combative, prickly like poison ivy grasping at their legs. Everyone looks up warily from their plates. The overhead light flickers, the wind howls through the windows.

'Anyone fancy taking a guess? Big news.' She taps her phone awake and a picture appears of a young Maia, arms clutched around the neck of a beautiful woman.

Shame drenches Colette. She takes a deep gulp of her wine and pictures the tines of her fork sinking deep into the soft flesh of Maia's throat.

'*The Daily Times* have just broken the story that Trent Halifax is having a baby!'

Eyes shift from Maia to Colette, then to the wine glass in her hand. She raises it at them in a silent cheers, before draining it in three deep gulps.

Desley begins to laugh, a high keening noise. 'That's just ridiculous,' she cries, jabbing her fork towards Colette. 'Colette is definitely not pregnant. I look more pregnant than Colette. In fact, she thought I was.'

Colette throttles the wine bottle as she tops up her glass, gripping it like it's Maia's throat, squeezing, squeezing, squeezing.

'Trent Halifax is having a baby. With his girlfriend … Jasmine.' Maia makes a show of checking her phone, lips pursed. As if she hasn't memorised every line of the article she's about to quote. 'A twenty-six-year-old production assistant on his TV show.'

Silence slams into the room. The rain continues to pound the windows, and the windows flicker with lightning that pops like camera flashbulbs. Like the paparazzi that have followed Colette since the rumour mill began.

She swirls the cheap wine in her mouth, enjoying the acidity of it. 'It's true. Trent and I have … we are no longer …' God, she still can't bring herself to say the words. 'They're having a baby.'

'Yuk. Who would have kids at our age?' Laurie says. 'Who would have them at all? Can't stand the noisy, smelly things. Enjoy your life, darls. Good riddance to him. And good luck. He'll need it.' He gestures to her with his wine.

For a moment, Colette is grateful to him for downplaying it like this, as if it's not world-ending. Like there might be a possibility of not waking in the night, turning over questions until she fears she might go mad. How long? Would he have told her if Jasmine hadn't fallen pregnant? And the one that cuts the deepest – *How could you?*

'I'm sorry,' Desley whispers and it's her pity that almost undoes Colette.

Pity! That overweight, badly dressed, frumpy woman pities *her*? Colette-bloody-Halifax?

'Don't be sorry. Laurie is right, who the hell wants kids this late in the game? I'm not sorry, I have an excellent life. She's welcome to him.' Her tone is caustic and its falseness clangs as loud as an iron bell.

Liar, liar, liar.

'A source close to the couple share that they're thrilled by the unexpected news,' Maia reads from her phone.

'Maia.' Tavis's voice is a low warning.

'What? I just think it's interesting that perfect Colette Halifax hasn't mentioned this? But you are a liar, aren't you, Colette. Lying just comes so easily to you.'

'You're being unkind,' Desley says.

'I'm being unkind?' Maia barks a laugh. 'Me? What kind of piece of shit says he can't stand kids? But Laurie, the Poet Laureate, gets to walk around saying, and doing, whatever the hell he likes, and *I'm* unkind?'

Colette frowns at the abrupt shift of attention.

'Yes, you are unkind. You were unkind to me, you're being unkind to Colette. And now Laurie,' Desley announces with a hiccup.

Laurie relaxes into the seat with a smirk as if to say – *yeah, stop being unkind to me.*

Colette reassesses Desley. She's drunk, that's clear from the flushed face and glazed eyes, but Colette is impressed. There's hidden depths to Desley. Colette wouldn't have thought she had a speech like that in her.

Colette's gaze flicks to Tavis. He is watching the table with an incredulous expression. Perhaps he hasn't had enough wine. Colette suddenly finds it all terribly amusing. She begins to laugh, maniacally.

'Is this funny to you?' Maia rounds on her.

'Is it funny to you? You're the one who started it. You're the one that wants the drama. Silly little girl.'

Maia leaps out of her chair, knocking it to the ground. As she plants her hands on the table between them, she knocks Tavis's plate, sending lasagne hurtling through the air. It lands on the table with a sloppy sounding squelch. There's something grotesque to the sound of it.

Maia's teeth are gritted, and she's almost snarling as she screams at Colette. 'You are a liar and a fraud. Don't you dare call me little girl.'

There is something about her rage, her loss of control, that pumps steel into Colette's spine. She straightens, leans back in the chair and smiles. She knows what Maia wants, but she also knows how badly it will annoy her if she doesn't get it.

'Are you okay, Maia? Do you have some medication you need to take?' Her voice is sweet concern, like honey on a fly trap.

'Don't. Don't you act like I'm crazy. You know what you've done. You are a fraud and a phony and a liar and a fake. You—'

Whatever she was going to say is muffled into Tavis's chest. He surges from his chair, throws Maia over his shoulder and stalks from the room, closing the door with a carefulness that feels more threatening than any of Maia's screaming did.

The silence rings in Colette's ears, full and loud like the ringing after a gunshot.

'Why would she keep saying that?' Desley's voice is little more than a whisper. 'That you're a liar.'

'Because I am one.' Colette drains her glass and arches a brow at Desley. 'Aren't we all?'

Desley's gaze sinks to the table, her already flushed face reddening further.

Interesting.

Colette storms from the room, no longer hungry.

Maia

'What the hell, Maia?'

He's put me down but holds me by the arms, as if I might try to run back down to the dining room. My mind is reeling, not just from the argument.

He carried me up the stairs.

Inappropriate but there's a heat between my legs I can't deny. It was sexy.

I yank my arm from his grip and rub a hand across my face. I probably seem like a complete pyscho. I *feel* like a complete pyscho.

'Let's go somewhere and calm down. Stay away from everyone for a bit, yeah?'

I nod and walk the hallway to my door, opening it and holding it for him. He gestures for me to enter first. Manners or trying to ensure I get inside without further drama?

I cringe, suddenly seeing myself as he must.

'Do you think I'm nuts?' I squeeze my eyes shut, as I can't bear to see his expression.

He doesn't say anything. The rain has passed its baton to the wind. It pummels through the trees, moans its way through the cracks in the windows while the frames shudder.

I crack an eye and meet his gaze.

His full lips are set in a grim line, unimpressed. As he should be.

'What was all that about? You've been at her from the moment we arrived and you ruined Desley's reading. She was almost in tears.'

I scoff.

He shakes his head. 'Come on, dude.'

I bite my lip, but I double down, refuse to accept the shame. 'No one wanted to listen to Desley's writing.'

He steps back. 'Why are you being such a bitch?'

His words slap me back to myself. 'Me, the bitch? If you knew what she'd done,' I splutter, but he interrupts me, arms across his chest.

'Mocking her husband having a baby with someone else? That's not cool. I don't care what she's done but you're better than that.'

If only he knew.

I'm not. I'm really not.

I am capable of the worst things.

'You don't even know me. And if you think that you get to demand I adhere to some patriarchal ideal of a good girl who never speaks up or says a word out of place, you have another th—'

He holds up his hand. 'Don't make this about gender.'

'Everything is about gender,' I screech. 'Everything!'

'Nope. What you did down there was cruel. I couldn't care less what's going on with you and Colette but Desley is nice and she was trying to read her work.'

I blink, skewered by the sharp edge of his truth.

Collateral damage.

To be honest, I hadn't even noticed Desley, let alone thought about her. So consumed by my thoughts of taking a shot at Colette.

Why was I so bothered by her? I told myself that it was protection of Lily, that I was furious about the way she'd wielded her privilege so carelessly. How she'd used another woman's skills and talents for her own gain. How she'd made Lily beg for the money that she was owed instead of paying her a fair and equitable wage. Lily had couch-surfed, unable to pay rent while Colette's name (husband's name anyway) ensured the book that Lily had written for her soared to the top of the charts. The way that she was such a 'pick me' girl, with her perfect hair and perfectly toned body, but it wasn't about her it was about ...

Laurie.

Me.

Mama.

'My mum died.' I trail off, hoping the spaces between the words will be enough to sum up what it all means.

He doesn't move.

'I don't know why I said that. It's just, Mama being dead is the reason for everything. All of it.' My face starts to tingle in the way it does before I cry.

'Mama is dead and I never had a dad ...'

'Yeah, I'm sorry your mum died. Truly. My dad was a deadshit who wanted nothing to do with his own kids. I never even met him until ...' He stops, reconsiders and restarts. 'That sucks. It all hurts but you don't get to walk around bleeding all over everyone like that. That's not cool.'

His refusal to accept my apology stings. I expected my words to crumple him, like they do me.

'You're right. I'll apologise to Desley.' My tongue is thick in my throat.

'And Colette?'

'No. No way. That cow doesn't deserve an apology. If you knew—'

'Stop it. I don't need to know but Jesus.' He rakes his hands through his hair. It sits up boyishly and suddenly, strangely, I want to kiss him. 'If you'd seen her face when you read that article aloud. She's heartbroken.'

'What? Colette? No chance. Women like her are never heartbroken. She probably only married him for his money. She would've known what he was like from the beginning, turned a blind eye to it for the lifestyle.'

He coughs a disbelieving laugh. 'Wow, and you, a feminist.'

What the hell does that mean? How dare he – a man – critique my feminism? 'Excuse me?'

'Listen to yourself. Hanging Colette by the neck for something her husband did. He had the affair but it's *her* fault?'

'Why are you defending her?' It hits me like a truck. He fancies her. Perfect princess Colette.

'You men are all the same. Can't you see it's all fake?'

'What is?'

'She's just had a nose job and no one with that little body fat has boobs that perky. Implants for sure.'

He sighs, looking disappointed. 'That's exactly what I'm talking about.'

I fold my arms across my chest. 'What? Tell me, all-knowing oracle, please mansplain it to me.'

'Whose business is it if she has surgery? Hers. Instead of looking at her life – a middle-aged woman who gave up a successful journalism career to support her husband's career, to raise the kids, and was left for a girl barely out of high school. But instead of critiquing *his* choices, you're stringing *her* up for them.'

A banging starts up, somewhere deep in the house.

'How do you know all that?'

Those full lips clench again. He's silent for so long I think he's not going to answer. 'I asked for the names of the other guests before I came.'

'And?'

'And I researched them.'

My stomach sinks. He's stalked us? He knew who I was before he arrived. My accolades spread out on a marble table for him to dissect.

'Who?'

'Huh?'

'Who did you research?'

His pause tells me everything. 'All of you.'

'Why?'

'Because that's what people do, isn't it? They look each other up on the internet.' His eyes slip to the left.

'Do they?'

He rounds on me. 'Didn't you?'

A puff of frosty air, as gentle as if someone was standing behind me, against my neck. I shiver.

Because, of course I did.

All of them except him. He wasn't supposed to be here. There was never supposed to be a fifth guest.

'How did you get here?' I hadn't seen him arrive the morning of the changeover. I'd watched the road, desperately searching for Laurie. The carpark is empty; he hadn't arrived by car.

His eyes slide away from mine again. 'How did you?'

I'm silent until he meets my gaze again and we stare at each other, the stillness between us swelling and swirling, kicking up debris.

I can't breathe. The walls creep closer. I slap at my neck, that puff of air again. My skin prickles as if someone is behind me, staring at me.

There is no one, I tell myself.

I lick my lips. 'Tavis …'

A crack of lightning illuminates him and then nothing. The house is thrown into blackness. I hold my breath and count. Five … six … seven …

The lights shudder back on.

'Shit,' Tavis says. 'I should've got the torch when you suggested it.'

I nod, unable to speak, my tongue too big for my throat, because there in the pitch black, with my back against the wall, I could've sworn I just felt someone run their fingers along my back.

Desley

'I don't know about you, Delicious Desley, but I need something to recover from that.'

Laurie pulls a joint from his back pocket and cocks a questioning eyebrow.

Desley shakes her head.

Laurie moves to the window, cracks it slightly and lights the joint. He inhales deeply, exhaling on a sigh. His eyes are closed, his expression peaceful and suddenly she wavers.

Born sensible, her mother always said. Desley had never experimented with drugs, not even while backpacking.

Desley thinks of Scott. The sharp comments, the unkindness, the frustration with her that is always at a simmering boil. The constant wheel of laundry, tidying, driving kids, packing, organising, arranging.

What can it hurt? One night of relaxing the tight grip of responsibility?

'Actually,' she says. 'I will share some of that, after all.'

Colette

The stairs scream as she marches up them. Anger shears through her. She can hear Tavis and Maia arguing in Maia's room.

Colette imagines kicking her door open, continuing their argument.

How dare she? The powerlessness of the last couple of months, the betrayal, the fucking baby! The complete and utter destruction of her entire life. The life that she worked so hard for. Ripped from her by a young, thoughtless, selfish girl – someone just like Maia. That generation are so arrogant, so careless.

She will not let Maia destroy her, not like Jasmine did. She will end her before she gets anywhere near Colette's career. It's the only thing she has left.

No more threats of Lily. She will call a lawyer. Her hand scrabbles at the door handle of her room and her thumbnail catches, bending backward, splitting at the seam, sending a hot stab of pain through her hand.

She bangs her fist against the door. The pain feels so good that she does it again. Imagines it's Maia's head. As she pounds it becomes Jasmine, then Trent.

The muffled voices she hears in Maia's room quiet.

There's a stack of leather-bound books on the shelf in her bedroom, reproductions made to look like first editions, thick brown spines covered in gilded cursive print. She picks up the top one and hefts it in her hand. It's heavy.

She hurls it at the wall.

The spine of it bends and creases.

The thump reverberates through the room, sending her products rattling against each other drunkenly. So much money sitting there on the desk. For what? To chase the inevitable aging away, but none of it works. Nothing ever works.

Another book from the stack, in two hands this time. She brings it over her head and slams it to the floor, over and over again until she is panting with the effort.

She grips her knees, bends and sucks in a breath and screams.

Over and over, until she can't breathe.

Wiping her sleeve across her eyes, careful to avoid her nose, she catches sight of herself in the cloudy mirror.

Her eyes are wild and bright, her hair dishevelled, jaw tight, teeth clenched. She looks insane.

But she feels better. Calmer. The *release* of it. She sucks in a breath and breathes out on a groan. Everything feels clearer, she feels steadier. The fear has gone and now she is left with only an anger that fizzes and pops beneath her skin.

They know now. Everyone knows. No more hiding, jumping at the phone notifications, waiting for the ping that tells her the story has broken and her humiliation will be complete. No, not complete, truly begun – ripped open, laid bare for all to feast on.

The whispered *did you know*s? The fake *I'm so sorry*s. The pitying looks.

It all lies ahead of her.

She sinks to the bed, feeling raw. He – they – have taken everything from her and now Maia, here of all places, is threatening the one thing she has left. Her career.

In this house, in the middle of nowhere, she is stripped of everything that keeps her afloat; schedules, parties, appointments, wi-fi, noise. All the things that hold her together.

Her eyes sting and her lip quivers. There's no air.

The floodgates rip open and what she's feared all along happens.

She was terrified if she ever let one tiny tear out, like a crack in a dam she would be overcome.

And she is.

The tears are streaming and her nose is running and she can't tell what's snot and what's tears and she doesn't even care. She sinks backwards onto the bed and lets it drip into her ears and hair. Her breath is stuck in her chest.

Let go.

She can't.

Dizzy, she forces herself to take one tiny inhale, wobbly like a toddler on new walking legs, but it does the trick. *Control it, don't let it control you.*

She's so hurt. And so sad.

She gave up everything for Trent. Sacrificed so much: her job, her values, her truth. She'd denied her feelings, buried them deep. What kind of mother resented her children? A terrible one, obviously, but Colette could never understand why she and Trent couldn't share the parenting load equally. Why couldn't she keep working? Why was she expected to do it all on her own? The kids. *God.* She loved them, of course she did, but sometimes she wondered how differently her life would have been if she hadn't been expected to play the role of perfect wife and mother.

Her whole adult life she watched what she ate, what she drank, worked out, slathered herself with fake tan, bought – and wore – sexy lingerie. Spent months planning the perfect birthday gifts, for him, his mother, his sister.

And it was all for nothing.

Because what she feared had happened anyway.

While her back was turned, so briefly, so carelessly, it all came crashing down. Maybe things would have been different if she'd stood up to him more, demanded he perform his share of household tasks, around the house, with the kids, instead of letting him sleep off hangover after hangover.

That familiar, bitter resentment. All that acquiescing had got her precisely nowhere, while his career had soared from strength to strength.

She was middle-aged and alone.

Abandoned.

Too old to find love again. Men her age were all dating twenty-eight-year-olds with perky breasts and a kid-free lifestyle. Just look at Trent. The only men that wanted Colette now were old enough to be her father. Not that she cared. The thought of getting naked with a stranger made her want to howl, but Shelly assured her she needed the attention from someone else (*believe me babe, nothing like getting under someone to get over someone*).

She sat, salt water draining from her ears like a receding tide, and with it, her sense of sadness. They were right, whoever *they* were, crying was cathartic. She should have done it months ago. Thumping her pillow, she scowls at the cobwebbed ceiling.

She is still in love with Trent.

After all of it.

She hadn't cried. Prided herself on not crying. Had a list of reasons why she hated his guts. She'd gleefully hired the most expensive lawyer with Trent's money – an immaculately dressed woman whose anger at her own husband was barely repressed – and told her *I want it all*.

He'd capitulated on nearly every request, no matter how petty.

The dog? Hers. The Royal Doulton tea set his aunt had given them for their wedding, which sat in a cupboard for two decades, dusty and forgotten? Hers. The coffee table they'd spent weekends trudging through furniture stores to find, Colette ripe and round as Jasper incubated inside her? Hers.

As if giving her every material possession would redeem him in some way. Or maybe the new girlfriend couldn't bear the constant reminder of his other family through furniture another woman had chosen.

Colette hadn't been able to bear the reminders herself.

Most of it had been sold cheaply on Marketplace, stacked in the boots of other people's cars, their incredulous looks at the low asking price, the quality of the item, so thrilled with their bargain, wads of cash pressed into her hand in case she changed her mind.

She didn't want any of it.

All of it reminders of a life that had been a lie.

She won't let it happen again.

Whatever Maia thinks she's going to do, Colette will do back to her twice as bad, and three times as quick.

She springs from the bed. Maia won't know what hit her. There is no way Colette is going to take this crap from her.

This is her life, and she's not going to let someone ruin it.

She'll kill someone before she lets that happen again.

Day Three

Desley

Her tongue is too big for her mouth. And there is a small child playing drums, right inside her head.

Bang, bang, bang, it goes.

A light flickers in her right eye.

She is hungover.

In fact, she is more hungover than she has ever been in her life.

Trying to swallow is impossible, the roof of her mouth is coated with something thick. She groans and rolls to her side. The threadbare sheets are like sand on her skin.

Why are they so thin?

It comes to her slowly, like a dripping roof.

She's at Rhamnusia, on a writing retreat, not at home in her comfortable bed with its hand-painted *Live, Laugh, Love* sign on the side table, nor the faux-velvet throw cushions that drive Scott crazy. This bed has a dip she has to work not to fall into. It also smells of old fabric and something musky, decaying.

A *ping* sounds in her brain.

She lurches to sitting. This isn't her room.

Desley clutches the thin sheet to her chest. Oh God, she's not even wearing a bra. Ever since she'd read that Halle Berry wore a bra to bed, she had too. Particularly after having babies, they never quite sat as they once had and she never wanted Scott to see them unleashed (not even in the shower).

The bed wobbles as the other person in it shifts, and she squeezes her eyes together.

No.

This can't be. Her stomach churns, maybe with dread, maybe a response to the alcohol, but regardless she sucks a breath and tries to stave off the wave of nausea.

'Alright, sleeping beauty?'

Oh God. She wants to die.

'I think …' She presses her hand to her mouth. 'I think I'm going to be sick.'

He leaps out of bed and shoves a bin under her face. There is a used tissue in the bottom that wrings her stomach.

Laurie.

She is naked. In Laurie's bed.

And she has no recollection of how she got there.

The bile rises in her throat. The discarded tissue. The smell of alcohol swimming back to her from her breath in the rubbish bin. She gags, stomach clenching, but nothing comes up. Tears begin to stream.

What has she done?

There's rustling and the floorboards creak as Laurie moves to the other side of the room. She risks a look. Thankfully he's wearing underpants. There is something so grotesque about the sight of him in them, and his naked body, so unlike Scott's (the only naked man's body she's ever seen) is enough to bring the bile back to her throat. There is something raw about him, he's like a baby bird not yet grown his feathers. Curls of silver hair colour his chest, his flabby stomach hangs over the waistband of the underpants, the crotch of the undies sagging sadly. She closes her eyes against the wave of pity the sight of him in his flaccid underpants inspires.

'Laurie.' Her voice is as rusty as an unopened door. 'Did we ... did I?'

Still clutching the sheet to her chest, she fumbles under the blankets, almost crying out with relief when her hands meet the elastic of her large and practical knickers.

That laugh. *Ha-ha.* 'Don't tell me you can't remember the best orgasms of your life, love? Five of them, one after the other. You were insatiable.'

A wave of relief.

They hadn't.

One of Scott's major gripes with her. She took so long to bring to orgasm that he'd given up trying.

She and Laurie clearly hadn't done anything. So why didn't the arsehole just put her out of her misery instead of pretending otherwise?

'Are you going to ...' He gestures to the bin she's still clutching.

She shakes her head and hands it over. He takes it gingerly, springing forward and hopping back like she's contagious.

She flops back onto the meagre pillow, head screaming.

'How did I end up here?'

'That age-old story, boy meets girl, girl meets wine, fun is had.'

He struts to the desk pressed against the far wall. She gazes about.

His room is bigger, brighter than hers. The bed is a double, whereas hers is a single. One wall is all-natural light, albeit dim and grey. In the corner of the room, a ladder stretches to a closed manhole, a series of black and white photos hang on the wall opposite it.

'Why is there a ladder in your room?' That felt like the safest question to ask. There are other questions, of course, far more pressing, but that one doesn't have the potential to ruin her entire life.

He shifts his gaze to it. 'This was Evelyn's room. That's why there's so many photos of her. The ladder leads to a little balcony. Nothing more than a roof space, really. I'm surprised they've left the ladder. Workplace health and safety would not sign off on that nowadays.'

His tone is disappointed, as if the black hats at workplace health and safety have a lot to answer for.

'Look behind you.'

She tilts her head gingerly.

'You were obsessed with that last night.'

She blinks. 'What?'

'Look.' He gestures behind her again.

Desley cranes her neck, the light flickering in her eye again. The room shifts sharply. She breathes in and out slowly, eyeing the strange shapes on the wooden bedhead until they come into focus.

Evelyn.

Someone has gouged the name into the wooden headboard. Her stomach pitches. Who? Why?

'You really don't remember anything?' His question feels loaded. He licks his lips, as if he's nervous.

She closes her eyes and shakes her head. 'It's not that I don't remember *anything*.'

Images appear like the words on a magic eight ball. Colette and Maia screaming at each other over Laurie's lap. Her precious, much laboured over papers, stained with wine as red as blood, trampled on. Maia's gleeful dropping of the Trent's new baby bomb, the wine that followed her shock pronouncement.

So. Much. Wine.

The joint.

And then ... nothing.

She hates herself. What a mess she is. A writers house is supposed to be inspiring and productive. Only she could end up making such a fool of herself.

'I might write a poem about this. Whispers of betrayal echo in her wake as she beckons me in, her willing mistake, her velvet peach, just within my reach. What do you think?'

She squeezes her eyes shut. How is she going to get out of his bed without him seeing her body? There is no way she can just fling the covers back. Jesus Christ. What if someone sees her leaving? Panic begins to rumble, mingling with hot humiliation. She wants to sob.

She needs to get out of here and into a scalding shower. Although it will take some scrubbing for her to ever feel right. If she ever will.

'What would your husband think of that one? I'll title it Delicious Desley.'

Her eyes fling open. There are handprints on the ceiling near where the ladder meets the plaster. A large spider web hangs in the corner, near the ladder. It's thick, almost like wool.

What kind of spider makes a web that size? And more importantly, where is it? Like the flies caught within it, she is stuck.

Is he threatening to tell Scott that she was in his bed? Her heart bangs. Sweat breaks out along her top lip, whether from organ failure, or fear, it's too soon to tell.

She prays it's organ failure.

Her therapist had explained fight or flight to her in one of their sessions. Had called the way she froze under pressure a *normal physiological response to stress*. She simply needed to witness it and allow it to pass through. There were some hacks to override it and get her body moving again but none of them come to her now.

All she can do is blink up at the ceiling. He is going to tell Scott. Her life is ruined. She'll lose her girls. Scott always threatened if she left, he'd go for full custody. His sister is a high-flying divorce lawyer in Sydney and regales them every Christmas with horrific stories designed to show her prowess as a lawyer but they horrified Desley. Such wanton destruction of people's lives. How could people be so cruel to someone they had once loved? It baffled her.

But marriage wasn't the idyll she'd been led to believe, all too often it felt like her husband was her enemy, rather than her biggest support. And she just accepted it. Had normalised it.

'Would he agree? That you taste like a peach?'

Desley tries to calm herself by taking deep breaths but they only give her a head rush.

Something begins to spark. What *would* Scott think if someone wrote a poem for Desley? He barely noticed her. Unless it was to criticise her housekeeping or organisational skills.

Wouldn't that give him a shock? He'd never believe that someone else could find her attractive, although whatever is happening here isn't about that.

Memories flash, the joint, the buzz of the wine, the light-headed laughter, Laurie's hand on her leg, her leaning in to kiss him, wanting to feel wanted, for just a moment. Hoping that someone wanting her might make her want herself. Love herself. Throwing it all to the wind because for the briefest of moments she felt desired, even if it was by a mean-spirited bully who is now threatening to blow her life up simply because he can.

And once again she's powerless.

She sits up, ensuring the blanket covers her modesty. The room swims and pitches and she screws her eyes against it.

'Are you threatening me?' There's a tremor in her voice.

'Threatening? *Ha-ha.* No. Just …' He leans back in the chair and eyes her. 'Weighing it all up. Wondering what it's worth.'

What does she have that he wants? Surely nothing. She longs to get out of this bed, this room, but her clothes. She can't see them anywhere.

Laurie licks his lips. 'Not a threat. Merely a question, Delicious Desley.' He holds his hands up to placate her, a *who, me?* expression on his face that she doesn't believe for a moment.

It's not cold in here, she realises with a shock. From the moment she entered the house her feet have been numb. But Laurie is walking about with nothing but his undies on. Hopefully her heater is now working too. She needs a hot shower, and then to lock herself in her room and sleep for a week. Suddenly, she doesn't care if he sees her body, he's seen it already, last night. She winces, although not being able to remember eases some of the shame. The humiliation of his eyes scanning and analysing all the ways her body fails her; stretch marks, sagging skin, acne scars, caesarean scars. He can look at it all, as long as she can get out of here.

'My clothes? Where are they?'

He looks at the ceiling. 'You were pretty wild last night, who knows where they are.'

She doesn't smile.

'Come on, love, lighten up. I'm just having a laugh with you.'

No, you're not, she wants to say. *You are revelling in my humiliation. You are using my error in judgement to bully and demean me.*

And I hate you for it.

One thing she can see … Her dress is crumpled like a dead body in the corner, stockings crouching like a wounded animal. One thing she can smell … Her stomach rolls. It would serve him right if she vomited all over his bed.

She can't stay here a second longer.

Sucking in a breath, she flings back the covers and leaps upon her clothes. Keeping her face averted, she kicks her legs into the dress, yanks it up and punches her arms through. The zip sticks and makes a tearing noise as she pulls. It doesn't matter because she will never wear this dress again. How could she? It's tainted with her mistakes, her idiocy.

'Come look at this.'

Laurie is standing at the window, still in nothing but his underpants, the curtain pinched aside. Desley doesn't care what he's looking at. She needs to get out of here, away from him, before anyone sees her, but when she catches sight of his face, she is drawn to him like he's pulling an invisible string. There is wonder, genuine wonder. All the ego and dramatics have fallen away, and he's ... just an old man standing in saggy undies by a window.

'Come.'

He leans away from her and pulls the curtain with him. The sky is a powdery grey and the lawn a blanket of white.

'Oh.'

Everything is blanketed in a thick sheet of snow.

Silent flakes cover everything, lending a mysterious beauty to the otherwise shabby yard. It whirls down in silent flurries that remind Desley of the Nutcracker ballet she took the girls to at Christmas.

A set of footsteps loops underneath the zombie arms of the dead beech tree, turning on themselves so that they appear to multiply, until there are four sets of prints, not one.

A clammy feeling squeezes her.

The narrow winding laneways that led to the house will be covered in snow as well. Even if a taxi would come collect her, which she doubts, she imagines the wheels spinning uselessly on black ice, the car careening out of control, ambulances unable to reach them.

She is trapped.

Laurie shifts, stepping closer to her. She jumps as he rests his hands on her hip and pulls her against his nearly naked body.

'Don't.' She pulls herself away from him, but he hangs on tight. The scent of him turns her stomach, cigarettes and unwashed hair.

'Come on, Delicious Desley, you didn't mind last night.' His fingers are digging into the soft flesh of her hip.

The desk is blocking her escape, he has her pressed up against it, his erection jabbing into her. His sour breath is against her neck as he nuzzles her. 'Come back to bed and let's finish what we started.'

Just say no. It's just a word, just say no. But the words stick in her throat. His hands are roaming, pinching, scratching, tearing at her dress.

She hits out, connecting with his chest, and although it's not hard, it's enough to make him stagger. Darting under his arm she is at the door before he even turns around. The cold of the hallway is like a slap in the face and Desley suddenly remembers that she is very, very hungover.

Her key. Has she left it in there? She cannot go back into the room with Laurie, not after that.

The hallway is still and silent, which is what she thought she wanted but instead of being a relief (no one will see her) it is ominous, threatening (no one will see her).

She'll have to throw herself on the mercy of Colette or Maia.

No, not them.

It'll have to be Tavis.

He's the only one she can trust.

They can't know what she did. They'll all know.

A sob bursts from her as she scrabbles at the handle of her door. Can she kick it down?

Something scuttles in the corner of the hallway.

The doorhandle turns under her sweaty hand. It wasn't locked.

She is inside, turning the lock and leaning against the door with tears streaming.

That's it. She's done. She gives up. Forget this retreat, hell, forget all this writing nonsense. She wants nothing more than to be home with her girls, even Scott, back in the comfortable, rose-scented house she had come to resent.

What she'd done – or nearly done – with Laurie.

Scott would never forgive her – she'll never forgive herself.

It could ruin her life. What if he did as he threatened and told Scott? Or sent Scott that poem about her? Panic races through her. What will she do? How can she stop him?

Because stop him she must, her entire life depends on it.

She won't have her whole life ruined by one thoughtless, drunken mistake.

Colette

A thud somewhere deep in the house wakes Colette.

She lies in bed listening to the silence. How strange it is to have nothing to do, nowhere to go. The rain has finally stopped, the near constant rattle of the windows finally ceased. She listens to the hissing of the wind in the trees and picks over the bones of last night.

What a nightmare.

And yet, there's a sense of relief that the news is out. That she no longer has to conceal the truth of her life. She'll never let anyone see her pain of course, but people can make their own judgements. Men leave their wives for younger women every day, of course they do, neither her nor Trent are anything special or unique in that regard. But not everyone has to have it splashed all over the pages of newspapers and gossip sites.

She sighs, drained. The door to her marriage slammed shut with the words 'she's having a baby'. If only she could stop staring at that closed door.

After throwing back the covers Colette leaves the warm comfort of the bed and moves to the window, gasping in surprise when she yanks back the curtains at the magical scene that is displayed.

The whistling in the trees isn't wind, it's snow. With her hand against her heart, she breathes a circle of fog against the glass. Drawing a small heart, she wonders at the small unfurling of joy.

She's not going anywhere now, but also, even if someone has followed her here, they won't be camping out trying to get photos.

For the first time in a long time, she feels safe. Cocooned here in this strange, noisy, cold, groaning house.

There is the slow clap of footsteps along the hall and Colette frowns as they stop, but no door opens.

There is silence.

Her heart begins to flutter with memories of last night's ugliness. Maia?

Maia, with her threats of Lily.

Maybe it's the hangover, but the anxiety she's felt so often over these last couple of months gurgles up again, taking her by surprise. It's all so out of her control.

That's not true, there is always something she can control.

Seeking escape from the chafe of her thoughts, she looks out at the canopy of trees, now tipped with snow, and allows the peace of the vista to enclose her. Resting her head against the frost-laced window she watches the flurries of snow, the silence of it all, the peace, and she can pretend she's the only person in the world.

Movement behind her snags her gaze in the dim reflection of the window. She turns, heart racing, but there's no one there.

Silence.

'Hello?'

A rustling noise at her door. She could've sworn she saw something. Striding to the door, she pulls it open and sticks her head in the doorway just as Desley throws open her own door. Her hair is dishevelled, her eyes bloodshot, wild. Like a woman being chased by something. Colette knows that look all too well. Desley slams her door shut without saying a word.

There's something unravelled about her that makes Colette uneasy. Returning to her room, she stands in the centre of it, gazing about at the sadness of it. The sagging ceiling; drab, discoloured paint. The whole place is depressing. She can't wait to leave. But first, she has things to do.

Colette boots up her laptop, her fingers tingling with anticipation.

She needs to order a new phone, and that's easy enough to arrange.

The rest of it is what causes the tremor in her chest.

Double clicking on the video-calling software, she brings up her list of contacts. The mouse icon hovers over Shelly's name. There's no point in calling her – the snow has scuppered her chance of escaping this house now.

And with the baby news released, this hidden house in the back of the woods is the best place for her. No prying eyes in the dining room, hidden photographers lying in wait for her, furtive photos snapped and uploaded to online gossip sites. She clicks on her agent's name.

Her stomach twists. With her phone out of action there is no way to tell if Lucinda has tried to call her back or if she's been cut loose. Agents are notorious for ghosting, perhaps even invented it, leaving you to work out that the unreturned phone calls and unanswered emails meant you no longer had a working relationship, rather than laying it out for you.

The ringtone sounds followed by the electronic burp that indicates her call has been answered.

'Hey, sweets.' Lucinda is only half in the screen as she moves from her desk to close the door behind her. She's in the office. Colette blinks.

Is it a weekday? She realises she has no idea what day it is.

Time moves differently here, thick like molasses, it feels almost as if they'd gone back in time, rather than forward.

Lucinda re-enters the frame and pushes her glasses onto her head, letting her honey blonde, razor-blunt hair frame her face.

'How are you?' Judging by her tone, she's seen the announcement.

How am I? Colette looks over the top of her laptop out to the concrete-coloured sky.

'I'm … all right.' And surprisingly she is. 'I feel better now it's out there.'

Lucinda arches a perfect brow. 'Right. How's the retreat?'

'Cold.'

She's never known cold like it. Frozen gusts of wind blast through the sepulchral garden, the trees stripped back to their bones by it. It seeps through the crooked windows and covers everything she's touched with a fine layer of damp. The eerie creaking of the house that too often sounds like footsteps, even though she knows they can't be.

'That's why I'm calling, actually. There's someone here. Maia McKenzie? Seems Lily Raiti has breached the conditions of her NDA.'

Lucinda makes a sound of irritation. 'Gen Z. They kill me.'

Her gaze shifts as she jots something on the electronic notepad she's never without.

'I'll get legal to send her a cease-and-desist and we'll sue her for the money back. Leave it with me, sweets. We'll scare the shit out of her.'

Colette smiles. Speaking with Lucinda makes her feel powerful, she's awe-inspiring. There's the usual talk about a woman in the position of power.

Robot, ball breaker. Bitch.

But Colette loves having someone like her in her corner.

'Thanks, Lulu,' she says, putting on the baby voice she uses when asking people to do things for her.

'I tried calling you. Do you want to release a statement? About the midlife crisis crap?'

From the outset that's how she referred to Trent and Jasmine. *The midlife crisis crap.*

Colette couldn't imagine the unmarried Lucinda putting up with any of the shit Colette has taken from Trent over the years. Lucinda probably ate the heads off her lovers when she was done with them, like a black widow spider.

'Do I need to?'

'Control the narrative, sweets,' Lucinda says firmly.

Colette nods. 'Okay, put something out. I don't care. Just as long as it's all over and done with by the time I'm released from this retreat.'

'I'll tee you up some interviews for the end of the week? I'll get Belinda to write you a script. We'll straddle betrayed wife and independent feminist reclaiming her power.'

'Sounds good. Speaking of – I've had an idea for the next book.'

'About time.'

Colette closes her eyes to fully picture it. 'Marriage. Women rebelling against the Disney-esque lie we've been sold. How our capitalist society doesn't want to pay us for the endless load of invisible work we do, so has brainwashed us into believing that doing it for free, sacrificing ourselves, raising the children by ourselves even in a partnered situation, is the definition of *motherhood.*'

Phew.

She releases a deep breath.

Lucinda taps her electronic pen against her lip, looking doubtful. 'I don't know about that, sweets. Feels a little … bitter, given everything that's going on.'

Bitter? Damn right it's bitter. How else is she expected to feel? Trent has blown her life up, taken everything she'd worked for, and given it to another.

Without a single consequence.

'Maybe tone it down a little? People will have a definite interest in your side of the story, so maybe we focus on finding oneself outside the marital bed? How the end of your marriage was the start of your relationship with yourself? Take yourself off to New York or Greece. Write it off on tax. I'm thinking *Eat, Pray, Love* but for the social media generation. Even better if you can find a new man by the end of it. Hotter than Trent, of course.'

Of course. As if a hot man were merely a rabbit pulled from a hat.

Colette nods, irritated at Lucinda's dismissal of her idea. She's tired of this narrative, that the only power women have is to take a holiday, reinventing themselves and starting a new relationship. Finding oneself is permissible, but only if it's palatable.

'I'll get Belinda to write up a proposal and we'll send it off. See if we get any nibbles.'

'I'd like to do that. The proposal. While I'm here.' If she's going to be stuck here, she might as well get something out of it.

Lucinda tries to screw her face up, but it's so Botoxed it barely moves. But Colette knows what the narrowed eyes and pursed lips means.

'You've got a lot on at the moment, sweets. Let's strike while the iron is hot. I'll get Belinda onto it now.'

Lucinda makes moves that indicate the conversation is over.

'One more thing before you go.' Colette inhales, striving for a casual tone. 'This Maia. What do you know about her?'

Lucinda makes a noise low in her throat. 'Untouchable. Literary genius. Gen Z publishing sensation et cetera, et cetera. Youth plus beauty plus all the buzzwords equals the hottest thing since *Yellowface*. Why do you ask?'

Colette swallows. 'She's threatening me.'

'Threatening you how?' Lucinda's tone is irritatingly calm. As if there are various grades of threats, some more acceptable than others.

'With this Lily stuff.'

Lucinda hums. Something she does when considering a particularly sticky situation. Colette had heard enough of Lucinda's humming to last her a lifetime, particularly lately.

'Leave it, sweets.'

'Leave it with you?' Lucinda's catchphrase. An all-encompassing phrase that means, at the core of it, *I'll sort it out for you.*

Lucinda shakes her head, just once. Her honey blond highlights shimmer like tinsel on a Christmas tree. 'She's untouchable, sweets. Let her say whatever she wants. Don't,' a hard inflection, '*inflame* it.'

'Wow. Nice victim-shaming, Lulu.'

Lucinda lifts a shoulder, her gaze drifting to the left. Colette has received enough of her precious time. 'Pick your battles. You won't win against her.'

'What? What does that mean? She's threatening to—'

But Lucinda is nodding to someone over the top of her computer. 'Sorry, sweets, got to go. I'll let you know what the publishers come back with re the proposal. Mwah.'

She air-kisses and starts her new conversation before they even disconnect.

Colette grinds her teeth, revelling in the sound of it. There is no way she is going to allow a kid to ruin the only thing she has left.

Jasmine had taken her entire life. Now Maia is trying to take her career.

Colette slaps her laptop closed. Maia might be a *voice of a generation* but there is no way she is just going to roll over and 'not inflame the situation'.

No chance.

Just because Lucinda can't help her doesn't mean there isn't anything she can do. She will not rest until she finds something on Maia that she can use as leverage to stop her. Colette's career is all she has left.

And Maia is about to find out how dangerous a woman with nothing to lose can be.

Maia

'When did your mum ... you know.'

'Die.'

I hate euphemisms. Nonsense like *How long ago did you lose her?* As if I'd placed her down somewhere and wandered off. Or I'd parked her in the IKEA carpark and couldn't remember the bay colour or number.

As if Mama had wandered away down a winding laneway with many forks and I'd chosen the wrong ones.

Which I had, of course.

We're lying in my bed, watching the snow fall outside the window. We hadn't got around to closing the curtains last night. The lights had gone out and when they came back on, I decided to just do it. To feel. To live again, however fleeting it may be. I'd grabbed his face in my hands and kissed him.

We'd lain together under the threadbare blankets, the chill of the room ignored as we explored each other's bodies. It had taken me by surprise how badly I wanted him. All the emotions from the argument with Colette, the lead-up to seeing Laurie, Mama's death bubbled over like a boiling pot and I'd thrown myself against him, into him, into *us*.

'Six months ago. And I'm warning you now, don't you dare tell me she's looking down on me, that she's everywhere or any bullshit like that.'

He raises a brow. 'But she is, right?'

'No, Tavis. She's not. She's fucking dead. My brilliant, kind, immensely loving Mama is dead. And no one can make her less dead by offering trite platitudes.'

My reflection had been the last thing I'd seen in my mother's dark eyes. But those beautiful eyes shut, and never reopened.

My mother is dead, and the world is unsafe.

'I agree she's dead. That's not up for debate but look around. The ground beneath you shivers with the force of billions of years of cosmic collisions. Sea waters rising and falling, and rising again. Freezing, shifting, hardening. Just so you can lie right here and speak your mother back into existence. Because that's what you do every time you say her name.'

I'm silent.

Fucking poets.

This guy must get laid a lot.

'Yvonne,' I whisper.

'Yvonne. Yvonne. Yvonne,' he repeats again and again. He flips onto his back and yells her name at the ceiling. 'Look outside.' He gestures to the window. 'Tell me Yvonne isn't in every one of those magical snowflakes.' He leaps out of bed. 'Yvonne! There she is, in the ice hanging from that ancient tree. In the beat of that bird's wing. Look.' He wraps his hand around my arm and yanks me to the window. 'See that last rattling leaf on the tree? That's Yvonne.'

I think of a baby bird, tapping its way out of its shell. Following the light. Following its instinct.

Birth and death go hand in hand.

How can the world go on? Now the most extraordinary woman it has ever seen is no longer here?

'Isn't that what this is all about?' he says.

'What?'

'Writing. Isn't it all just to prove we can bear the unbearable? That we're all connected, through grief, pain, loss, birth, death, joy.'

'I can't,' I whisper. 'I can't bear it.'

He traces his finger along my eyebrow, down my cheek, across my jaw until it reaches the soft indentation behind my ear. I close my eyes, basking in his touch.

'What would your mother say?'

My lip begins to tremble. *Mama.* 'She was so wise,' I choke out. 'She would say what was right, what was true. Always. She was so expansive, so loving. Just so good.'

As good as Tavis, almost too good to be true.

And I'm the opposite.

I'm sullied by what I planned to do here.

It hits me then, and I almost fall to my knees. She would have said exactly what Tavis just said. That I could bear the unbearable.

I had clutched her skeletal hand and sobbed against her tissue-thin skin. 'How will I go on, Mama? Without you? I can't.'

'You will, my darling girl. You will keep putting one foot in front of the other. And I'll be beside you, every step of the way. In the rustle of the wind through the leaves, the waves crashing against the beach, the laughter of a small child. My love, I'll be everywhere. And one day you'll look into your own baby's eyes and there I'll be.'

I had told her, vowed, that I couldn't and wouldn't bear it.

But, as always, she'd been right.

Grief held my head underwater just long enough for me to fear I'd drown, but a bubble of oxygen would appear just as it all became too much.

My hand sweeps along Tavis's arm, tracing the hills and valleys until it comes to his hand. I weave my fingers between his. Perhaps he is an oxygen bubble.

'I have a confession.' The words stall on my lips. 'Laurie.'

Tavis's gaze is at the window, out into the garden.

'Yeah, that guy is such a dick.'

'He is.' I lick my lips, trying to find the right words.

'Ugh. Those bright orange trainers. Man.' He laughs.

My stomach clenches.

'He's such a clown.'

'Tavis.'

'The finger thing he does.' Tavis pretends to shoot her. 'So cringe.'

'Tavis.'

'Such a sleazebag as well. He's always staring at your …'

'Tavis!'

He turns puzzled eyes to me.

I pull away and walk to the door to delay having to speak the words into truth. 'I think … he's my father.'

'What? Your what?'

He slumps onto the bed heavily. It might've been comical if it wasn't for the insignificant fact that this is my life. My only remaining parent is very probably the sleazebag, the *dick*, that Tavis has just described.

Tavis looks as shocked as if I've just told him that Laurie is *his* father.

'For real?'

I shrug. 'I don't know for sure. But …'

How do I explain this next bit without coming across like a complete lunatic? It's probably impossible.

'It was always just me and Mama growing up. No father. Not really any boyfriends either. Just us. I'd asked occasionally, but she'd tell me she would always love him for giving her me, but that he wasn't very nice. We moved around a lot. And I always had the sense that we were hiding from him and then something my aunt said at Mama's funeral confirmed it. I'd asked if she knew his name. She said she didn't, but that he was some poet Mama met while on a writers retreat here. My aunt said if she ever met him, she would kill him, because he had tried to kill my mother.'

Tavis screws up his nose. 'Laurie?'

I tense, waiting for the line men deliver for each other, even when they haven't earned it.

He doesn't seem like that kind of bloke, I just can't see it, he's weird, but harmless. He's never done anything like that to me. Of course he hasn't, you're not a woman.

But thankfully he doesn't give me any of that 'not all men' crap. He closes his eyes and breathes out deeply as if considering something. When he is done with whatever that something is, he opens his eyes, strides towards me, taking my hands in his.

'Do you want to talk about it?'

I find that I do. I nod.

'I did some research. Contacted Mama's old friends. Went through photos, archives. You name it. I was a woman possessed. One name kept coming up. Alan 'Laurie' Lawrence.'

Tavis bites his lip. 'Okay. And then what?'

I hear a slow, soft drumbeat rolling through the house, not my heart, it seems to come directly from the house itself.

'Then,' I stutteringly explain, 'I called Eliza here and asked her to offer Laurie a spot.' I wince at the memory. I'd all but blackmailed, and definitely bullied, Eliza into doing it. Made promises of write-ups and free advertising, online reviews and referrals.

'That makes sense. You wanted to meet him. Get to know him. Ask him about your mum.'

I press my lips together and continue. Quieter now. 'Not exactly.'

Normally I can lay my thoughts out like a dinner setting. Each one in its rightful place, clearly marked. But I don't know how I feel about anything anymore. My emotions are messy, all over the place.

I had been so clear on what I wanted to do while I was here but when faced with it, faced with Colette, with Tavis …

Tavis.

The last thing I'd expected to find was this.

But what is this?

A man who makes me feel exposed, precious, fragile.

And I like it. I like *him*.

The anger of last night has eased and I'm left hollow.

'My research about Laurie brought up similar types of stories. Whispered accusations, people unwilling to put anything on record, but the same kinds of stories, over and over. Grooming, groping, to outright assaults, and in my mother's case, an attempted murder.'

Tavis's jaw drops and his eyes widen. 'Seriously?'

I nod. 'Seriously.' For months me and my staff have been researching, cross-referencing and are weeks away from a Weinstein-style exposé of Laurie. 'I arranged for him to be here this week. Not only to determine if he's my father, but to try and get an admission from him, or something that I can use. I'm planning to destroy him.'

Tavis doesn't say anything, just nods once, slowly.

'I told everyone it was about justice, for the women. But it's not. It's revenge. Pure and simple.'

I swallow, the admission swiftly followed by a burning shame. 'I'll let you think about that. I'm going to shower,' I say, turning away before I see what I fear I will in his eyes.

That he's seen the truth of me, the ugliness, and is repelled by it. I flee the room to the safety of the bathroom. My clothes are on the floor and I'm under the water in the space of a minute.

Standing in the airless cubicle reminds me of the mildewed greenhouse hidden in the back garden of the house we lived in for a time in Tasmania. A weird place, that house, so damp I'd wondered if I'd ever feel dry again. I'd believed fairies were in the garden, that the tiny mushrooms that would appear overnight, as if by magic, were signs of their nighttime activities.

I tip my face into the pathetic trickle of water and exhale, letting the heat blur the edges of memory. The water streams down my face, masking the world beyond the shower's hiss – until a sound slices through it.

A baby crying.

I freeze. The cry sharpens, urgent and high-pitched. My breath catches as I fumble to shut off the taps with a metallic clunk. Silence rushes in, as thick and heavy as the freezing air through the open window.

I step out onto the bathmat, where two sodden footprints bloom. I heard it. I know I heard it. But now there's nothing.

I cock my head, straining for the sound again. Nothing. Just the drip of the shower.

I've officially lost the plot.

The bathroom's freezing air seems to mock me, seeping through the inch-high crack of the nailed-open window. I lean towards it, peering out. Snow blankets the ground, muffling everything. No neighbours. No animals. Just the endless, silent white.

Maybe it was the pipes. Everything here is ancient. But in the weeks I've been here, I've never heard anything like it.

I grab my towel (the one I brought from home, I learnt my lesson last stay) and rub it briskly along my legs. A cold gust blasts through the room, swirling steam against the mirror. I shiver again, harder this time.

When I turn back to the mirror, the fog is gone, replaced by something impossible. Words, dripping with condensation, scrawled across the glass:

Leave.

Or else.

I swipe at it, my hand making a screeching noise against the glass.

Anyone could have written that, at any time. I think of the wet footprints on the bathmat. There was no way to know who would come into the shower next.

This has to be the work of Colette. I can't imagine that cream puff Desley writing spitefully on the mirror for someone to find. Tavis had been with me. Although he'd left at some stage during the night to use the bathroom. He wouldn't have written this.

It has to be Colette. The more I think about it the more certain I become. It's just the sort of crazy, spiteful, messed-up thing someone like her would do.

Pathetic. A grown woman.

All the murky feelings dug up by my conversation about Laurie and Mama thrash through me. The unsteadiness I'd felt, the wavering as to what I am capable of, gone. Replaced by rage. Tucking the towel beneath my arms I storm to her door and batter it like it's her face.

She fractures the door open and peers at me through the gap.

'Did you write something in the bathroom?'

Colette blinks, slowly. Is she medicated?

'What are you on about now?'

There's something in the way she says *now* that infuriates me.

Her words kick me right back to the school yard, where I'd been a nuisance. In the way. Didn't know the rules of the games all the others knew. Loitering at the adult entrance of the tuck shop, where the kind ladies shared food with me.

The poor girl, the new girl.

I straighten my spine. That's not true anymore. I am powerful and I will use my power to stand up for the powerless – for the small helpless girl that I once was, for the women Laurie took advantage of and for people like Lily who are used by people like Colette.

I place my hand on her door and step forward. She narrows her eyes and her knuckles whiten around the edge of the door. It quivers beneath my palm.

Her room smells expensive, scented with oils and lotions and creams that probably cost more than most people make in a week.

I think about her black eyes when she'd arrived, her perfectly straight nose. How much did things like that cost? If you don't like something, just change it.

'If you think you can intimidate me, you're wrong,' I snarl.

Colette raises her eyebrows. 'I'm not the one stropping about like a teenager, banging on people's doors. I have the right to privacy while I work and,' she smirks, 'I believe the house rules are we must not interrupt other writers while they are working.'

Something crackles between us.

'You wouldn't want to get asked to leave, would you?' Her voice is saccharine.

I bark a laugh. 'You think you could get me kicked out of here? Try it.'

She widens the gap, and steps forward, so close that I take an involuntary step backward. 'You think you can intimidate me, little girl? I've dealt with so many people like you that I can do it with my eyes closed. I'm warning you. You do not want to mess with me. I'll take you to places you can't even imagine.'

I step back once more. Her eyes are narrowed, her voice little more than a hiss. She is sparking an energy that makes me feel unsettled. Have I misjudged her? She seems … unhinged. Capable of anything.

'I will destroy you,' she spits. 'Do you hear me? If you breathe a word about Lily to anyone, I will make your life a living hell. You'll wish you'd never met me.'

Jesus. I recoil as a lump of spittle flies from her mouth and lands on my cheek.

'Do you need to take your medication, Colette?' is all I can think to say, mimicking her insult last night.

Truthfully, I'm scared.

My anger brought me to her door, but this woman is not what I was expecting.

I swallow and remind myself, *I am powerful. I won't back down*.

'Try it. But if you pull any more shit like that message in the bathroom, I'll tell the world about Lily. About what you did.'

'I don't know what you're talking about.'

There is something about the glint in her eyes.

I know with every fibre of my being that she's lying.

Desley

Desley presses her freezing fingertips to her eyelids, basking in their icy touch. Who needs eye masks and patches when you can just come to Rhamnusia and freeze your extremities? *Built-in cooling patches.* And lord knows, she needs a cooling patch today.

There's been no writing, of course, she hadn't expected there would be. The nausea finally subsided around lunchtime but Desley hadn't done much more than lie in bed and wallow in self-hatred.

Apart from some noise earlier, the house is as still as a grave. She'd dragged herself to the shower, turning the tap as hot as it could go, and stayed under the water until it had gone cold. But she still feels dirty, tainted. Her laptop glowers at her from the desk.

There is no way she can bear to stay. Not now. As soon as the snow eases, she'll book the first flight out of here. Hell, she'll hire a car and drive all the way home if that's what it takes. If her stomach hadn't been growling for the last two hours with increasing ferocity, she wouldn't bother with dinner either.

The thought of seeing Laurie brings the nausea straight back.

She isn't sure who she hates more – herself, or him.

All she can think of is getting home, back to her girls, and putting this nightmare behind her.

Heaving herself from the bed with a groan, Desley lurches to the window and stares out at the snow, which has become a full-on blizzard. She bites the inside of her cheek, trying not to cry as she watches the flurry of ice whitewash the lawn. Thick banks of snow cover the office – it looks like a gingerbread house. She is hit by a pang of regret. Her hopes had been so high for this week but nothing had gone the way she'd imagined. It's over. She has to let her dream go.

All she can do now is email her publisher, tell her there would be no book two, pay back her advance if they want it and get a boring office job working for a soulless corporation.

No thinking required.

And no feeling.

She's had enough of feelings for a lifetime. She sighs. The hangover has dulled somewhat but has left her hollowed out, like an empty jug.

Although she's been an empty jug for some time.

A gust of damp air rattles the window and lifts the hair on her nape. She shivers. A figure appears in the yard below.

A black mackintosh pulled up high, shrouding their face. A hat pulled low. Their head is faced towards the ground as if searching for something. A crumpled shape lies in the corner of the garden, under the tree.

Desley gasps and squints. It looks like the misshapen figure of a person.

The wind howls.

It can't be.

She rubs her hand against the glass, squints. It's just a log.

Fat, foolish … enough.

Turning from the window, Desley snatches her scarf from the back of the door and strides through the doorway.

Locking the door, she cocks her head. Maia's door is ajar and she can hear voices within. Peering through the crack, she's surprised to see Maia and Tavis in an embrace. They jump apart when they see her.

'Sorry. I was just wondering if you're going down to dinner?' She can't bear to face it alone. What if Laurie is down there already? She can't be alone with him. Ever.

Her memory had reappeared in humiliating flashes and although it reassured her that she and Laurie hadn't had intercourse, what she had remembered was almost worse.

The mood in Maia's room is charged. She turns defiantly towards Desley, a hand on her hip. She has a spiky energy and Desley's already jittering heart beats faster.

'We are.' Tavis gives Maia a look like he expects her to object.

She bares her teeth at Desley. 'Can't wait. Another exciting night at Rhamnusia. What delightful surprises lie in store for us tonight?'

Desley's shoulders creep up towards her ears as her stomach growls like a beast woken.

Tavis places a hand on Maia's arm and they share a look. Desley's cheeks heat. There's an intimacy between them that makes her feel like a pervert peeking through a window. She should go downstairs instead of standing here like a complete lump but she's too scared to move.

If her choices are standing here like a weirdo or encountering Laurie alone in the dining room, she would choose to stand here all night.

'I'll walk down with you?' Desley says hopefully.

Tavis strides from the room, tugging Maia through the doorway, closing the door firmly behind her. Desley fingers the key in her pocket.

Tavis hasn't locked Maia's door.

'How did the writing go today?'

Desley winces.

'That good, huh?'

'I'm giving it all up. Writing.'

The announcement feels so momentous she expects the floor to open beneath them but Tavis and Maia keep walking along the dim hallway.

Tavis pauses at the top of the stairs and gestures for Desley to go before him. Maia is already stomping her way down.

'I get it. It's not for everyone,' he says with a casualness that is breathtaking.

Not for everyone.

The words are like a blade. How badly she had wanted it to be for her. Had believed it her destiny to write. Not just to write – to be a novelist.

Writing is the beating heart of her.

Or at least she'd believed it was. To give up her dream feels like a kind of death but neither Maia nor Tavis have even blinked.

Has someone said something to them about her first book? The shame of the emails from her publisher: *This book just doesn't work, Desleigh. The first one didn't sell as well as we'd hoped. We can try to jump genres, see if that helps. Shift your positioning in the marketplace, perhaps. Have you considered writing Crime?*

Desley would never, could never, read a book again. She would curdle with jealousy every time she picked up a new release.

To stop writing would be like sawing a limb from a tree. It wouldn't grow back, but perhaps the foliage would eventually cover what was lost.

She clears her throat. 'Yes. Perhaps it's not for me.'

'What you read the other night was great though,' Tavis says as the stairs scream underfoot. 'I'd be happy to workshop with you, if you need someone to bounce ideas off? Or you can use my ChatGPT account? It's the full version. That's what I use to do all my writing. Just tell it what you want, and off it goes.'

Desley presses her lips together. He uses AI to write his poems? Isn't he successful, famous on the internet? Where's the art? The passion? She shakes her head. 'Thanks for the offer but I'm done.'

Her heart is pounding as they walk into the lounge and when Laurie turns from the fire towards them, she thinks, *I'm screwed.*

He's going to tell everyone.

Bile burns in her throat and she almost vomits on the floor right then.

'Are you all right?' Tavis is peering at her, his face contorted with concern.

He really is a lovely man. She's so grateful he's here. Without him there wouldn't be a single person offering safety. But he feels safe to her.

Desley is surprised to find she is clutching his arm so tightly her knuckles have paled. His gaze shifts from her colourless hands to Laurie, who is watching them with an air of smugness.

The wind is shrill outside, and the fireplace coughs a bellow of smoke into the room, tainted with the odour of cigarettes and decaying foliage. The snow, hardened now into ice, tap, taps on the windows.

Desley shivers.

Fear snakes through her. The hissing and popping of the fire feels like an ominous warning.

The curtains are parted and the windows beyond reflect a shiny black endlessness. She thinks back to that day in the forest. When the ledge slipped out beneath her. Laurie's hands wrapped so tightly around her wrists that his fingerprints had remained for a whole day. The feel of those same fingers against her hip as she twisted from his grasp and ran from the room.

Was it only this morning? It feels like a lifetime ago.

'Alright, Delicious Desley?' Laurie hollers from the fireplace.

She is a worm on his hook and he is going to make her squirm. She nods, gaze fixed on the table.

'Feeling better?'

She nods again.

'Dinner,' Maia exclaims. 'Eliza won't be out in this, surely?'

'She was. I saw her. Earlier.'

Three heads swivel towards Desley. 'When? Where?' Doubting tones.

'Outside. In the garden. She seemed to be looking for something,' Desley says. 'At least, I thought it was her.' She's not so sure now.

'In that?' Maia jerks a thumb at the window and the storm gathering speed beyond it.

Desley is bone-weary of being dismissed by these people. 'I'm just telling you what I saw.' Her tone is a shard of broken glass.

Maia cocks a brow and Desley is pathetically pleased to have wrong-footed her. Her and her smooth skin, tight abs and literary genius can go jump in the lake. She's done with being nice to these utterly horrible people. Not Tavis, of course. But everyone else can just bugger off.

With a rush of cold air Colette saunters in.

'Let's check the kitchen for dinner,' Maia mutters to Tavis.

'Where's the wine, Laurie Lawrence?' Colette's voice is high and hard, like she's been drinking already.

Her eyes are glassy and two spots of colour are high on her cheeks but her hair is perfect. Not a strand out of place. How does she do that?

'Got one ready for you, darling.' The wine splutters into the glass, trickling along the stem and pooling at the base. It splatters on the carpet as he hands it to her.

Desley walks towards the window and peers out into the sooty wall of darkness. Placing a hand on the cool glass she fancies she feels it tremor. The forest appears closer than ever, the inky fingers of the trees reaching towards her. There's movement out in the forest. She stares.

There *is* movement, it's not just the wind in the trees. An animal perhaps? But what would be out there, in this weather?

A flurry of snow splatters against the window and she jumps.

Her scalp prickles and the sense of being watched increases. Hands trembling, she snatches the curtains closed. She sucks in a breath, bunching the fabric in her hands.

She returns to her self-soothing mantra. *One thing she can feel* – the arctic chill of the weather outside. *One thing she can smell* – it smells dead in here. Old. Musty. As if something died in here, long ago, and the smell never left. She thinks then of the Thorne family. How one, or all, had perhaps stood in this exact spot and stared out the window into the dark forest on the night they died. Perhaps they too were thinking about their unrealised dreams and aspirations. How terrified Evelyn must have been when she returned home to find them all dead.

And Byron Jackovic. The monstrosities he committed out there in that very forest. The horror all those women must have felt as they realised their lives would end amongst the trees. As fanciful as she is, Desley cannot imagine the horror of it.

And yet. Here they are.

Life moves on. The house fills with writers, time and time again. People stack their books on the shelves, scratch names into the headboard of the furniture.

Because that can't have been anything other than a sick joke played by an unstable artist.

But suddenly, she's not so sure. What if all the creaks and shuffling noises, the disturbed air and flickering lights, really are Evelyn Thorne?

'Desley?'

Laurie and Colette are staring at her with matching expressions that tell her they have been trying to get her attention for some time. Laurie extends a glass of wine, so full it might overflow at the slightest nudge. Her mouth waters unpleasantly at the sight. 'No,' she coughs and shakes her head.

Laurie releases that fake belly laugh. 'Overdid it last night, didn't you, Delicious Desley.' He winks at her and slurps at the wine to empty it some before placing it on the table. 'More for us, Colette.'

He pronounces it with an affected French accent. Cool-ett.

'I wonder what's for dinner tonight,' Colette says as she sinks into the armchair. She gulps her wine. 'I can't believe Eliza made it. The snow looks knee-high.'

Desley frowns. That much?

Laurie's eyes burn and linger on her, like the pain of fingertips on a hot pot.

'Do you think it will clear by tomorrow? Only, I need to get back. One of my girls …' She trails off. What kind of mother fakes an illness upon her child?

One that drank too much and woke up in a stranger's bed.

Shame claws through her. She is a terrible person. Eyes screwed shut, she wishes she could lose herself in the wine tonight. Drink it all away, make it not true.

By tomorrow evening she needs to be enclosed back in her life, in her house. She needs to be Mum again. Mrs Armstrong. The energy of motherhood and its demands closing around her like Harry Potter's invisibility cloak.

'I doubt you'll get back tomorrow.' Colette speaks to Desley but her gaze is trained on the murky reflection of the mirror above the fireplace.

It shows the hallway. Empty.

'I'm leaving too,' Colette announces. 'As *fun* as this has been, I want to get back to civilisation.'

It hasn't been fun for anyone, Desley thinks. It's been awful. Thank God this will be her last night. She takes no pleasure in the thought that it cannot get any worse than last night.

'Consider this our last supper then,' Laurie says, thrusting his glass towards his mouth.

Desley looks away. Her fingers tremble. Trains are safe to use in the snow, aren't they? She sees steel twisting like ribbon, sparks exploding in violent bursts of orange, scorched metal, shattered glass. Her mouth is dry and she taps her thumb to rid her mind of the horror show it replays over and over.

Laurie refills Colette's glass with a leer and Desley shivers. How awful he seems to her now. How predatory his gaze is. How unkind his eyes are. It's difficult to think that this is the same man who saved her life when the cliff had collapsed beneath her.

Her mind flicks back to those terrifying moments in his room, like a clock stuck at midnight. Over and over it jolts back to her. Had she overreacted? If she'd just said no, would he have released her and allowed her to leave the room? The fear feels a world away now but at the time ... She pushes her chair back.

'I need water.'

The coolness of the hallway is satisfying after the close heat of the dining room and she is grateful for the dim lighting. Her cheeks are burning. Her heart skitters.

He won't say anything, surely. But she's not sure at all.

She rounds the corner and almost collides with Maia.

'Watch out.' Maia is holding a large carving knife.

It seems to pulse between them.

The dim light of the bare overhead bulb flickers, catching the metal. Maia hasn't lowered it.

'What are you doing?' Desley can't catch her breath.

The alcohol has ruined her nervous system. She's frantic, on edge. Maia hadn't meant to almost stab her, but why hasn't she lowered the knife? Or apologised. Instead she's gazing blindly at it, as if hypnotised.

As if also wondering why she is holding a large knife. She lifts her gaze and fixes it on the dining-room door.

Her dark eyes are bottomless pits.

'Maia? Are you alright, hun?'

Maia shakes herself from her trance and locks eyes with Desley. 'You're nice, Desley.' It doesn't sound like a compliment. 'Too nice for this crap.' She stabs the knife towards the dining room. 'For them.' Her voice is venomous.

'They're okay,' Desley says, backing away slowly.

'No, they're not. They are egotistical, maniacal, liars, thieves.'

'Thieves?' Desley asks, confused – why would she call them thieves?

There is clattering from the kitchen. Situations like this are beyond Desley. She never knows the right thing to say or do, particularly under pressure and this … this is pressure.

The pressure that has been building for days, too big for the house to hold.

Boom.

The lights flicker off and Desley holds her breath. When the lights stutter back on Maia seems to have come to her senses. She shakes her head.

'Maia?' Tavis calls from the kitchen. 'I need help with this curry. The pot is hot.'

Desley bites her lip and stares at the lights. Are they dimmer? They feel dimmer. She sniffs the air; is that the acrid smell of melting plastic, metal? The air feels heavy, laden with the weight of impending disaster, thick and suffocating as she struggles to catch her breath. She imagines she hears the hiss of electricity as the fuse box blows, spitting sparks, smoke curling into every dark corner of the house.

'I need a glass of water.' She is suddenly desperately thirsty. As if every cell in her body has withered away.

She will take the torch off the wall on her way back into the kitchen. The storm is gathering, she doesn't want to have to come and find it in the dark if they lose electricity.

'Here, give me the knife, go and get a glass of wine,' Desley says matter-of-factly.

Maia hands the knife over, eyes blank. As soon as Desley's hand curls around it, she takes off towards the kitchen. Her slippers scuff along the ancient lino and she skids to a stop in the doorway. Tavis glances up with a look of surprise.

His eyebrows furrow when he catches sight of the knife. 'Where did you get that?' he says, gesturing with his eyes to the knife in her hand.

'Maia had it ... I was ... water.'

She dumps the knife into the sink, fingers hovering over it. She turns the tap on full. Running her wrists under the freezing water feels so good, all those dehydrated cells spring back to life, and she twists her face beneath it.

Sucking at the stream of water, gulping, letting it run along her cheek into her ear. She can't get enough. When she has finished, she rights herself, panting as if having run a great distance.

Tavis is staring at her, mouth open, eyes wide. Water runs along her face and drips onto her collar.

Does she seem crazy? Well, she'd just caught Maia wandering the hall with a carving knife, so if Desley is crazy (and she might well be) she certainly isn't the *craziest* of them here.

'Right,' she says brightly. 'What's for dinner? I'm starving.' Her stomach growls on cue.

Tavis lifts a corner of his mouth and, thankfully, chooses to move on without comment.

A clap of thunder and a flash of light.

Desley screws her eyes shut. The storm sounds so close.

They'll be safe here. She taps her thumb. That feels like a lie. She doesn't feel safe.

'Can you hold the bowl still? I need two hands for the pot.'

Tavis tips a thick, fragrant curry into a bone-white bowl. There's a crack on the edge of it, like a chipped tooth. Thick chunks of chicken plop into the liquid with a disturbing sound.

It smells amazing.

The wind whistles at the window. A scratch along the glass. Her heart pounds. It's just a branch, she tells herself, but she can't look.

'Tavis.' Desley's voice trembles.

He runs a spatula around the base of the pan, collecting the thick paste of curry. 'Mmm?'

She pauses, unsure of what she really wants to say. 'I'm leaving tomorrow. And I wanted to say … thanks for being so kind to me.'

He looks up from the pot, solemn. 'You're leaving?'

'I can't bear it.'

His lips curl slightly, as if her words have reminded him of something.

'I don't think you'll be leaving tomorrow, unless this weather clears up.'

Another gust of wind whistles through the window and the lace curtain lifts, as if a hand hides behind it.

Desley catches sight of herself in the window. Her eyes are bloodshot, her skin is grey, her hair wild. She looks as shit as she feels.

And she feels particularly shit.

'I don't think the weather can be as bad as last night. That was the worst of it, surely.'

Another thought chases her words.

They haven't seen the worst of it yet.

Colette

Maia blows into the dining room, like the snowy gusts beating against the window. Her eyes are filament bright.

'Hello again, Colette,' she says.

Colette's ready for her this time. She leans back in her seat. The alcohol has mixed with the Xanax she took earlier, dulling some of the fizzing that has electrified her since she overheard that conversation earlier this afternoon.

Checkmate, bitch. She eyes Maia darkly. *This ends tonight.*

'I am so looking forward to tonight. Barb's special chicken curry,' Maia says.

There's an edge to her tone. A murky sense that she could do or say anything. Laurie, for once, says nothing. The room is silent.

The proverbial calm before the storm.

Enjoy it while it lasts, Colette thinks. *Because I am the storm.*

Desley and Tavis enter with dinner, the trolley rattling like a train. Colette studies Maia as she flirts with Tavis, smiling and laughing, filling her plate with the fragrant chicken curry, like she doesn't have a care in the world.

Like she isn't trying to ruin Colette's life.

Rage rumbles to a boil.

Dishes are filled, rice passed from hand to hand, glasses topped up. Colette sips her wine, waiting for her moment. It needs to be right, to be perfect.

Thunder smashes against lightning, so quick it's almost impossible to tell them apart. The house quivers as wind shrieks through the trees, batters the house, strikes at the windows.

Finally, everyone is seated, and silence falls like snow over the table.

Colette smiles. 'I heard something interesting today. In the hallway. Your door was open.'

Maia's gaze stabs towards Laurie. For the first time since Colette encountered her on the stairs, Maia looks her age.

I've got you.

Like a hound hunting a fox, Colette has hold and will not let go.

'What I heard is just *so* interesting.' She mimics Maia's words from last night.

'Girls,' Laurie starts. 'Can we just—'

'Wait.' Colette holds up a finger. Her voice is loud, strong. 'Since the very minute I arrived, Maia has been threatening me.'

'What?' Maia yells, all wide eyes and faux indignation.

'You have.' Colette points an accusing finger in her direction.

The curtains shiver.

'I will not tolerate it. You're lucky my phone is broken or I would have got my lawyer involved. You'll be lucky if I don't sue the arse off you.'

Maia scoffs. 'What a rich person thing to say. Sue me for what? Telling the truth?'

'Maia is threatening to tell people I used a ghostwriter to write *Kindred*. Big deal. Plenty of authors use ghostwriters. I paid market rates and I'm sorry if Lily didn't get paid in a timely manner, but that isn't my fault. The business side of things is handled by my agent.'

'Cop-out,' Maia coughs into her glass.

Colette licks her lips. 'But what about you? What about your little secret?'

Maia kicks the chair out from under her and stands, eyes flaring. 'You fucking psycho. Don't you dare.'

'Why not, Maia? Why are you the only one that gets to push people around and spill their secrets like wine?'

Maia is leaning across the table, looking as if she might make a grab for her. Colette leans back, just a little.

'What I heard was shocking. But so interesting. I just can't wait to tell everyone; I am as excited as you were to share my news.'

The room is silent, even the wind has paused, waiting. Then it comes out, fast, the words falling like ice.

'Turns out Laurie here is your dad, isn't he?'

Her words ricochet around the room.

A crack of thunder shakes the house, the wind, as if channelling the energy in the room, begins to surge. Something – sleet? Snow? – strikes the window.

Is there a noun for synchronised intakes of breath? A slice, a sledge, a sheath, a deceit? All of them here, in this room, tonight.

It's a slam-dunk. The atmosphere in the room becomes electric.

The air dips, swells and then smashes to pieces.

Laurie groans, a long low noise that sounds like the words *not another*. His gaze flicks from Maia's breasts to her face and he swallows hard. 'No offence but I don't think so, love.'

Maia rounds on him. 'It's true. My mother is Yvonne McKenzie.'

The truth is there, right in the fullness of their lips, such a particular shape, the slant of their eyes. It's true.

Laurie downs the remainder of his wine. 'I don't know any Yvonne.'

Maia is fumbling in her pocket. 'Oh no, you don't. You don't get to pretend not to know Yvonne. You spent too long pretending not to know her. To know me.'

'Look, love, people say all sorts of things when you're famous. You get used to it, but this ... you can't be my daughter.'

'Why not?'

'I just ... it's not ... I don't remember any Yvonne.'

It's as if Maia is a balloon and Laurie a pin. The air deflates from her slowly and she slumps into her chair.

'She was an artist. A poet, but not like you. She just embodied art in every form. You met here, in the late nineties.'

Laurie pulls a rueful face. 'I've lived a life, honey,' he says by way of explanation.

Maia huffs a pained laugh. 'You've lived a life.'

Laurie rubs his hand across his eyes. When he lifts them, there's a light in them. Colette smirks.

He's lying. He knows exactly who Yvonne is. Dirty dog. He can't even be honest now.

'Here.' Maia slaps her phone on the table.

A photo of a smiling woman, a brightly patterned scarf tied around her head, shines brightly on the screen.

Laurie stares at the photo, unspeaking.

The silence stretches on.

'Anyone for water?' Desley asks, as bright as broken glass. She refills her own and offers the jug around.

'No?' Desley confirms, as they all gulp their wine. She drains her glass like she wishes it was alcohol.

'Of course Laurie knows who Yvonne is. He's not stupid, no matter how he acts,' Colette says.

His head jerks towards her. 'Hey.'

Colette pauses, waits until she has everyone's attention. Then drops her bomb. 'The real question is, how much is me keeping silent about this, about your *story*, worth to you?'

Maia's mouth drops open. 'Are you blackmailing me?'

'Yes. I am. Keep your mouth shut about Lily and I won't go to the papers. I heard *everything* you told Tavis.'

It's been years but Colette can still remember the desperate rush to be the one to break a story. The frantic, secretive calls, codewords and long late nights working to pull it all together, get it through legal and keep it all under wraps until the editor gave the go-ahead. Colette knows how hard Maia and her team will have worked, how badly they won't want to lose the scoop.

'Hey,' Laurie exclaims again, indignant, as if he can't believe he's been dragged into such petty drama. Men like him can never take responsibility.

Trent: *Honestly, Coll, I didn't mean for this to happen.* Like having sex with and impregnating a girl half his age was a slip. Like socks on a tiled floor. *Whoops, there I go, having sex with someone who's not my wife of almost twenty years.*

Laurie's rubbing his face again and when he lifts his head, he's aged a decade. He studies Maia hard and seems to come to some kind of decision.

'I don't know what you want from me, but you're not going to get it.' His voice is hard and low. 'You're not my kid. She might've told you that, or maybe two plus two equals five, but—' He shakes his head. 'I'll tell you what I told the others. You're not going to get anything from me. Clear?'

Colette looks at Laurie, surprised at his response. She'd assumed he would be shocked, anyone would be, but he's angry.

Not angry.

Furious.

Maia's face crumples.

'Maybe we should talk about this later.' Tavis, as always, the voice of reason.

'Nothing to talk about, *Travis*.' Laurie slops a spoonful of chicken curry into his bowl. It splatters onto the tablecloth, the sauce blooming like blood. There is a barely repressed violence in his movements.

'It's just ...' Maia starts.

'No,' Laurie yells. He bangs his hand on the table, shaking the crockery, startling them all.

'Mate, calm down.' Tavis again.

'Keep out of it, boy.' Laurie's face is flushed. 'You don't know your arse from your elbow.'

Like a slap, it occurs to Colette she's opened the lid of a box and she is going to be very, *very* sorry.

'Mate—'

'Shut up,' Laurie roars. 'I'm not your mate.'

Tavis stands. 'No, you're not my mate. I wouldn't be mates with someone like you. You're scum. I won't have you speaking to Maia like that.'

Colette meets Desley's wide eyes with raised eyebrows. What's with the knight in shining armour performance?

Laurie is shovelling the chicken curry into his mouth like a starving man while the rest of them sit in stunned silence. More for something to do, rather than hunger, Colette gets up and transfers the vegetarian curry from the dinner trolley to the table.

The fire fizzes and crackles and thick smoke corkscrews into the room. Tavis is still standing.

Maia gives Colette a hard look. She smiles widely in return.

'You think this is funny?'

'Funny, no. What you deserve? Yes.'

'There's something wrong with you. No wonder your husband left you.'

And that's it.

THE FINAL CHAPTER

The final straw.

Those words. The words that pursue her like a ghost. That appear in the deepest, darkest hours. When sleep eludes her, they run round and round in her head. Like an animal digging its burrow those thoughts invade everything she does. That she is faulty, defective in some way. She couldn't keep her marriage together. Everywhere she looks, she's surrounded by happy families and there is something wrong with her because she couldn't keep her husband.

The rage and hurt bubble over and Colette is no longer in control of herself.

She picks up her glass of wine and jerks it towards Maia.

The cherry-red liquid arcs through the air in slow motion. There's something beautiful about it, for a moment at least, as it hangs like mercury between them.

The moment is gone as soon as it connects with Maia's face. It stains her white top, swelling and spreading, drips along her chin.

Desley shrieks as it splatters along her cheek.

A roll of thunder shakes the house.

Maia wipes the wine from her eyes. Her head lifts slowly and when their gazes meet, Colette experiences a shiver of fear. The lights flicker as a crack of lightning pierces the silence.

Maia leaps towards Colette, sending crockery and cutlery flying. Her hands are clawed, like branches of the zombie tree in the front garden.

'I'm going to kill you,' she screams.

Colette leaps from her chair, knocking it to the floor.

Desley begins to shriek, a high-pitched animal sound.

Tavis body-blocks Colette, shielding her physically from Maia.

Even with the table and Tavis between them, Colette has no doubt it will come to blows. The tension between them is a road train sliding on black ice.

It is inevitable.

Part of her wants it, the release of it. Somewhere to put all this anger.

'I'm going to fucking kill you, Colette.' Maia's voice is low, dangerous.

'I'll kill you first,' Colette bites back.

'Come on, girlies, unless there's a jelly pit, I'm not interested in watching women fight.'

'Shut up, dick,' Tavis growls.

'You shut up,' Laurie mutters into his wine glass.

Colette doesn't take her eyes from Maia. Like a dangerous dog, she's clearly calculating the best way to get to Colette.

'Colette.' Tavis shoves her with his hip. 'I suggest you go to your room. Now.'

She hesitates, not willing to back down. Why should she be the one to leave the room? Why shouldn't Maia be the one to leave, tail between her legs?

She catches Maia's murderous look, the wine now as purple as a bruise. The colour reminds her of the bruising beneath her eyes. Her nose. She can't risk it.

'With pleasure.'

Fuck this. She's absolutely had it. Done.

As she reaches the doorway, she turns and points a finger at Maia. 'You're going to regret messing with me.'

Her shoes are hammers on the stairs. She kicks her door open, revelling in the thump of it against the wall. She slams it closed, so hard the window rattles.

She strikes the lock closed. And the clunk of the lock turning unlocks something in her. A great trembling shakes her. Ripping her clothes from hangers, she shoves them into her suitcase without a thought for their care instructions or delicate fabric. Sweeping her products from the bookcase into her make-up bag, she throws it into the case and slams the lid.

Her fingers tremble as she opens her laptop and boots it up. She has enough shit to deal with without putting up with this bunch of idiots and their problems. She plans to get out of here at first light. She'll take the first train back to Sydney, and get very, very drunk in the privacy of her own home.

She would rather face paparazzi camped outside her door than put up with these losers.

A few unflattering photos to go with what she's certain will be unflattering articles. Aren't they always? A grainy photo, a bad angle of the abandoned wife, the thinly veiled misogyny – *no wonder he left her, she let herself go!* – with a smaller, more flattering photo of the young mistress. An article full of nothingness and nonsense handily delivered by some nameless 'friend of the couple'.

The storm outside gains momentum. As the wind shifts from moan to scream, ice-cold air flutes through the room.

No connection.

She opens another tab, tries another web address.

No connection.

Her heart sinks. She needs to get out of here.

Another roll of thunder punches through the house, and she knows.

She won't be leaving. At least not now.

Usually being inside on a stormy night is comforting, but this feels ominous. Like calamity is merely moments away – a tree might collapse on the house, or parts of the roof will peel off, like an onion. The house groans with the effort to stay strong against the barrage.

Something bangs lower in the house, causing the boards to shudder under her feet. The rasp of tin against iron. It sounds too much like a screaming woman.

There's someone in the hallway.

Colette's skin prickles. She blinks, her vision impaired by the negative image of her laptop screen seared onto her lids.

The hallway is creaky, the house is old, it's unavoidable. You can walk as quietly as you like, but the floor betrays.

Colette cocks her head.

Creeping from her chair, she presses her ear against the doorjamb. Muffled footsteps. Her hands tingle. A door clicks open and closed again.

Colette waits for a beat, listening in the silence. Although it's not silent. It's blowing a bloody gale. The windows shudder, the house creaks and groans. Something bangs.

A crack of lightning so loud it feels biblical. Fire and brimstone. It's immediately followed by a roll of thunder that rattles the house. The wind dies down with the speed of a magician pulling a tablecloth from under crockery.

Then an explosion, and the lights go out.

Maia

Colette has left the room, but the energy remains the same. It's dangerous. Hot enough to burn. Thick enough to choke.

'I've met a lot of people, darls. You can't expect me to remember all their names,' Laurie says, but the muscle spasm in his jaw, the tiny flicker in his eye tells me he remembers. I open the microphone app and press record, clicking the screen off before placing the phone on the table between us.

'What about the ones you sexually assault?'

It is as if a tree has crashed through the roof. The silence is as dense and dank as the forest beyond the window. A draught shudders the ill-fitting windows, and there it is, the moist, rotting smell of the decaying foliage beyond.

Strangely, he looks at Desley. Why is he looking at her? He should be looking at me.

His expression is pained as he shakes his head. 'Look, all right. It was a bad joke.' He holds his hands up, as if surrendering. 'Nothing happened, okay? I was joking.'

He's still talking to Desley. I don't understand.

Tavis shifts suddenly, thrusting his chair back so quickly it clatters to the floor. The noise shakes everyone awake and the tableau, so frozen, restarts.

Tavis moves to the bureau and the wine bottles. Desley is shaking her head, swaying in her seat, looking shell-shocked.

'My mother—'

'Look, I don't know what your problem is. I don't know your mother. I've apologised to Desley. I put my hand up. It was a bad joke. No harm done, eh?'

Desley's face is ashen, waxy and, shit, she's crying. The words I'd spoken had been on repeat so long in my mind that I hadn't paid any attention to anything else going on around me. I rewind memories, like pressing a button on a remote.

He and Desley on the walk. Her furtive looks, her terrified jump whenever I came upon her in the hall. The red eyes, the strange half conversations.

'What did you do?' My hands are on the table between us, I'm leaning towards him, yelling it now. 'What did you do to Desley?'

A small white bubble of spit flies between us, landing on his face. Finally he recoils.

Not at anything he's done, but instead at what I've done. By being touched by something he's done.

Me.

Tavis's hand is pressing down on my shoulder, lightly, but enough to bring me to the seat. Tavis sloshes wine in my glass with such haste it spills on the tablecloth.

'What did he do?' I ask Desley.

She's making a small keening sound, like a wounded animal. Tears have worn a track through her flaky make-up. Underneath her skin is lush, peach. I wish I could tell her that. That she doesn't need to hide the truth of herself.

Her hand is cold under mine. I rub my thumb along hers. 'What did he do?'

'Nothing.' She raises her eyebrows. 'You heard him. A bad joke. That's me, isn't it?' She pulls her hand away. 'That's how you all see me.'

She grabs my drink, downs it and snatches the bottle from Tavis's hand. 'Fat, foolish Desley.'

I shake my head. 'That's not how we—'

'Don't lie!' She's screaming. It's her turn to rage now but at who? My head is jumbled and I can't think straight. There are too many threads and I can't grab hold of one. But I have the feeling that when I do, the whole sad tapestry is going to pull apart.

'You didn't even offer me,' she thumps her chest, 'the respect to listen to my opening chapter. Five minutes. I'm not important enough, am I? Not literary enough for you. Not famous enough for you.'

'Des.' Tavis speaks low and soft. 'I loved your chapter.'

Her fingers play with the stem of the glass. 'You're the only one who bothered to listen.'

My stomach sinks. She's right. I'd been so focused on Laurie, on Colette, on finding ways to destroy them that I hadn't given her a thought.

'I'm sorry,' I say, shaking my head. 'I'm so sorry, you're right. I had some things going on. It wasn't about you at all. Believe me.'

Desley shakes her head and takes another deep drink of my wine. 'It never is.'

It's all been about me. And the father-sized hole in my life.

I'd never wanted to know him. Until Mama died, I couldn't have cared less.

But losing her untethered me, set me adrift in a way that made me want to destroy him, like I was destroyed.

Knowing Laurie, finding out about him at least, is important to me. Like some part of my history will be revealed to me.

Questions at the doctors; Family history? Unknown.

Is my second toe being longer than my first a common family trait?

Is my dust allergy something he shares? My avoidant nature, my love of words, of flowers, of dogs.

Are these parts of his DNA laddering through me?

I stare at him. He stares at the chicken flesh on his plate.

How can he not want to know? How can he not want to know me? His own daughter.

'You're a terrible person,' I tell him.

He nods wearily. 'Not the first time I've heard that. Won't be the last.' There's no fire in his voice. He doesn't care what I think of him.

'I know what you did.'

His head jerks up, bloodshot eyes wary.

'You tried to kill my mother.'

His eyes harden. Another roll of thunder, a clap of lightning following instantly. The rain pounds on the roof, so loud it's almost impossible to hear myself.

I list the facts as I know them. 'In March 1997 you met Yvonne McKenzie here at Rhamnusia. You began a relationship and lived at an artists' colony called Montségur. When she told you she was pregnant with me, you pressured her to have an abortion. When she refused, you set the building you lived in on fire, hoping to kill her.'

He says nothing. Just stares at me flatly.

'I have five women willing to go on record to state you sexually assaulted them. It looks like I can add Desley to the list.' Another guess, but it adds up.

Desley gasps.

Laurie scoffs, eyebrows pulled together. 'Bullshit.'

'I was drunk and then that joint ...' Desley wails. 'I shouldn't have. And you ... you ...' She's really sobbing now.

I circle my hand on her back.

She inhales on a hiccup. 'You threatened to tell my husband about it.'

Laurie scoffs again. 'Piss off. You should be so lucky. You're not my type, sweetheart.' He eyes her cruelly. 'I prefer my sausages not so overstuffed.'

'That's enough.' Tavis stands. 'Go back to your room.'

Laurie leans back in his chair. 'You don't get to tell me what to do, Travis. You're not so squeaky clean, are you? You're not the only one who can throw out accusations.'

What does he mean? I spin a glance to Tavis. He is staring at Laurie with a look of disgust that I share. I wrap my arm around Desley's shaking shoulder, overcome with hatred. How could we share the same blood? The thought makes me want to open a vein.

'You know what, Laurie? You're right. You're not my father. I don't care if you donated your sperm and played some part in my creation. You are not my father. I don't want anything to do with you. You make me sick.'

'You're just like her,' he says, and there's a cruelty to the lift of his lip. 'Think the world owes you something.'

He's describing himself, not me or Mama. I smirk. 'Everything I have, I earned. I have never had to force myself on anyone, Laurie. They give themselves to me willingly.'

'Fuck you,' he shouts. He winds his arm back like he's going to hit me.

Tavis leaps between us, grabs Laurie's arm and twists it behind his back. The glass falls from Laurie's other hand as he hits out at Tavis.

But Tavis is quicker, younger, more sober, and manoeuvres out of the way easily.

'Come on.' Laurie is breathing heavily. 'Young punk. You want to make out you're some big hero? Sticking up for your whore?'

I can see it's a step too far for Tavis. His expression changes, his face contorting with fury, and he yanks on Laurie's arm with force. 'Get the fuck out of here.'

Laurie stumbles. A frisson of fear shoots through me, this is quickly getting out of control.

'Come on, Travis!' Laurie yells. 'Are you scared? I'll show you what a real man looks like, not some tight-jean-wearing pansy boy.'

Tavis hauls him to the doorway, a muscle in his jaw pulsing. Laurie's feet drag along the floor behind, ruching up the rug.

Desley buries her face into my shoulder.

Tavis grunts, twisting Laurie's arm again as he shoves him through the doorway. Laurie sprawls on the floor, hitting his shoulder against the stand.

'What the hell is wrong with you?' Tavis asks, arms spread wide. 'Seriously. You've just been given an opportunity to right some wrongs. Repent. You don't deserve her fucking forgiveness, after all you've done. You're lucky she didn't stab you in your sleep. Despite you, you piece of shit, your daughter is incredible. You don't deserve her.'

I can't help the thrill of pleasure his words give me.

He thinks I'm incredible.

Desley gives me a little squeeze. Laurie lurches to his feet and throws a punch. Tavis ducks it, and grabs Laurie.

They stumble, clutching each other in a strange dance, and land against the door, exploding into the chill night.

Tavis remains upright, banging heavily into the wall, but Laurie slips down the steps, and tumbles into the snow.

'Had enough, old man?' Tavis asks, as Laurie struggles to get upright.

If it wasn't so pathetic, it would be sad, watching Laurie scramble about in the snow.

But I feel nothing.

The wind is brutally cold and stings my face with tiny pieces of ice that feel like glass.

Tavis only has socks on, no shoes or boots.

'Leave him, Tav,' I call. 'He's not worth it.'

And he's not. He's a miserable, disgusting old man. That's all the closure I need. There is nothing he can tell me about Mama, or their time together.

I don't want anything more to do with him.

Tavis and Laurie face each other, circling warily in the snow. Their feet leave deep marks.

Laurie is swaying slightly. From the ankle-high snow, or is he really drunk? It's hard to tell with him.

The hairs on my arms prickle, not just from the cold. Drunk or not, there is a sense of menace about Laurie. A dangerous edge.

'Be careful,' I call.

Tavis glances at me and Laurie takes advantage of his distraction, charging at him, low and hard like a front rower's tackle. Tavis staggers but doesn't fall. He grips Laurie by the shoulders and wrenches him off, sending him heavily onto his back in the snow. A gasp of air is shaken from him as he lands, and he lies there, stunned.

'You're a dick,' Tavis shoots at him as he strides towards us and steps inside, shaking his head. 'Let's get inside. I'm bloody freezing.'

The bottom of his pants and socks are sodden and he's shivering. His lips are almost as blue as his eyes.

I'm tempted to lock Laurie out, but I just push the door closed and leave it off the latch. Maybe the cold air will sober him up.

Tavis sniffs and wipes his sleeve across his nose, which has started to drip. 'Damn, I'm cold.'

Desley springs into mum mode. 'Take off your damp clothes and jump into a hot shower before you catch the death of yourself.'

I freeze. 'Mama used to say that.'

'Did she?' Desley rolls her eyes. 'I cringe every time I hear myself say it. I'm turning into my mother. Don't we all?'

I smile. 'I hope so. Come on.' I take Tavis's hand in mine – it's ice cold. 'Let's go up before Laurie comes back in. Let's just leave it. Leave him.'

We walk up the stairs together, pausing at Desley's door. 'I'll meet you in my room,' I say to Tavis. When he's out of earshot, I grip Desley's arm.

'Are you okay? Do you want to go to the police?'

She stares at my hand on her arm, like she's never been touched before. 'He didn't … We didn't. He … couldn't. Like he said, I'm not his type.'

She looks so anguished that my heart hurts. I don't know what to say. 'What he said back there, it's not okay. You're better than him. He's a piece of shit. At the very least, let's meet with Eliza tomorrow and ask to have him sent home. He needs to be held accountable for his behaviour.'

She smiles and pats my hand. 'Really. It's fine. It's my own fault. I shouldn't have drunk so much. And …' She grimaces. 'Turns out middle age isn't the best time to start experimenting with drugs. I just want to go home myself, please just let it go.'

I study her. She seems to genuinely want to put it all behind her. Imagine being the type of person who lets things go, instead of burning the world down when wronged, I think with a little wonder. That's not for me, and I don't want it for her, but it's not my place to push it.

'Let me know if you change your mind.'

I'll be asking Eliza to have him kicked out even if Desley does leave. After everything that's gone on tonight, we can't all stay here together.

I say goodbye to Desley. Tavis is standing at my desk looking over my book notes. I slide my hand up his back and he turns to me. 'Come back to my room? After your shower?'

He nods. I squeal as he cups my face with his hands. He smiles, sliding his icy fingers along my neck.

'Sorry,' he says, resting his forehead against mine. 'That wasn't cool. I've been trying to work on my temper lately … sometimes I …' He closes his eyes. 'The things that guy's done, y'know? He's a piece of shit.'

I slide my hands under his shirt and he shivers. 'You don't have anything to apologise for. It's him. The saddest part is Desley is blaming herself. But I'm not going to let him get away with it.'

'He sucks,' Tavis says.

I nod. 'He sucks.'

'I should go out and end him.'

I smile. 'Not worth it.'

'Sorry if he is your dad.' Tavis says.

He is my father, I feel that in some secret part of my body. A deep biological recognition pulses within me.

But the need to know him, to understand him and why he did the things he did no longer burns inside me. There is just no understanding some people. He's done terrible things because he's a terrible person. No amount of 'understanding his motivations' will change that.

Tavis presses his lips against mine, hard and brief. 'I have to get in this shower.'

'Okay, okay, go,' I say, kissing him back hard as I push him out my door.

My room is silent and bleak. I fumble with the radiator. The dial is open all the way but the heat it emits is pathetic and my time outside has chilled me. Parking my butt on the top, I sit and release a sigh.

What a night.

My head is spinning. It feels impossible to come back from this.

The ugliness with Colette that spewed over into everything and everyone.

Desley's face when she shared what Laurie had done.

The fight between him and Tavis.

We all have secrets.

A spark of lightning and the lights flicker.

I'd been obsessed, I can see that now, with the idea of coming here and confronting Laurie, to have him confess. Now, having met him, I can't ever see that happening. He will never confess or take accountability. I see now that the takedown article I'd planned to humiliate him with will achieve nothing because that man feels nothing, and there isn't a thing I can say to him to make him feel sorry for what he did.

A door opens along the hall and I pause, ear cocked. The rumble of the pipes tells me the shower is still on, so it isn't Tavis.

I spring up and place my hand against the door to keep it closed. My skin prickles as footsteps sound along the hallway. I press my ear against the door. A soft, even rasp of breath comes from the other side. Surely my imagination but I turn the lock.

A beat, and then the soft sound of feet along the runner. I turn the lock again and snatch the door open but there is nothing, no one in the hallway.

But the air is unsettled, as if something has just disturbed it.

I close the door again, my heart pounding. This house is beginning to get to me. The walls seem closer than they were yesterday, their angles tilting just slightly wrong. The noises it makes are all wrong. Just an old house moving in strong weather, I tell myself, but the thought doesn't settle the trembling in my chest. The room feels too still, the kind of stillness that makes you second-guess the spaces behind doors and under beds.

'I'm not afraid of you,' I whisper into the darkness, listening for some kind of response, and I swear I feel the door shiver beneath my hand.

* * *

My head is on Tavis's shoulder, my leg tucked between his. It all fits perfectly. Tugging the blanket under my chin, I sigh a contented breath.

'I like this,' I say, my voice muffled into his skin, which is slick with sweat.

And I do. Which surprises me. Cuddling after sex usually gives me the ick. Get it in and get out is my motto but not with Tavis.

He strokes my hair.

'Are you cold?' I ask.

He shakes his head. It's pitch black but I feel it.

He came straight to my room from the shower, skin puckering in the cold, that threadbare towel low on his hips, and I'd never felt desire like it. Like a punch to the gut, I needed him, immediately.

We still haven't talked about what happened with Laurie.

'Thank you for tonight,' I say. 'With Laurie.'

'Man. So embarrassing.'

I laugh. 'For sure. But not for you. Him.'

'Yeah, totally for him. It's just not a good look, y'know? I don't subscribe to all that alpha-toxic-battering-each-other-because-we're-blokes sort of crap.'

'He does.'

'Yeah, but he's ancient. And a dickhead.'

Outside, the storm is raging but the bed is warm, his body is comforting.

We'll need to talk about things in the cold light of day, of course, but right now I'm content with this. A spark of lightning hits and is followed so quickly by thunder that I jump.

'Christ,' Tavis whispers.

Then an explosion, and the lights go out.

Desley

Desley is shaking when she gets into her room.

Anger, fear.

But underneath is something else.

She'd spoken up. Had pulled what he'd done into the light and, by doing so, unlocked something in herself.

She feels lighter, stronger.

Tavis and Maia's response when she told them what Laurie had done changed something for her. Her self doubt had her believing that she'd made it up, or blown it out of proportion. Laurie's mocking voice in her head sneering, '... not my type.'

She'd told Maia she wants to let it go but as she's blindly snatching clothes from hangers and shoving them into her suitcase, rage rips through her, setting her fingertips on fire.

How degrading that had been. To hear Laurie speaking out her worst, deepest insecurities. That she was too ugly, too overweight for anyone to find attractive. The mantra that dogged her every footstep since teenage-hood, when she'd noticed all the girls around her growing taller, while she just seemed to grow wider. It was why she'd ended up with Scott, truth be told. She was just so piteously grateful to be shown some attention.

Even now, when the attention had waned (unless it was turned on her flaws and failings), she still couldn't bear to admit that she wanted to leave him because otherwise she would die alone, she just knew it. He would move on with some tight-bodied, younger woman, maybe even have more children like Colette's husband, take her daughters, the only thing truly of any value in her life, and move on. Discard her like an apple core left to shrivel away in the sun. She swipes at the tears collecting on her chin.

She hates Laurie so much.

Every negative thought she's ever had about herself, every nasty comment ever made to her was reflected back to her tonight in his cruelty.

He humiliated her tonight in the dining room. Like she was some kind of desperate fool. Rage flaps and flails inside her, overtaking the shock and grief of what she'd done. She had kissed him, but he had kissed her back. Had wanted to kiss her. Had groaned in her ear and called her *Delicious Desley*. Made her feel wanted for a moment. Only to have her stupid (stupid!) behaviour thrown back at her like that in front of all the other writers. She wants to smash something, to rip and tear and punch and kick.

Anything for a physical release from the fury that blossoms behind her ribs.

Sometimes, she wishes she were braver. That she could get the people that hurt her back. That the thread that connected her to others, that made her care so much about what others thought of her, didn't exist.

That, like a wart, she could excise it with a sharp blade.

Her fingers tingle.

She stares at the wall that divides her room from Laurie's and thinks about the Thorne family who died here.

She could do with a sharp blade now.

Instead she grabs a notebook and begins to write.

Desley's room is above the front door of the house. Sandwiched between Laurie and Colette, she feels squeezed by their energy.

Fearful and intimidated by them both, she can't wait to be back in her laundry detergent–scented bed, with its myriad cushions, and the balmy Queensland weather.

She signs her name with a flourish. Her therapist said writing things down could help organise anxious thoughts, and it has.

The page is filled with black writing.

I hate you, I hate you, I hate you, I hate you.

The words cover the entire page. In some spots she's pressed so hard the pen has ripped a gash, right through to the pages below.

It's childish, and quite possibly, okay definitely, unstable. But she feels better for it. The rage that had electrified her has shifted from a raging river to a mere trickle. She still feels shame, but the writing has brought a sense of peace as well. She is leaving tomorrow, back to real life.

Back to her babies. And Scott.

Just thinking his name brings a twist of nausea. He's texted tonight, but she hasn't had the energy, after everything that happened downstairs earlier, to read them.

There will be enough time to deal with the recriminations and demands. On her return home, she's sure they'll tumble into their old habits soon enough.

Scott will sulk for a few days, punish her with the silent treatment (hopefully – his idea of *talking* is to harangue her until she feels she might go mad). She's learned over the years that all he wants is an apology, but lately he accuses her of offering insincere apologies (correct) and deflecting from the issue at hand (also, correct). But mostly because the 'issue at hand' is how Scott feels hard done by.

A concept she just can't accept.

She struggles to understand how a man, who arrives home from work at six thirty, if not later, to find his two daughters ferried from school to scheduled activity and back, fed a homemade nutritious dinner (one egg allergy, one extreme distrust of anything green), showered, homework done, hair brushed or deloused, combed, plaited, clean and gorgeous in that way freshly washed children off to bed are, can possibly feel hard done by.

Lately she'd been working her way through Scott's favourite Ottolenghi recipes, all of which have a minimum of seventy-four steps and require a solid five-hour hands-on cooking time. Which he eats silently, leaves his dirty plate on the bench, stretches and retires to the couch to watch television while she cleans up.

No wonder she's knackered.

This time at Rhamnusia has shown her just how invisible she and her needs have become. Maybe when she gets home, she'll make a list of things Scott can do around the house and they'll make some changes.

She closes her notebook with a sharp slap and cocks her head at a sound.

The front door opening?

Of course it isn't, she tells herself with a shake of her head.

The shriek of the creaky stair, footsteps.

Then an explosion, and the lights go out.

Day Four

Colette

Colette's eyes slice open. First thought: *Fuck this.*

She's fully dressed and lying under the covers in bed. Her face, the only thing out of the blankets, is freezing. The switchboard tripped sometime during the night and the house is still and dark.

She kicks the covers off and springs out of bed. Thrusting the curtain aside, she sighs at the endless sea of white that greets her.

Too bad.

She'll put her Louis Vuitton on her head and walk like the African ladies do with their water buckets.

Not exactly the same, but the sentiment is similar.

If they can do it, so can she.

She snatches her trench from the hook on the back of the door and shrugs into it.

Everything about this place makes her skin crawl.

All night long the house had creaked and groaned, shaken and shuddered through the storm. She needs a long soak in a scented bath, a sheet mask, low calorie protein and six litres of filtered, chilled water.

And silence.

Silence for days.

The argument with Maia ran on an endless loop through her mind long into the night. Thinking up snappy retorts and nasty put-downs. Very nearly said some of it too, when she'd heard them come up the hallway.

She hadn't in the end.

In the end, she'd packed her bag, got dressed and lain under the sandpapery sheets and stewed in her self-righteous hatred.

The first thing she would do after she'd washed her hair would be to call Lucinda and have her blackball Lily from the agency. Hell, the industry. Followed by a call to her shark of a lawyer and a promise to sue her for every last penny she made from the book.

Then she was going to open a fake Goodreads account and one star every single one of Maia's books. She would cut and paste the unkindest reviews she'd received on her own book and add them to Maia's.

Maia was probably too cool to fall down the review hole like the rest of the authors Colette knew, herself included. It was unlikely she would look, but if she did, Colette wanted Maia to see the copied comments from Colette's worst reviews and know with certainty that it was Colette that had put them there.

A warning that she would not go quietly. A warning for Jasmine too. If she thinks she can push Colette around, selling stories to the media, like a bird of prey, pick, pick, picking at Colette's life until she had destroyed it, she has another think coming.

Heaving the suitcase into her arms, she tests it for weight. There is no way she can walk with that. She will leave it here. Eliza could arrange to have it sent on. The cost means nothing to her.

She stares out the window. The snow looks deep in some places but has finally stopped falling.

She'd watched from this window as Tavis and Laurie carried on like a pair of idiots last night. Laurie is in his sixties for God's sake. Outside screaming and yelling and trying to fight a man half his age. Over what? His treatment of his alleged bastard baby?

Pathetic.

The house is silent as she moves into the hallway. Everyone's sleeping off their hangovers probably. Although she's not feeling too good herself. Wine and Xanax are never a great mix, and she'd added a sleeping tablet to it all around midnight.

She slams the door to her bedroom hard enough to make the house shake.

Rise and shine, fuckers.

A gust of cold air hits her as she reaches the top of the stairs and she gasps. Her room was cold, but this is proper freezing.

Someone has left the front door open, and the air is as cold as her mother-in-law's heart. Jasmine's problem now.

Colette smirks. *Good luck, babe*, she sends out into the ether to Jasmine, *you'll need it.*

She rubs her arms and wonders if she will be able to make it into town. Colette peers out the door. The office is dark, the door closed.

She doesn't remember ever seeing it open, not that she has really looked. It suddenly occurs to her that she doesn't know if Eliza lives on site or not. No matter, Colette will email to ask her to send the bag on.

She flips her collar up against the cold and sets off, her feet unsteady in the ankle-high snow.

For a fleeting moment she smiles, thinking of a family holiday they'd taken to the Swiss Alps when the kids were small. Trent had taken off along the slopes and she'd stayed back with Jasper and Willa, on the kids' slopes, making snow angels and sliding down a tiny slope on a toboggan. They'd whooped and howled with laughter all afternoon and slipped into the bar afterwards, bright-eyed and wild-haired, hearts full.

The kids slurped thick hot chocolates – for once she'd relaxed and let the barista top them with cream and sprinkles – and they'd spent the evening in front of the fire, she and Trent with hot toddies, playing board games and laughing as if they were immune to tragedy.

It had felt as if life would never, could never, get better than that moment.

The memory sucker punches her. She doubles over, breathless.

That was gone forever. Trent had taken that from her and she could never, would never, get it back.

The panic that has dogged her since her diagnosis is back. Her breath comes in ragged gasps, her chest tightening, tightening, tightening – a band of iron around her ribcage. Her heart pounds a chaotic rhythm, and she scrabbles at her throat, trying to loosen her coat as if that will help. Her vision narrows, tunnelling, edges blurring and wavering. She stumbles, collapsing to the ground.

She will never have a day like that again. Trent will go skiing with his girlfriend and *their* child, and the idea of it makes her want to howl. Her thoughts are a chaotic and deafening spiral of dread.

Maia's words last night are a blade in her side. *No wonder he left you.*

All of Colette's secret, deepest fears realised.

She is unlovable.

She isn't worthy of a man like Trent.

No amount of Botox or fillers or Pilates or fake tan or eyelash extensions or painted nails could hide it. It all might have distracted Trent for twenty years, but he'd discovered it, eventually.

She releases a slow low moan. She longs to lie here and never get up. Let the snow fall around her and disappear into the blackness.

Colette can't live without him. Doesn't want to. She loves him more than she's ever loved anyone and he's left her.

What do you want? – I don't know. – Do you love her? – I don't know.

He didn't even know if he loved Jasmine, but he'd chosen to leave Colette for her. The unknown was more attractive than the known – the sacred oaths they'd taken, the family they'd created. Everything he and Colette had built together.

What a bloody mess her life is.

And then a sound – a crack, barely perceptible over the wind – snaps her head up. She is hurtled back to herself, and the panic twists away as quickly as it appeared.

She's lying in the snow in the garden.

In full view of all the rooms and the office.

She must look crazy. She feels crazy.

And sad.

So fucking sad.

Struggling to her feet, she stumbles trying to get her footing and topples sideways, landing against something soft. Her hands come away red.

Recoiling, she stares at the stain of crimson snow. Kicking out, she sweeps snow from the heaped pile.

A flash of colour, of fabric.

Her mind can't make sense of it.

Colette's back in the snow on her knees, sweeping the snow frantically, her hands burning with the chill.

A glassy eye.

Blue-lipped mouth.

Like the evening before, Colette screams, over and over and over. Her mouth as wide as the gaping maw of Laurie's dead corpse lying in the snow at her feet.

Maia

Tavis and I stare at each other, wide-eyed, frozen.

Someone is screaming in the front yard. A blood-curdling, spine-chilling scream.

What now?

What else can possibly go wrong?

Tavis leaps from the bed and rushes to the window. 'Shit,' he says, attacking his clothes on the floor.

He hops one leg into his jeans, then the other, stumbling in his haste. As his hand connects with the wall, he turns to me. His face is a mask, so blank that a chill skitters along my skin.

'Tav?'

I'm scared.

'Stay here.'

And then he's gone.

I don't, of course. Stay put. I'm at the window, shivering, staring out at the snow before he's made it down the noisy stairs.

But I can't see anything.

Dressing quickly, I run through the hallway and tumble down the last couple of stairs.

Tavis stands on the front door mat, his bare toes curled against the cold.

'Stop,' he says. 'Don't. Don't look.'

I do though.

I look at Colette first. She's stopped screaming, but the expression on her face tells me she's still screaming inside.

What has she done?

Her hands are covered in blood.

My gaze falls to the misshapen lump beside her.

I blunder forward, shoving past Tavis.

He's right – I shouldn't have looked.

But I did. And now I would give anything to take it back.

That last image of my father will never leave me: grey, lifeless face, lips as lilac as a bruise, sightless eyes fixed on the sky above us.

Hands clutching my knees, I vomit. It melts the snow, creating a steam bath of foul smells. My whole body is trembling. I'm dimly aware of Tavis and Colette speaking. He's trying to help her to stand, but she's clutching at him like a drowning person.

He heaves her into his arms and carries her into the house.

I sink to my haunches.

Snow begins to fall, and I tip my face towards it. Its glacial touch as gentle as a mother's kiss. I vomit again. It doesn't make me feel any better.

This feeling of sickness cannot be alleviated.

What we've done here will stay until it poisons me.

Desley

Through the *I am* affirmation meditation track, Desley hears screaming.

Her stomach clenches.

Again?

Surely not.

On leaden legs, she makes her way to the window. The angle of it hides most of the grounds below. She can't see too much but she sees Tavis is lifting Colette into his arms and making his way towards the house. Maia is hunched over something in the snow.

A flash of colour is all Desley can make out.

She taps her thumb, but the anxiety is too strong. The door bangs and Desley jumps.

'Desley,' Tavis calls from downstairs.

She stares at the door, thumb forgotten. What does he want with her?

Even once she'd jammed the chair from the writing desk under the handle of the door she'd still lain awake all night, listening to the house breathing, swelling as it shifted on its foundations as if a huge underground dwelling monster was stretching awake beneath them.

The ghost stories of the taxi driver had hovered around her head. Even with the light on she'd convinced herself she could hear breathing that wasn't hers, feel a gossamer touch on her face.

'Desley,' Tavis hollers.

A spike of fear shoots through her at his tone. It's enough to spur her into action and she's in the hallway, blinking into its dim light like an animal above ground after a long winter of hibernation.

'Yes?' Clearing her throat, she tries again. 'Yes, Tavis?'

Her footsteps are muffled as she treads the runner to the banister. Tavis and Colette look at her with wild eyes. Colette is soaking wet and shivering like Desley's dog, Crumpet, does after a bath. She wishes Crumpet was here, to hold in her arms, bury her face in his warm fur. To feel safe. Loved. To distract her from the horrors of this house.

Tavis is dishevelled, his face ashen.

'Get Colette into the shower. She needs to warm up.'

'What's happening?' Desley asks, although she doesn't want them to say it out loud. She's leaving today. Leaving all of this drama behind.

'It's Laurie,' Tavis says.

What now? Desley thinks, dread swirling in her stomach.

But she already knows.

'He's dead.'

Colette

Of course, there's no hot water.

The switchboard tripped, the boiler is probably on the blink too.

Colette looks at her legs, blue and goose fleshed, and decides to forget about the shower, and just put dry clothes on. Wrapping herself in the threadbare towel, she shuts off the tap and opens the bathroom door.

Desley is slumped against the wall and startles when she sees Colette.

'Hi, sorry, I was just ... waiting. In case you needed something.'

Colette eyes her. There's an edge to her voice.

Fear?

Somewhere between the front door and the shower, Colette has managed to convince herself that it's all a bad dream.

A trick. A practical joke. Laurie's idea of teaching them a lesson.

Colette scrubs her eyes. 'Tell me this isn't real?' she pleads. 'Laurie isn't really dead?'

Desley pales. She studies her nails and blinks rapidly. 'I ... I don't know. What did you see?'

Colette closes her eyes and the unwanted image becomes clear. Laurie's purple face, those cloudy eyes.

And the blood.

So much blood.

'He's dead,' Colette says with certainty.

Desley releases a breath. 'How? I mean, what was he doing out there? It was hectic last night.'

They share a look. 'I meant the storm, but …'

They giggle. Colette presses her hand against her lips. 'How can I laugh at a time like this? What's wrong with me?'

'I think it might be shock,' Desley says between hiccupping laughter. 'It's not funny at all. Is this a prank?'

Colette shivers. 'I wish.'

Desley jumps. 'Oh! You're cold. Do you need something from your room? Before you shower?'

'There's no hot water. I'll just get dressed.'

Desley nods. They stare at each other for a moment. 'Will you come in with me?' Colette asks. She's too scared to go in her room, any room, alone.

Desley nods again.

They walk in together, leaving the door open, and stand at the window, so close they're touching. Colette welcomes the body heat as well as the comfort the closeness of Desley's body brings.

Maia and Tavis are still outside. Near the shape. She can't think of it as Laurie, even though she's seen it with her own eyes.

Tavis is pacing, his phone to his ear, Maia is tapping at hers with a look of frustration. She holds it up to the sky and moves it back down.

'No reception,' Colette whispers to the glass.

The wind picks up, shuffling through the trees, pressing Maia's and Tavis's clothes against them, shifting Laurie's clothes too. Giving the impression of twitching or jerking.

Desley gasps. 'He's moving. I just saw him.'

Colette narrows her eyes.

THE FINAL CHAPTER

She hadn't checked for a pulse. None of them had.

She bangs against the glass. Tavis glances up. His hair shifts as the wind moves around him.

Colette lowers her hand.

It's merely the wind.

She'd seen Laurie's ghastly face. There's no way he is still alive.

'Nothing,' she mouths with a shake of her head, gazing at the still shape of clothes that hid Laurie. Who, while repugnant, repulsive, disgusting, merely hours ago, had been vibrantly, definitely alive.

Who is now definitely dead.

There's no grief. She barely knew the man and hadn't liked him but she can't believe that he's dead.

'What happened?' Desley asks, her gaze fixed on the treetops. 'Do you think he wandered out and got lost? He was quite drunk.'

Something claws at the corner of Colette's mind. She closes her eyes, trying to bring it into focus.

The blood. A hole in the back of his head. He hadn't fallen and hit his head. He'd been hit on the back of the head and then fallen.

Someone had hit him on the head.

Colette steps sideways, away from Desley, and studies her.

The roads are impassable. Although the snow has stopped, there are no car tracks, nor footprints, around his body.

Whoever did it hadn't left any tracks.

Or, they'd covered them.

Colette swallows as an icy hand runs up her spine.

One of them here is a murderer.

Maia

I stare at Laurie's body. Commit it to memory. It feels important for some reason. A reason I'm not willing to excavate right now.

So I stare.

His legs, splayed at an unnatural angle, head twisted, vacant sightless eyes, so sharp in life, are now sightless, empty.

Vacant.

Whoever had been behind them was gone.

His mouth is ajar, as if in a soundless scream. I see he's missing a molar at the back of his mouth.

And the blood.

It makes me think of the frozen drinks you can buy at the fair. Crushed ice, with coloured flavouring on top.

Only it's my father's blood.

I retch. Thankfully there is nothing left.

'Fuck,' Tavis mutters again. It's all he's said since Colette has gone inside.

He's hammering on the office door. The lights are off. There's no answer.

'There's no reception. I can't even get an SOS call.' He holds his phone to the sky, as if that will help.

I cough out a laugh. He looks at me.

'Holding your phone up like that. I did that too. As if the bars are out there,' I wave my phone in a circle above my head, 'and we just need to capture them.'

He lowers his phone with a wry smile and takes my phone from my hand. 'Yeah, I guess you're right. It's just … Fuck. I can't believe this.' He studies the screen of my phone as if it holds an answer.

I clench and unclench my hands. They're frozen.

'We should go inside.' As if my words have raised my body's awareness, I begin to shiver uncontrollably. My teeth begin to chatter.

'Of course, yeah. Come here.' He slides my phone into his pocket before he pulls me up and into his arms. His body heat makes me realise how cold, how damp I am. 'Are you okay?' he whispers as he runs his hand along the back of my head. He's so tall, I feel as if I am tucked beneath his arm like a child.

I nod. 'Tavis?'

'Yeah?'

'What happened?'

'Huh?' He pulls away, ducks his head to meet my gaze.

'Is this … Did you … last night?'

Tavis expels a rough breath. 'No. I don't know.'

I think back to last night. As I'd walked inside I'd turned and stared directly into Laurie's eyes. 'Did he hit his head when he fell? And we didn't notice?'

Bloodshot eyes, surly expression, struggling into a sitting position.

There hadn't been any blood.

It was dark of course.

But would I have noticed? I would have noticed — there's so much blood. 'I don't understand,' I say.

But of course I do.

I just wish I didn't.
Someone has hit Laurie on the head and killed him.
And it can't have been anyone except one of us.
My blood chills at the thought.

Desley

They sit huddled together around the dying embers of the fire. Not one of them has got up to stoke it. They can't do anything but sit and turn the events of last night over and over like a stone in their palms.

Who saw Laurie last? How had he looked? Every little noise, creak, groan of the house pulled apart and analysed. The switchboard – what time did it blow? Had anyone seen anything, heard anything? They'd all said they'd seen nothing, heard nothing apart from the sound of the switchboard blowing up.

Desley hadn't said a word.

She picked at her thumbnail, the tip stained with something dark. Despite the words that flowed between them, they were struck by a terrible inertia. Too scared to do anything.

'The switchboard,' Maia says, finally. 'We need to check it. Reset it, get some electricity. We need to get the wi-fi working, call the police, find Eliza and let her know what's happened. We can't just leave him out there.'

Everyone nods but it's clear they're all thinking *what else can we do?*

'Two of us need to go find Eliza, and two for the switchboard,' Tavis says.

Safety in numbers.

Desley grimaces. There is no way she is going back down to the dungeon. She can tell everyone feels the same and she's read enough crime novels to know they'll all be under suspicion. Now is the time to act normal, or as normal as possible, to avoid any tricky questions later.

Colette voices it. 'I can't go down there. Last time …'

They're silent, thinking about her panic attack.

'Let's you and I go find Eliza then,' Desley says.

After the argument between Maia and Colette last night, it's unlikely they can go together. And venturing into the snow, as unattractive as it is, is a more attractive proposition than going down into the bowels of the house.

'Eliza will have a landline, or the office will. She can call the police. They'll need everything to be left just as it is. Nobody touch anything they don't have to and—' Tavis pauses, swallows hard, '—stick together.'

Desley eyes him.

He's pale, as the rest of them are, but there is a calmness about him too. Maia is barely holding it together, she's far more upset than Desley expected any of them to be. It's a strange sort of devastation. She hardly knew him, and it's not like he was a nice person. He was awful, and while she'd never say it out loud, if anyone deserved a violent death, it was him.

'Let's get dressed in warm clothes and go now,' Colette says.

Desley nods, chewing her lip. A thought has begun to niggle, and she can't let it go.

Laurie's spiteful threat about the poem he would send to Scott. Had he written it?

She nods in what she hopes are the right places but all she can think is: she needs to get into Laurie's room and find his notebook.

If he's written anything she'll rip it out, and no one will know. All will be contained. She hadn't meant to say anything last night but the stress of all the arguing … it just spilled out. Although she's changed her mind now, at the time she wanted the world to know just what kind of man Laurie was. Listening to him deny Maia's reality had made her as angry as she'd been the morning she had awoken in his bed.

He was a terrible person, and she isn't sorry at all that he's dead.

She, who cries at toilet adverts on the telly, much to Scott's disgust *(crying again, over what?)*, who cannot see another person cry without shedding a tear herself, cannot summon one for Laurie.

Even in death, she despises him.

'Let's go now,' she says, standing.

The look on the others' faces tells her that she's interrupted their conversation but she needs to get into Laurie's room before the police arrive.

She desperately needs that secret to stay between these walls.

Desley has surprised herself with just how much she wants to keep her life the way it is. What she is willing to do to ensure it stays exactly the way it's always been. Isn't something, even something terrible, better than nothing?

'I'll meet you back down here in—' How long will she need? 'Five minutes?'

Colette stands and they walk together up the stairs in silence, each lost in their own thoughts. Desley nods a goodbye as they reach her door.

Once inside she's frantic, pulling her coat from the wardrobe, the scarf, her gloves. Clothes scatter like seeds as she rifles through her suitcase.

Pressing her ear to the door, she listens for movement. None. She creeps out her door, pulling it quietly closed. She needs to be careful, the walls are so thin, Colette can't know she's left her room and come looking for her. Her hands are trembling as she tests the handle of Laurie's door.

The handle depresses with a squeak and she slips inside.

It's still and eerie.

A sad-looking pair of pants, just stepped out of, lies on the floor. Lumps of clothes are strewn around the room. His jacket hangs on the back of the chair, waiting for him to return.

With the force of a fist, it occurs to Desley he isn't coming back for any of it.

Her stomach twists and like the last time she was in his room, she tries not to vomit. Even in her wildest fancies, she could never have imagined this. Any of this.

A hand to her chest, a deep inhale. She can do this. Opening her eyes, she gazes around.

Unlike the rest of his room, the desk is tidy. An angular Montblanc pen lies next to an olive leather notebook. Nothing else. She picks up the notebook and flips to the last page of writing.

There are ten lines of scrawled ink, some unfinished, some scored through.

Speak her name. Resurrect her. Paint the dusk sky the exact shade of her shadow.

Scour the floorboards she haunts. Who turned your smile into his—

Tell me, who sliced out your tongue, who began with delight and ended like a fist in the gut. Yvonne. A light that shone upon my worst errors, now blinds with its—

Desley places the notebook back onto the desk and closes her eyes. Not a word about her. No mention of peaches, betrayal, Scott.

The sickness that twisted her stomach now twists her heart.

No one knows. No one will know. Her greatest mistake died with Laurie.

She releases a breath that is thick with relief. She is free. *Safe.*

The creaky step shrieks.

Footsteps make their way along the hall. Her heart begins to punch in her chest again.

Creeping towards the door, she presses herself against the wall.

No one will come in here, surely?

She holds her breath. When whoever it is passes by, she will creep out into the hallway and wait for Colette downstairs.

Then, when they've found Eliza, she'll call Scott. He'll make the necessary arrangements for her to get home.

The footsteps pause at the door.

And the door handle begins to move.

Colette

For the first time in her life, Colette wishes she owned one of those horrendous puffy jackets that unfashionable people wear. She's never understood why anyone would willingly purchase something that makes them look like a Teletubby.

As far as she's concerned, it's fashion over comfort, always. During cold weather, her preference is for natural fabrics, and layering. Nothing could convince her that a plastic jacket, and that intolerable rustling noise they make, is superior in any way to a Merino Stella McCartney coat.

But now, as she peers out into what can only be described as a blizzard, she gets it.

She sighs. Her boots are going to be ruined. Vintage Celine, picked up on her last trip to Paris.

Unzipping her suitcase, she begins to layer. This season's The Row turtleneck over Alaïa cashmere. Even now, she'd rather be cold than badly dressed.

Out of habit she slides her finger along the trackpad of her laptop to wake it up. Logging in, she checks the wi-fi.

Nothing.

She pauses.

It's utterly unbelievable that Laurie is lying outside dead in the snow.

It's like some wires have come loose in her head. Her thoughts are scrambled. She understands what's happened, but whatever connects her thoughts to her body is disconnected.

There's no feeling behind the thought that runs on a loop like one of those motorised car racing tracks Jasper used to love.

Laurie is dead. Laurie is dead. Laurie is dead.

And one of them has killed him.

It has to have been one of them. There's no alternative.

Maybe the three of them did? Is Desley covering for Maia and Tavis? Did he fall and hit his head during the fight?

But the way he was lying ... the hole in the back of his head. It doesn't make sense.

Perhaps he was walking away from the fight when Maia hit him on the head and Tavis and Desley are covering for her?

Was it just a mistake? An accident?

She feels excluded. On the outer.

She was in her room but they were together. All she can do is take their word that when they last saw Laurie, he was alive.

How does she know that's the truth?

She can't know.

Trust strangers who have proven themselves utterly untrustworthy?

Maia would go as low as she could, she'd proven that.

Tavis, maybe protecting his new love after being rejected by her father? He's a big guy. Is he violent? He'd got physical with Laurie, that's proof that he could be. He's large enough to finish someone with one punch.

But.

If he'd fallen, or been hit with something during the fight, would they have come inside and gone to their rooms as quietly as they had?

She can't shake the look on Maia's face.

As absolute as her dislike for the girl is, she can't deny that she appears distraught. But is she shaken because she'd played a part in her father's death? Or even killed him herself?

Rolling the cuff of her sleeve and shrugging into her trench, Colette considers.

Desley. Out of all of them, Desley is the one Colette thought would go to pieces over a dead body.

The woman who twitched and shuddered as if electrocuted, jumping at the slightest noise, is now as calm as anyone Colette has ever seen.

Certainly the calmest she'd ever seen her.

Not that she really knew her, but her impressions of Desley over these last few days were of a fragile, skittish woman.

Colette hesitates as she belts her coat. The fabric is silken under her fingertips. Dead body or not, she can't ruin this out in the snow. The boots are bad enough. She remembers seeing a macintosh hanging on the wall at the back door.

She'll wear that instead.

Two pairs of socks, her boots zipped, and she's in the hallway but jerks to a stop.

Returning to her door, she locks it and slips the key into her pocket, Eliza's warning ringing in her ears.

Did she know something Colette didn't? If she felt someone was a danger to any of them, surely she had a duty to inform them?

This was the problem with places like this; no board of directors to answer to. Everyone complained about shareholders, but at least they ensured people didn't get murdered on retreat.

Christ. One of them has murdered Laurie.

There is no way to call the police and they are moments away from being snowed in. Trapped.

The house feels still and watchful. Although the noise of the storm kept her awake all night, she longs for it now. It's too quiet. Eerie in its silence.

Colette swallows hard, the weight of the silence in the house pressing on her like a hand around her throat.

She needs to get the hell out of here, as soon as humanly possible.

Maia

I'm officially an orphan.

The last rattling leaf on the tree. The idea swirls around my head like the snow outside.

I'll never know the truth. The past is always a mysterious beast, both malleable and unshapeable, but now ... it is nothing.

I am free to make of it whatever I wish.

My dead parents might have been in love once. Made a joint decision to bring me into the world, their own worlds slowly growing apart, with love.

But the truth hovers.

Its ghostly presence dogs my every step.

Laurie was most likely my father.

He was a terrible person.

And now his human vessel lies dead, abandoned, in the snow outside.

I rub my face. Tavis moves towards me and I lean into his embrace.

'I can't believe he's dead,' I say into his shirt.

'Hmm.' His chest rumbles like last night's thunder. 'Would you like to stay up here while I go look at the switchboard?' he asks.

I shake my head. I do not want to be alone right now but with Desley and Colette out of the house and Tavis downstairs it gives me an opportunity to explore Laurie's bedroom.

For what?

I don't know.

A memento? One last sense of him, who he was. Something that might prove he wasn't a terrible person. That if his DNA is half mine, some of it is worthy?

It doesn't make sense, but it feels right.

I can't get the image of him out of my head. The gaping wound at the back of his head, those cloudy, sightless eyes, the face, blue with cold. I need to replace it with something warm, something real.

Surely that can't be real. What I saw outside.

'Actually.' I pull away from Tavis and meet his gaze with wide eyes. 'I might have a lie down. I'm not feeling great.'

He nods, concerned, and I feel like a shit for lying to him like that but I need some space.

I think of last night. The fight between him and Laurie. He was alive when we went inside, I would bet my life on it. As we walked inside our gazes met. His, bloodshot and angry, but alive. Something happened afterwards.

Tavis was wet, cold. Needed a shower.

And yet, his skin had been cold when he'd come into my room. *After* the shower. I'd mentioned it and he'd brushed it off.

Did he have time to go outside after Desley and I had returned to our bedrooms?

'Babe.' He brushes my hair back and stares hard into my eyes. 'Lock the door behind you until I come back.'

I smile and nod. What was I thinking?

It was Laurie that had been angry, spoiling for a fight, not Tavis. Tavis had remained calm. I stand on my tiptoes and pull his face towards mine, crushing my lips against his. Whoever it was, it wasn't Tavis.

'Be careful down there,' I say.

He widens his eyes at me. 'It kinda feels like the safest place at the moment.' We laugh. 'And that's saying something because that basement is from a horror movie.'

'Go,' I say, pushing him out of the room. 'Let's get the switchboard sorted and the police out here.'

God knows how they will make it out in this snow but I assume they have their ways.

I watch Tavis as he disappears into the gloom of the hallway and then I run up the stairs, my heart banging in time with my feet. My socks slide on the floorboards as I take the sharp turn into the hallway.

Laurie's door is unlocked and I press the handle down but stop before pushing the door open.

What am I hoping to find in here?

It feels like a betrayal, an invasion of privacy. Which it is, of course.

But he isn't here to care and once the police come through this will be my last chance.

Once Tavis gets the electricity back working and Desley and Colette find Eliza, this room will be monitored.

This is my only chance.

Desley

Desley shrieks and grabs her medallion.

'Jesus Christ,' Maia says, her own hand at her chest.

They stare at each other a long moment. The strangeness of the situation paralysing them both.

Heat floods Desley's cheeks. She's been caught in a dead man's bedroom.

Thankfully Maia came in now, and not while Desley was rummaging through his notebook. That would have been harder to explain.

'I ... I ...'

Maia's face is tight. The door closes behind her with a snip.

Desley begins to sweat. There's something in Maia's face that makes her uncomfortable. She still hasn't said anything.

'I don't know what I'm doing in here,' Desley bursts out.

The expression shifts and Maia nods, gazing about the room. 'I get it,' she says. After all, she's in here too. 'I don't know what I'm doing in here either. I just ...'

Her face crumples, and she's crying. Desley is taken aback. Maia has been unflappable, self-contained in a way that both terrifies and impresses Desley. Mature, self-reliant beyond her years. Even last night as she'd discussed her mother, shared her secret with

Laurie only to have him respond so cruelly, she'd handled it with a mature grace.

Desley reaches out slowly, unsure of how Maia will react, but she throws herself into Desley's arms and begins to sob loudly.

Around and around her hand goes on Maia's back, and she's not thinking about Laurie and his lifeless body outside, his cruel words, his mocking dismissal of her, but instead, she's thinking of her girls. How she'd rubbed their backs like this when they were little. How expanded her heart had felt, as if she were connected to the entire universe.

As if she'd finally found her reason to exist.

And how she would do anything to protect them.

Desley snaps back to the room. The longer they linger, the harder this will be to explain. Colette will be downstairs waiting for Desley. They are supposed to be finding Eliza.

The police.

The police will be called and will question them all.

There will be an investigation, questions to answer. Her blood seems to slow and her hands tremble.

'Can we get out of here?' she asks.

Maia hesitates, gazing about the room, but nods.

'Wait.' She grips Desley's arm. She tries to pull away but Maia increases her tension. 'What happened between you and Laurie … last night … did you?'

Desley thinks of the last page in Laurie's notebook. The way he had attacked Maia, denied knowing her mother. But that poem. *Yvonne.* He'd known exactly who she was talking about. Perhaps from the very moment he'd seen Maia – but he hadn't cared at all. Again she is struck by a feeling of dislike for him. Suddenly the meaning of Maia's words fall into place.

'Are you asking me if I hit Laurie on the head?' The laugh that escapes is high-pitched and, even to her ears, desperate.

Keep cool, Desperate Desley.

'You saw me go into my room.' Desley forces herself to leave it at that. The more you talk the more people think you're lying, everyone knows that.

Maia stares hard into her eyes for a beat. Her full lips press into a tight line and she releases Desley's arm.

'Sorry, of course. Go ahead.' She gestures to the door. 'I want to … sit for a bit.'

There's no lingering suspicion in her voice but she's no longer looking at Desley, which makes it hard to read her expression. The ceiling feels low, the warmth of the room is cloying, the sense of Laurie, all around them, is too much for her.

Evelyn's room, haunted by her, now haunted by Laurie.

Colette

The door to Laurie's room opens and Desley strolls out like she's not walking out of a murdered man's room.

Colette's mouth falls open.

Desley shudders to a stop, pulling the door closed behind her. But instead of releasing the handle, she grips it so tightly her dimpled knuckles whiten.

'I thought we were meeting downstairs?' Colette says.

What she wants to say is – what the hell are you doing in Laurie's room?

Desley's wearing a coat – of course a puffer – but carrying nothing and although it's hard to tell with all that feathery bulk, it doesn't appear that she's taken anything from Laurie's room.

But, Colette stares hard at her through narrowed eyes, what was she doing in there?

Desley shifts and there is something new in her expression. Something Colette doesn't have time to analyse before it's gone.

'You don't have a coat. The weather, you'll need one,' Desley says. 'I'll wait here for you?'

'I'm going to use the old mac. The one at the kitchen door. I don't have anything appropriate for this.' Colette waves her hand towards the windows.

'Okay, let's go then,' Desley says.

But she doesn't move. Just stands there with her hand squeezing the door handle like she's wringing a chicken's neck, a rictus grin fixed to her face.

The hallway is dim and airless and as cold as steel in winter, and standing in front of a dead man's room gives Colette the creeps. She heads to the stairs, not caring if Desley follows or not.

Colette has shrugged the macintosh on and is buttoning it by the time Desley makes it into the kitchen.

The coat smells like the forest. Dank, damp, rotten. But it will have to do. She folds the sleeves up and prays it isn't Laurie's jacket.

Wasn't. She cringes at the thought.

There is no sign of Tavis or Maia and again the house is cloaked in that watchful silence. She throws the kitchen door open.

The sky is squid-ink black and the air below freezing. The wind has stopped, finally, but in its place is a chill air that is so cold it burns Colette's face. She shivers and flicks the collar of the macintosh up around her neck.

'Bloody hell,' she murmurs. 'Right, where do we start?'

The quicker they find Eliza, the quicker she can hand this over to someone and get the hell out of this place.

Laurie's body lies in the snow at the front of the house. If they start in that direction, they'll need to walk past him. The thought is too horrifying.

She thinks about that sightless, screaming face.

Evidently Desley is thinking the same thing as she looks at Colette with large frightened eyes. Tears gather along her lids like the storm clouds on the horizon. Colette looks away.

If Desley starts crying, Colette will follow suit. She breathes deep and clamps down on any feeling. She can't let go right now, none of them can.

While Laurie wasn't the most likeable character, his death was so unexpected. So unpleasant.

The uncertainty is so unsettling.

Yesterday she would have said Desley was incapable of hurting a fly but today …

Colette gazes at her.

Today she's not so sure.

'That way?' Desley gestures to behind the office where the property stretches on.

The sense of unease that has sat, as hard as a rock, in her stomach since the gruesome discovery increases as they begin to move towards the office. The feeling she's had since arriving, the sense of being watched, of something malign stalking her, increases. There's movement she can't decipher at the edge of her vision, but each time she turns her head, there's nothing.

'Behind the office, into the garden. Perhaps there's an old stable block and caretaker's cottage that way.'

Colette realises she never paid much attention to Eliza. It felt as if, like some kind of macabre jack-in-the-box, she just popped up in random places as the whim took her. Colette had never seen her come, or go.

Desley nods as she zips up that awful jacket. She looks like a marshmallow. Colette probably doesn't look much better. The macintosh is for someone much taller, it hangs shapelessly to her knees, and although she's rolled the sleeves twice, they still graze her knuckles.

They aim towards a small break in the overgrown garden behind the office. The snow has obliterated everything. There's no path, no clear direction in which they should head. The only thing driving them forward is that this way means they don't have to walk past Laurie.

There isn't a single noise – no cars, no birds, no planes.

No people.

Another time Colette might have considered it blissfully quiet but the still air only serves to unsettle her.

Dread lifts its head like a snake and strikes. 'Do we know for certain Eliza lives onsite?'

Desley blinks into the chill air. The tip of her nose has reddened and begun to drip. 'I don't know. She scares me. I avoided her mostly.'

Colette smiles. 'She's seriously weird. She asked me to keep tabs on who was using all the internet.'

'What?' Desley's head snaps around, her expression incredulous.

'I know.' Colette's exhaled breath is a puff of smoke. 'Said we were using too much.' Colette thinks back to Eliza silently waiting for her in the hallway. 'She has to be onsite somewhere. She's worked here for years, she told me.'

On the horizon, another storm is spreading like a stain. The breeze has returned, rustling at the leaves above them. Colette hoped last night was the worst of the weather. They need to find Eliza and get her to call the police so she can leave. The police won't need long with her, what she knows is cut and dry. She can answer their questions over a dry martini in the hotel bar.

The clouds scud overhead, too fast. Fear rises up. What if the storm hits and they are still out walking around looking for the stupid caretaker's cottage? Her boots would be ruined.

Another, darker thought chases that. What if there really is someone associated with Jackovic living in the forest? Ridiculous. Impossible. This weather is just too bad. But a cold sliver of fear snakes along her back.

'Should we go back?' Desley's voice is a tremor. 'Maybe Tavis has the electricity back on and we can call the police. Let them find Eliza.'

Yes, Colette longs to say. But her need to handball this problem onto Eliza is too great. She wants rid of it all. Preferably as soon as possible.

'Five minutes,' she says, punching her hands into the pockets of the mac.

Something rustles, sharp against her knuckles. Colette pulls it out. Her eyes move over the handwritten note with its black spidery writing, heart rising impossibly high in her throat.

'What is it?' Desley asks.

Colette hands the scrunched paper to Desley wordlessly.

Desley's eyes move left to right, then again, and widen. Her teeth catch her bottom lip.

'Oh my God,' she mutters.

Desley

The wind is bitterly cold. It's picked up and is stinging Desley's face. The overgrown garden has led them back to the forest, it seems to surround the house. They pause at that rotting sign, hanging drunkenly on its screws at the start of the forest path.

Forest path this way. Beware of ...

As they study it, Desley has the sense of being watched, a nettle prickling along her skin. Her gaze darts about uneasily, but there is nothing but the skeletons of the ancient oaks reaching towards them. Lots of places for a murderer to hide.

She clutches Colette's arm, suddenly breathless.

Colette looks at her. The cold has reddened Colette's cheeks becomingly. Desley hates to even think about how she looks. Her nose is dripping, and she's sure her pink beanie makes her face look rounder than usual.

'Let's go right,' she whispers.

'Right.' Colette offers a brisk nod and sets off to the right. Eliza's house, if she lives onsite, isn't likely to be in the forest.

Desley closes her hand around the note in her pocket.

You should leave. Now.

Desley had struggled to understand. Who had put it in the coat pocket? And why? Who was it intended for? No one could have guessed that Colette would use that macintosh.

'Whose coat is this?' Colette had asked, checking the other pockets and coming up empty-handed.

Desley didn't know.

She couldn't remember seeing anyone wear it but she'd only ever been outside the once. With Laurie.

It hung on the peg on the back of the door for as long as she'd been here.

It's big. Worn. Too big to be Maia's. Big enough to be Tavis's but too uncool? Him with his black puffer over black hoodie, over black jeans. But if there was one thing Desley knew for sure, it was that she didn't know these people and the outward-facing appearance of people and their lives was never what it appeared to be.

They walk under a low-hanging tree and she remembers that first day walking up the driveway. *Go back*, *go back* the trees had seemed to whisper. Now they tugged at her coat, wound their fingers in her hair, discarded branches and vines clinging to her ankles as if urging her to stay.

Or stopping her from leaving. She's trapped.

Panic suddenly grips her by the throat.

One thing she can see ... but the trees are ominous and threatening. Broken stumps hunch in waiting for her to pass, rocky crags hide crazed note writers, killers. One thing she can smell ... The damp smell of the forest clings to her nostrils, decay and rot. Desley squeezes her eyes shut. She slips, landing heavily on her knee. She steadies herself by clutching at a rotting stump. Snow melts and drips into her sleeve, trickling along her arm with an icy touch.

'Are you okay?' Colette yanks her to her feet.

Desley shakes the water from her sleeve and presses her hand to her head. No. She can't hide it any longer. She's far from okay. The ground is unstable beneath her feet, rotten, sodden, bitterly cold. The wind begins to howl through the treetops and they sway, as unsteadily as she. Snow falls in clumps to the ground, shaken from the branches.

She cannot go on. It all seems too horrible, too surreal.

'What if this isn't the right way? We might get lost. No one will be able to find us and we'll have to eat each other like that movie. Remember that? The boys in the snow?' Her voice has risen, both in tempo and pitch.

Colette stares at her a long silent moment. 'We can't eat each other,' she says drolly. 'One of us would be dead.'

Desley stares at her. How can she joke in a situation like this?

'Look,' Colette says, her tone kinder. 'Someone will come find us. Tavis would anyway,' she says wryly. 'Maia would probably leave us out here to die.'

Desley doesn't laugh.

Colette continues. 'Eliza is here somewhere. If we don't find her, Tavis will get the electricity back up and we'll be fine. The police will come and we'll go home and forget this ever happened.'

Desley nods but as they restart their walk along the track she wonders, will she ever forget what's happened here?

She doubts it.

The path they walk on has been mostly protected from the snow by the canopy of trees above. Small banks of snow line the sides but it's more mud and slush than snow. Large, shapeless footprints show in the mud.

The trees part and a small brick cottage with a sharply pitched roof appears. Desley lets out a gasp of relief. The curtains are drawn but a sliver of light shows through the crack in the front room.

Colette sucks in a breath that tells Desley she isn't as confident as she'd acted. 'This has to be where Eliza lives.'

A squat fence snakes the perimeter of the boundary. Rotting palings hang like crooked teeth. Lurid green moss creeps along the decaying wood. Ivy strangles the corners of the house, almost completely obliterating the top window.

Desley swallows and as the gate squeals open, she stops, unable to go forward. There is something otherworldly about the cottage.

It makes her think of witches baking motherless children in ovens.

'Colette,' she whispers.

Colette has paused at the threshold of the property. One foot on the forest path, the other on the slick-looking cobblestone path that leads to the house. She is gazing at the house with a stricken expression.

A shiver creeps along Desley's spine.

The curtain in the front room twitches.

Colette

A muscle under her left eye begins to pulse.

Her feet are numb and she wants wine. Lots and lots of wine. She doesn't care if it's morning. Alcohol is the only thing that is going to dull the horror of this trip. Colette longs to turn back. But they've come this far.

She swallows. 'Let's just go. Get this over with.' She grabs Desley's hand, more to make sure she gets to the door than for comfort.

Desley is acting strange. Shock, sure, but there's something about it that unnerves Colette. There's another layer to it.

Desley knew Laurie as well as the rest of them but she's like a zombie. All glazed eyes and desperate twitching. She's falling to pieces.

Colette pauses.

The front door is open.

In this weather?

Desley squeezes Colette's hand so tightly her knuckles crack.

'Hello? Eliza?' Colette takes a step forward and stops. She's not going into a creepy house in the middle of nowhere with only Dumpy Desley for protection.

'Let's just go back,' Desley says, pulling on Colette's hand. 'If we can't get the power on we can walk into town and call the police from there.'

Colette can't stop staring at the door. It's been open for some time judging by the snow banking around the bottom of it.

The image of Laurie's caved-in skull jolts through Colette like an electric shock. Colette drags in a breath and feels herself sway. She's about to turn to leave when something draws her gaze. The sole of a sturdy walking boot can be seen just behind the open door. She swallows hard and steps forward. It's just a boot but there's something about the angle of it that draws her nearer.

You're seeing things.

But she isn't. There is a leg attached to the boot, splayed at an unnatural angle. Desley's hand is gripping her tight, pulling her back. She registers Desley saying something but all she can hear is the roaring of blood in her ears.

Flicking Desley's hand off, she jerks toward the crooked veranda. One boot on the bottom step. Two. She leans closer to get a better look, stumbling back when her gaze collides with Eliza's blank cloud-coloured eyes.

Magenta-coloured blood has pooled beneath her head. A gash, similar in size to the one in Laurie's head, rips her hairline apart.

Colette retches, her stomach twisting, knotted, but nothing comes up.

Eliza is dead. Even if she could have survived that much blood loss, the grey, waxy tinge to her skin tells Colette it's too late.

Stepping backwards as slowly as if she's moving through thick mud, she turns and stares at Desley.

Desley is frozen on the path, her thumb doing that strange tap, tap, tap against the palm of her glove. The look she gives Colette is strangely disquieting. Desperate, pleading. Like she already knows the horror that lies inside the door without Colette saying a word.

Colette turns, pauses at the top of the steps. 'We need to get out of here. Now.'

Snow begins to drift gently, and bizarrely, Colette finds herself awed by the beauty of it. In spite of humans and their petty obsessions and squabbles, nature keeps doing what it does.

She feels as if she's floating outside herself, watching the snow fall while Eliza lies inside. Another dead body but Colette just feels numb.

Shock. It must be.

Desley opens her mouth to speak but pauses, as if thinking better of it. She blinks, long and slow, her gaze flicking to the open door.

'Don't look,' Colette croaks. 'Don't look.'

But Desley lurches forward, up the stairs, to stand mutely at the open door, gaze unreadable. Her lower lip begins to tremble.

Colette clasps the sleeve of Desley's coat and yanks her onto the path.

They try to break out into a run but their feet can't get any purchase on the sludgy ground. As quickly as she can amongst the slush, Colette begins to inch towards the forest path. That stinging sense of being watched begins again.

Desley slips, her hand falling from Colette's.

Crack.

A great force strikes her from behind and she falls to the ground.

Maia

Shit.

I stare around the room. What the hell was Desley doing in Laurie's room?

It's a dumpster fire in here. Clothes strewn everywhere, pants lying on the floor, clothes hanging on the back of the chair, his towel crumpled in the corner. The sheets are rumpled.

I can't help but think of Desley's accusation last night.

I've got a rule. Believe victims, always. Without fail. There's nothing lower than victim shaming and blaming.

But suddenly I get why people might find the truth so unpalatable that they deny its existence, no matter the evidence.

My dad.

Shit.

The house shudders awake. The light overhead flicks on. Thank God. I clutch the desk with relief, my hand knocking against a notebook. My mouth is dry. Blood is roaring in my ears. I stare at the notebook.

I'm a writer. I know how writers are. We own multiple notebooks, each more beautiful and ornate than the last. As if the beauty of a cover or a blank page will keep the braying wolves of writers block away.

Or, we just own one.

We cherish that one, fill every page, worry about losing it, mind it like a child, ensuring we know where it is at all times.

The *one* holds the deepest, darkest secrets of our hearts.

I swallow and trace my hand along the cover. It's smooth, soft. Well loved. Darker at the edge where the oil from Laurie's skin has stained the leather.

I hesitate. What does it matter if I destroy his privacy while he lies dead, outside in the snow? I pick it up, still considering. Or pretending to consider.

I'll open it. That's a given.

There's a loud bang and I jump.

Tavis will be looking for me now the switchboard is back on. The internet will restart and we'll contact the police. They'll close this room off. The notebook will go to Laurie's next of kin. There's no long-term love, or other children, at least not acknowledged. This notebook will be put in a box somewhere, as evidence perhaps.

Half completed poems, forever ellipses. His last thoughts, his genius, lost forever.

Pressing it against my chest, I come to a decision. I'm going to take it, this notebook belonging to my father. As I slip it in my waistband, a piece of paper spills from it.

A plain piece of printer paper, sharply creased. So banal looking that I almost leave it on the desk but a sixth sense has me picking it up, opening it.

I stare at it. Uncomprehending.

A photo of Tavis stares back at me – a photocopy of his driver's licence.

What the fuck is Laurie doing with a photocopy of Tavis's driver's licence?

Tavis's hair is shorter, darker; similar in colour to mine. His face a little rounder, younger. There is something about him that feels familiar. Despite the changes age brings, it's still him. Those full lips, sharp eyes. I scan the details, my eyebrows raising when I see he's exactly nine months younger than me.

My fingers press along the crease, closing it, but freeze as something flashes through my mind. I reopen the paper and scan it.

Travis.

His name is Travis.

A chill sweeps through the room that has nothing to do with the cold air outside.

He's lied about his name. What else has he lied about?

A bang from somewhere deep below pulses through the house.

Colette

Colette stumbles to her knees, hands splayed in the icy snow, winded.

A hand is on her back, her elbow, hauling her to standing. Her stomach is clenched, her face heats as she struggles for air. Her fingers claw at her throat.

Desley's face appears in her shimmering vision.

'What the hell?' Colette wheezes, when her breath returns.

'A branch fell and hit you.' Desley gestures over her shoulder. A thick branch lies crookedly in the snow.

Colette looks overhead to the giant wind-gnarled hawthorn tree, its branches quivering under the weight of the snow heaped upon them.

'Jesus Christ,' she mutters, rubbing her back. 'This fucking place.'

She glances back to the branch. Sees how its edge is jagged and torn. An accident? Merely bad luck? But hadn't Desley dropped her hand at just the right moment? She'd pushed her. Colette had thought she'd slipped but she pushed her. Into the path of the branch or away from it?

The primal fear she'd felt lying as still as a corpse in the MRI machine at the hospital claws its way back. Sharper and crueller now. She'd survived a tumour, surgeries, endless sterile corridors,

Trent's betrayal, the loss of her family, her entire identity. For what? To freeze to death in this godforsaken place, surrounded by liars and lunatics? Her breath catches, the panic swelling like a wave. Colette clenches her fists and inhales a sharp breath. No, she won't let it take her. She didn't fall apart then, she certainly won't do it here with these badly dressed losers. If she's going down, she's going down swinging.

'Let's get back to the house.'

Desley nods. 'We need to tell the others. Get to town. Get to the police.' Her tone is strong and clear. More steady than Colette has heard all week. Desley wraps her arm around Colette's waist and pulls her close, and despite Colette's misgivings about Desley's behaviour she's grateful for the warmth. Her back aches and her feet are numb, but she can feel the adrenaline sharpening her edges, lending her a sense of clarity and strength that cuts clean through the fog of fear. She's Colette-bloody-Halifax!

They'll get back to the house and contact the police. In a town like this it shouldn't take long. Then she's going to lock herself in her room until they arrive.

Soon it will all be over.

They head back towards the forest path. One thought spins around in Colette's head like a broken record.

Get back to the house, get back to the house. Before something else happens.

She feels that something else stalking her, creeping along behind her, waiting for its moment to pounce.

Maia

I slip from Laurie's room into the hallway just as I hear Tavis climbing the stairs. I rush into my room, stuffing the book between the mattress and the bed frame. I'm straightening up as Tavis rushes into the room. He brings the musty scent of the basement with him, his fingertips black with grime.

We stare at each other.

'The door,' he says. At my blank look: 'I told you to lock it. I could've been the murderer.'

There's a loaded pause as we stare at each other. His words sink into the surrounding air and my heart is in my mouth. The missing minutes between his shower and my bedroom hang heavily in the air between us.

'Are you?' My voice trembles. I move towards the window, a little farther from his reach.

The corners of his lips twist. 'Are *you*?'

I stay silent.

I could have been. I'd spent weeks and weeks fantasising about it. Maybe years. The man who almost killed my mother. Whose ghost chased her, and me, around the country. How I hated him. The way he'd denied even knowing Mama's name after everything he'd done to her. I'd never hated anyone more than I hated him in that moment.

Of course, I'm not happy he's dead. I'm shaken and shocked. And shock does funny things to your brain. Part of me is wondering if I *did* do it and blanked it out. Like a traumatic event, a general feeling of something malignant lingers, but you have no memory of it.

I can see myself, rock in hand, following Laurie outside and bringing it down on his head. How I felt when I saw him for the first time. Thoughts of retribution for what he did to Mama had been in my head for so long it seems unbelievable now that I didn't somehow bring his death to fruition.

But I smile and shake my head at Tavis. 'You got the electricity back on. We need to call the police.'

He hesitates. It's fleeting but I catch it. His phone is in his hand and he gestures with it. 'I already tried. No reception. And the wi-fi isn't working so I can't WhatsApp.'

'The wi-fi hasn't come on yet?'

He shrugs. 'I don't know where the router is. It might need to be switched back on manually or reset. We'll have to wait for the girls to get back with Eliza.'

'Women,' I say absentmindedly.

'Sorry?'

'They're women, not girls. Don't infantilise them.'

My phone, I think suddenly. I shove the pillows aside, toss the blanket to the floor. It's gone. My phone is missing.

My scalp prickles. There's a strange light coming through the window; green, electric. Another storm on the way. It haloes around Tavis and I am struck by how handsome he is. Magnetic, incandescent. Tall, broad shoulders. Those strong hands.

Those missing minutes.

He can't have killed Laurie, I reassure myself.

I think of his cool self-possession last night at dinner. We were all raging like the storm outside. But not Tavis. He'd sat perfectly still and silent at the end of the table, like a marble bust of a Roman god. He'd dispatched Laurie like it was merely an unpleasant task – biting the nasty onion, my Finnish friend Aino calls it. When you have an unpleasant job to do, you knuckle down and get it done. No fanfare, or applause. No dragging it out before or after, just tick, done, move on.

But he's lied about his name.

He stares at me. His blue eyes are cold in the eerie green light and despite last night's intimacy, I realise I don't know this man at all. The wind picks up outside and I'm suddenly aware that we are completely alone.

Something small and scared inside me comes loose.

Tavis takes a step towards me. I tense and step backwards. His eyebrows furrow, just slightly, and he doesn't come any closer.

'I'm going to walk into town. We can't wait any longer. We need to get the police out here as quickly as possible.'

I nod. Movement out the window catches my eye.

'Here they are.' Relief. Safety in numbers.

Their heads are bent against the snow which has started to fall faster now. Colette is wearing a dark rain jacket that comes to her knees. Desley sways like a drunk person. They look like returning soldiers, exhausted, wrung out. Where is Eliza?

I turn. Tavis is at the door. I hadn't heard him move. His expression is blank, but it feels studied, like he's trying to hide his thoughts.

'I've got to go now, before this snow really starts to come down. Otherwise I won't make it.' He presses his lips together, gives me one last dark look. 'See you soon.'

He pulls his hood up and walks from the room. My shoulders release when he leaves. I study the women as they approach the house. The path is ankle-high, deeper in some places, and judging by the way Desley is clinging to Colette, it's hard going. They're making slow progress at any rate.

I keep my gaze averted from the other direction. The driveway Tavis will be heading towards. Past Laurie.

A shadow moves in the forest, but when I look all I see is trees. The house begins to wake, creaking and groaning like an ancient slumbering monster awakening. The roof above me cracks loudly, making me jump. I think of Evelyn Thorne. Her ghost, or the idea of it anyway, lingers here. The death of her family and her discovery of them clings to the curtains, is soaked deep into the carpet. Rises like dust from the furnishings.

The stair squeals.

The hairs on my neck prickle. I can still see the two women making their way towards the house.

I cock an ear. I hadn't watched to see if Tavis did leave. I'd heard the front door but he could have opened it and stayed in the house.

Terror claws at me. There is no way to get downstairs without using the stairs.

The stair squeals again.

Desley

Desley has never been so cold in her life.

It's not just her sodden boots or damp jacket. This chill goes deep into her bones. She'll never get warm again.

A great trembling has overtaken her. Her teeth rattle in her head. Hands shake in her pockets like she's a puppet and her master is very drunk indeed.

Laurie. The note. Eliza.

Oh God.

Her stomach twists. Her face is numb, in fact her whole body is numb. She is walking, one foot in front of the other, but she wonders if she too is dead. Panic bubbles up but is quickly replaced by an empty blank feeling. She is trapped in a nightmare. Even in her most fanciful imaginings she can't have conjured up the horrors of this stay.

The feelings she has here, of someone watching her, the shuffling in the walls, the rasp of a breath. The cold breeze that seems to follow her from room to room. It is impossible to believe now that it is all in her head.

It's not just one of her fancies. There is someone – or something – here that wishes ill upon them.

She shoots a glance at Colette, who is limping slightly. The tree branch hit her hard. Desley can't stop replaying it. If it had been inches either way, it would have knocked Colette out, perhaps even killed her.

Another layer to the horror that just keeps coming.

Colette stumbles to a stop, her nails digging into Desley's arm through her puffer jacket.

'Look.' Her eyes are wide and fixed on something at the far edge of the property.

A dark figure is moving away from the house. A flash of black and then it's gone. Swallowed by the darkness of the trees that line the driveway.

'Who the hell is that?'

A bang brings their attention to the house. A fist against the window. Maia's face appears, contorted with terror.

'Help,' she mouths before disappearing from view.

Colette

It must've been a second, maybe two, but it feels to Colette like they'd stood frozen for an eternity, gazing up at Maia's window.

Her senses are in hyperdrive. A body's response to fear, she supposes. Everything seems louder, brighter.

She can hear the wind gathering speed. Feel the temperature drop as the snow increases in both speed and ferocity. The icy shards of it gather on her face, each tiny pinprick like a slap. The whiteness of the snow, so much snow, is blinding. Desley's raspy breath is like a saw on fresh wood. In, out, in.

Her mouth is dry, it is impossible to swallow. Maia looked seriously scared.

And now, Colette realises, so is she.

Scientists say fight or flight is the body's primal response to fear. Adrenaline drops into the body, flooding the system, overriding the brain. Colette's body breaks into a run before her mind has time to consider why. She throws open the screen door, letting it slam against the wall.

'Maia,' she calls out. 'We're here.'

She pauses, one foot on the bottom tread of the stairs, and is suddenly thrust back to the first day here. Her concerns about the cleanliness of the house. What she wouldn't give to care only about a few dust bunnies now.

'Maia?'

She throws a glance over her shoulder, expecting to find Desley behind her. But she's standing at the foot of the stairs, staring at the shoe iron on the hallway table with the strangest expression.

Colette pauses, watching as Desley lifts it and turns it in her hands.

The unwanted image of Laurie's battered head flashes through her mind.

The shoe iron is sharp, angled and a rusty stain stretches along one side of it.

Fear sparks like the lightning that had flashed all night long.

Desley stares at it, eyes wide but unseeing. Colette's skin prickles as a thought occurs to her. The flat of Desley's palm on her back just before the branch fell. The way she'd lingered on the path, appearing to know Eliza was dead without walking up the stairs. The pitch of her voice as she'd levelled her accusation at Laurie, only for him to turn up dead the following morning. The expression of desperation on her face as they stared at each other in the snow. How far would that desperation take her? Suddenly Colette isn't sure.

Colette holds a hand towards the shoe iron. 'Hey, Des, why don't you give me that.'

Desley snatches it to her chest and gazes at Colette through narrowed eyes. 'Why?'

'What do you mean, why?'

Silence shivers through the house.

'Please, Desley. Just give me the shoe iron.'

Desley's gaze flicks from Colette's outstretched hand to her face. Her eyebrows pull together. 'You don't trust me?'

Colette turns to fully face Desley and takes a backward step up the stairs. There's nowhere else to go but up, towards Maia and whatever horrors she is battling.

'That's not it.' Colette forces her voice to stay calm. 'I think it might be what was used to kill Laurie. Look at it. It's got blood on it.' As Desley looks down at the shoe iron, Colette adds, 'It's evidence. We shouldn't touch it.'

Desley stares at Colette, mouth open, eyes wide, but she still doesn't hand over the shoe iron.

Colette's blood chills. She doesn't trust Desley, she doesn't trust any of them.

'Desley.' Colette's using the tone she used with her kids when they were toddlers and she was exhausted and desperate to stave off another tantrum. 'Just give me that. Please.'

Desley begins to laugh. An awful high-pitched sound that is closer to hysterical crying than laughing. 'You think I killed Laurie? Eliza? With this?' She waves it between them wildly.

'I didn't say that.' Colette edges backwards up the stairs.

Could she throw herself on Desley and wrestle it from her hands?

Her mind is as wild as the trees in the wind. Desley couldn't kill her *and* Maia. Could she? If she had killed Laurie and Eliza then she was capable of anything.

'Maia,' she calls, not shifting her gaze from Desley.

A buzzing has taken up in her ears; she needs to know what the hell is going on here.

Her legs are soft, like the snow they've just tramped through, and her hands tremble. The house seems to loom above her, never terribly welcoming, it now has a chilling atmosphere.

Desley tilts her head and gazes up at Colette with a decidedly un-Desley-like stare.

It's pinched, flat. Gone is the sweet, motherly, dowdy air. In its place is something hard.

'What a funny feeling. You being scared of me. It's rather powerful.' Desley's mouth presses into a line. 'You see, I've never felt powerful before. Sad, isn't it. I bet you feel powerful all the time. Colette *Halifax*.'

Her tone is as sour as bitter berries. Desley hasn't moved towards Colette, but she is blocking the way out of the house. The only way is up.

Colette blinks as a light begins to flicker in her left eye. A panic attack is on its way. She sucks in a breath. Not right now. She can fall to pieces afterwards, but right now she needs to get that shoe iron from Desley and then she's getting the hell out of here. Maia's terrified face flashes in her mind. Dammit. Pain in the ass or not, there's no way she can leave without making sure Maia is okay.

'Maia?' she calls.

Desley blinks and shakes her head, as if waking from a trance. 'Don't yell. I think—'

But whatever it is she thinks is cut off by the sound of footsteps pounding on the hallway above them.

Desley's gaze shifts.

It's now or never.

Colette throws herself at Desley.

Maia

There's a thick thud from downstairs.

Like a body hitting the floor.

I pause at the bend that leads to the staircase. My heart is in my throat but my legs won't move. I'm so fucking scared of what I'll find down there. I'd completely lost it when I saw Desley and Colette through the window.

What I'd found in Laurie's room, what I thought I'd heard in the hallway ... I can hear scuffling, and grunting. What if Tavis is hurting the women? Picking us off, one by one? He's so big, we don't stand a chance.

But there are four of us against him.

The thought of other people in the house causes my fear, so paralysing, to dissipate like smoke. Braver now, I run along the hallway.

'What the actual eff?'

Colette is lying on Desley at the bottom of the stairs. They're scrambling about like children. Only, this doesn't look like fun. Colette is pulling at something in Desley's arms and Desley's making an awful keening noise that makes my hair stand on end.

'What is going on? Get off her.' My sock's loose and I slip on the last stair, my ankle twisting painfully. I land hard on one knee.

Colette's foot kicks out, connecting with my sore ankle. I grasp her foot and yank. She turns and meets my eye. She kicks out again.

'Stop it,' I grunt, trying to pull her off Desley and avoid being kicked at the same time.

My heart's racing. Why is she attacking poor Desley?

Although, surprise strikes through me to find Desley is giving as good as she's getting. I hadn't thought she'd have it in her, but it's clear neither are going to let up.

I hobble to standing, lean over and wind my fingers into Colette's hair. It's as soft as it looks. I tighten my fingers until she freezes. 'Let go,' I order. 'Now.'

Desley scrambles backwards, openly sobbing, clutching that object to her chest. What the hell is it?

A gust of wind through the open door drags my attention outside. A woman I recognise as the other Rhamnusia employee, Jane, is standing in the snow. My breath is a white scroll of smoke. It's freezing.

'Jane!' I call. 'Thank god you're here.'

Eliza must have called her, let her know what has happened. Jane lives in town, I remember her telling me, she would have a car. The roads must be open. She might have already called the police. The relief is enough to make my knees weak.

Colette digs her nails into my hand but I don't release her.

'If I let you go, you can't go anywhere near Desley,' I warn.

She responds by digging her nails deeper into my wrist. I tug her hair until she stops.

'Fine,' she gasps. 'But—'

'Maia. Help me.' Desley is openly sobbing now, hysterical.

Colette inhales to speak but I shush her. 'Not another word from you.'

I release Colette's hair and hobble over to Desley. She has crawled to the corner of the room and is crouched against the wall, cradling the object. It looks like the shoe iron from the shelf. I bend to her. 'It's okay. Jane is here. She works here. It's alright. We're going to be okay. Do you think you can get up?'

She nods wordlessly but stays where she is.

Outside the snow swirls, luminous against the dull sky. Jane is no longer visible through the doorway. She must be in the office, fixing the router or waiting for the police with Eliza.

'Eliza. Eliza is ... oh god, Colette and I found her. She's dead. Someone killed her. Colette thinks it was me. With this.' Desley hands the shoe iron to me. It's heavier than it looks. I study it. A corner of it is stained with something rust coloured. Blood?

'Wait, what? What the fuck are you talking about? Eliza?' I glance to the empty doorway. 'Jane,' I scream. 'Jane!'

There is no answer except the increasing moan of the wind.

My head is reeling. I look to Colette, expecting her to laugh, to tell me they're pranking, but I already know they're not.

I swallow hard, step away from Desley. 'Why does Colette think you killed Laurie and Eliza?'

Desley widens her eyes at me. 'I wanted to kill Laurie,' she whispers quietly. 'I could never have. I'm not brave enough. And Eliza.' She wets her lips. 'She terrified me.'

I put the iron on the ancient-looking sideboard and grip Desley's elbows, pulling her to standing. My ankle screams in agony at the extra weight and a hiss of breath is pulled from my lips.

'Are you hurt?' she asks kindly, ever the caring mother. I almost smile. How could anyone think Desley capable of murder?

'My ankle. I twisted it coming down the stairs.'

Her eyes widen. 'We saw you. We thought you were calling for help.'

The sounds on the stairs. The brush of breath against my neck. All this chaos had lulled me into a false sense of security.

But ... something doesn't add up. I'd seen the women. The two of them in the snow. I'd mouthed the words *help me*. I'd heard the stairs creaking before that.

Where has Jane gone?

I swallow, fear shearing through me like a knife. 'I think there's someone else in the house.'

Jane – That Night

Tonight has been the worst of it.

Drawn to the office window by the yelling, I stand and watch as the two men crash through the door. Not a shred of respect shown for the wooden screen door, handmade by Evelyn's father. Out into the snow.

I watch them all.

Maia and Desley hover in the doorway.

A flash of light glimmers behind the women. Too quick to make it out, but I don't need to see it fully formed.

I already know it's Evelyn.

I've seen her in fleeting glimpses over the years and have come to recognise her presence. Most of the time through tingling fingertips or gooseflesh scuttling along my arms. Other times in flashes of light, the faint scent of honeysuckle regardless of season.

She is unhappy with this behaviour.

And when Evelyn is unhappy, I'm unhappy.

They can never help themselves. The writers.

The drink, the ego, the hubris.

The stupidity.

Just take these two, for example.

Laurie, self-important twit he is, is flat on his back in the snow. The other man, young enough to be his son, is standing over him, face contorted.

Maia screams something from the doorway.

Lightning sparks in the sky like a flickering bulb.

The charge in the air is building, building, building.

And so is my anger.

How dare they disrespect Thorne House and Evelyn in this way?

I hate having Laurie here. Have avoided it for years, since the last time he came. That young woman … she left a letter before she'd gone about what he'd done to her. The same thing I'd heard Maia accuse him of doing to her mother, to Desley too.

I'd waited for news of his arrest, or for charges to be laid, but nothing appeared, except articles trumpeting his various successes.

While she had disappeared.

I'd personally read her application for Rhamnusia, chosen her myself. And her words had transported me.

Her application had sung with the language of hope.

She'd been planning to write about Evelyn, which had thrilled me. We'd talk for hours about the house, about Evelyn. I'd shown her the secret spots in the garden that Evelyn had loved. I'd even shown her one of Evelyn's diaries.

Not the ones with the incriminating details about her family's death; of how she had grown to despise their prudish, controlling ways, and how she had finally freed herself from their cruel reign. No, there was no way I would share Evelyn's deepest secret, that was between her and me. But there was no harm in sharing Evelyn's beautiful writing about her love of the house and gardens with *her*. Not when she was planning to write so beautifully, so respectfully, about Evelyn.

Laurie is on his feet now, charging towards Tavis with a roar.

I watch as they tussle on the ground. This feels inevitable, has done since I'd discovered we'd made the error of booking two, male, poets at the same time. Evelyn understood people, had made the rule herself. One of the commandments she had set, that the entire structure of Rhamnusia was built on. I had vowed to fix it, to make it right. Laurie had fixated on Tavis, pestering me with questions about him, asking to read his application, pretending to be interested in his poetry. I knew it was jealousy though. A younger, more handsome, *better* man comes and usurps your precarious position on the throne. When I'd refused, he'd stolen Tavis's application from my desk. Oh, he thought he was so clever, so slippery, but there isn't a thing that happens here that I don't know about.

Take that first girl for example. I'd sent her a letter a couple of years later, following up on her manuscript, with an invitation to return and read more of Evelyn's private letters.

She'd replied with a vague, unhappy missive informing me she'd given up on writing. Lost her passion for it, she'd said.

But I knew it had been because of what Laurie had done.

Another shout and they head back inside, leaving Laurie prone in the snow.

He's ridiculous. An embarrassment.

He lies there for a few moments before heaving himself from the ground, brushing thick chunks of snow from his clothing and stumbling back toward the house.

Like the trees that have lined the driveway to Rhamnusia for over a hundred years, I sit, still and silent. And watch.

Lights flick on, one by one. The bedrooms. The bathroom. Then, a flash of light on the rooftop balcony outside Evelyn's bedroom.

And that's when I feel her. Evelyn. She is the soft touch of air on my neck.

It would be easy to follow Laurie out onto the roof. Press a hand to the small of his back.

I know every inch of this house and can creep throughout it, as silently as a mouse.

He wouldn't hear me coming. No one would.

As drunk as he is, it will be easily written off as an accident. The barrier is low, the roof slippery. But would the fall be enough to kill him? I would need assurance.

The orange spark of his cigarette beckons.

Go, Evelyn whispers.

It's now or never.

And so I go.

Out into the snow.

Towards Evelyn's bedroom, with its ladder to the roof.

Collecting the shoe iron from the hallway table as I pass it.

Desley

Of course there's someone else in the house.

There's been someone, or something, here since they'd arrived.

The shuffling noises within the walls, the constant, thorny sense of being watched.

The way Eliza came and went silently. The only sign she'd been there the dinner in the kitchen, or a fresh hand towel in the downstairs toilet. There were secret entrances and exits that revealed themselves only to those who knew to look for them.

'Everybody into the dining room. Now.' Jane stands in the doorway, an expression on her face so fierce they are terrified into shuffling obedience.

'Something terrible has happened,' Maia starts, but Jane tuts her, cutting her off, and waves her into the dining room.

The room is a mess. Books lie on the floor, the plates from last night still spread on the table. Wine stains the tablecloth. The air is close, thick with the scent of spoiling curry.

Desley bends to collect the books. Covers are folded, some are torn. She attempts to smooth the dog-eared pages, tidy them quickly, but she can sense Jane has noticed. Shame floods her. How badly they have behaved.

'Leave it,' Jane spits, closing the door behind her.

'Sorry,' Desley murmurs as she stacks them on the side table. Taking care to line them up neatly, to show Jane she had nothing to do with this mess.

What relief. Jane is here now and will fix it all. Desley just wants to go home. It's all too much for her.

Maia hobbles to the armchair and sinks into it with a grimace. Colette studies her nails on the sofa.

Desley decides to stand near the window, next to the bookcase.

Jane blocks the doorway, glaring at them all in turn.

'Jane,' Maia begins again. 'We need help. Someone has killed Laurie and Eliza. I'm so sorry.'

Instead of the expected shock and dismay, Jane simply gazes around the room unhappily.

The curtains are still pulled, perhaps that's why the room is so warm. Desley shrugs out of her jacket and folds it over the back of the chair. As she pulls at her collar, a trickle of sweat snakes along her neck. Her vision is suddenly blurry. All that exertion.

'Did you hear me? Someone has—'

'Yes, yes, killed Laurie and Eliza. I heard,' Jane replies, her gaze still cataloguing the destruction of the room.

A laugh bursts out. Desley's never been in a fight in her life. Imagine what Scott will say when she tells him.

She tries to imagine the conversation, no one would believe her about what's gone on here. It's beyond ridiculous.

'Is something amusing?' Jane asks.

Desley tries to focus but Jane keeps shifting. Has she called the police? Jane. Why is she so angry. Desley blinks. It's like she's trying to make sense of a kaleidoscope image.

'I'm ... I'm not feeling well.' Desley leans against the bookcase, legs trembling.

'The police,' Maia says. She sounds as if she's underwater. Muffled. A bit slurred. Has she been drinking? The thought amuses Desley for some reason.

'Laurie. We need to call the police. The wi-fi is out,' Desley says between giggles.

Jane gazes about the room with a curled lip. 'I know. I turned the wi-fi off. And the switchboard.'

The mood shifts dangerously.

'It costs money to run this house. A house that has been thoughtfully dedicated to writers. For writers to write. But no one here is interested in writing, are they?'

Desley lifts her head. Jane comes into blurry focus but the edges of her are vague, which gives her a ghostly, malevolent hue.

Maia's head is in her hands. Colette's head droops towards her chest, jolting occasionally like she's trying to stay awake.

'What's happening?' Desley's breath catches. She presses a hand to her throat.

There isn't enough air. Why is it so hot in here? She's not been able to get warm since arriving at the house but now the room is as hot as an oven.

'I saw it all. All the drinking. All the yelling. Every light in the house left on. No respect.'

She scrutinises them coldly.

'You make me want to retch,' she snaps. Her lips are pulled back, showing teeth, grey and crooked like gravestones.

'None of you are here because you want to write. None of you are here because you want to honour Evelyn Thorne's memory. Even the women roll about on the floor like badly behaved children.'

Desley's heart crashes to her stomach. Jane's anger is hot, corrosive. Why isn't she upset about the deaths? Laurie she can understand, but Eliza?

Maia opens her mouth to speak but Jane holds a finger up and makes a sound at the back of her throat like she's reprimanding a dog.

Colette is slouched on the sofa, mouth slack, chin resting on her chest. Sleeping? Five minutes ago she'd been wide awake, battling Desley for the shoe iron.

The shoe iron. The rust-coloured mark.

'Laurie,' Desley gasps.

Jane smiles. A horrific twist of her mouth. 'Finally, one of you so-called writers uses your brain. Yes, Laurie. I hit him on the head and pushed him from the balcony. Believe me, it was nothing that man didn't deserve.'

A wave of nausea churns. Desley clutches for the back of the chair but it's not where she expects it to be. Her hand meets air and she stumbles, knocking the edge of the table. It's difficult to right herself. Her legs are soft and trembly.

'But Eliza? She ... she ...' Desley couldn't connect the words.

Jane grimaces. 'Had to be done. She wanted to stop me. Of all people. She should have known how important the rules are. The commandments. But she wouldn't send one home. Tried to stop me. Stop. Stop. Stop.' Jane presses the heels of her hands against her eyes and begins to rock.

Her rocking unsettles Desley and she staggers backwards, knocking into the mantle. Hands against the wall to right herself but she's suddenly so tired.

Why bother standing?

She slides down the wall until she's resting on the floor.

Jane is still speaking but the words are like bees. Desley swipes at the air. A droning sound reverberates through her head. Louder, and louder.

'... thought he was untouchable. That he would get away with it ...'

It's starting to hurt. Her head aches.

Maybe she'll just lie down and have a little sleep.

'... looks like an accident. Smoking marijuana. Drunk, as usual. Unsteady on his feet ... An accident, just like the Thorne family. Just like you three in here.'

Desley forces an eyelid open as a thought batters against her skull.

Jane said something important but Desley can't remember what. The light is too bright. She doesn't want to open her eyes. But she must.

Someone is at her shoulder.

Open your eyes. Open your eyes.

She forces her eyes open. Jane looms above her, fists against her hips. A power pose, Desley's therapist had called that. A gurgle of laughter. Hers? Surely not.

Her chest is so tight.

Look.

Jane at the door, a bone-white handkerchief against her mouth, watching Maia with a narrowed gaze. Desley follows her eyes. Maia is convulsing, writhing on the floor.

Her blinks become longer, it's harder to open her eyes.

A man appears in her vision. He's shadowy, hazy. She recognises him from the family photo on the dining-room wall.

Evelyn Thorne's brother.

Gas.

The Thorne family died from carbon monoxide poisoning while Evelyn Thorne was out one night.

Or was she?

A series of images, like broken crockery.

All the heaters in the bedrooms, stuck at zero. Except Laurie's. Evelyn Thorne's old bedroom. That heater is safe.

The heat in here, although there is no fire in the grate. The heating is on. To turn the heaters on, you must turn the gas on.

It occurs to Desley with a slap that every heater, except the one in Laurie's room – Evelyn's room – leaks.

A gas leak associated with the heaters is what killed the Thorne family... it never occurred to Desley that the issue wouldn't have been repaired.

Jane is trying to kill them like Evelyn Thorne killed her family.

Desley blinks. Jane is gone. The door shut tight behind her.

Her breath is stuck in her chest, like her lungs have expanded and no longer fit.

She thinks of her girls. Desley has never loved anyone, or anything, as much as she does her daughters. The first time she'd smelled Chloe's head she thought she might explode from the love that overwhelmed her.

The love that had eluded her, her whole life, had finally become hers. She isn't going to die here and leave those beautiful girls alone with Scott.

Her hands fist into the carpet. She just needs to get to the door. Fresh air. One mouthful and the fog that clouds her brain will clear.

There's a gurgling sound. She twists her head. Can only open one eye. The other simply won't move.

Maia is vomiting.

Desley needs to get to that door. Now.

Using every last ounce of strength she has, she shifts onto her knees. She's unsteady as the floor beneath her tips and jerks like she's on a boat.

I can do this.

It might be the last thing she ever does, getting to that door, but if it is, she wants her girls to know that she fought.

She isn't just fat, foolish Desley.

Her girls need to know she didn't lie down and wait to die. Mummy fought to see them again. She didn't just give up.

Her heart is pounding so fast, her breath as loud as a chainsaw.

Suddenly she is outside herself.

She sees herself wobble on her knees, shuffling forward, slowly but with purpose. One knee after one hand.

Finally her hand hits something hard. She lets out a mewl of relief.

The door.

She's reached the door.

Her hand scrabbles, seeking purchase, but she can't find any. The door is closed. The handle is too high for her to reach.

She would have to stand to reach it but her legs are no longer working.

Sorry girls, she sends a silent prayer to them. *I'm sorry I couldn't do it.*

She'll try again in a bit, she thinks. So tired. The carpet is scratchy against her face as she places it on the floor. Sleep closes around her, like the snow falling outside. Soft, blissful, warm.

A breath of cold air tickles her cheek.

Air.

Her lids slide open. The gap between the worn carpet and the door is nearly an inch. This old house has rattled and quivered in the gust and gale of the storm. Nothing quite as tightly fitting as it had been in its youth, gaps appearing over the years as its wood sagged and aged, curved and gnarled.

The wind that always seems to find its way in. Including the space between worn carpet and door.

Tilting her head, Desley sucks at the sweet cool air flowing under the door.

Adrenaline surges through her muscles as they prime.

If she can get this door open, she can release the gas from the confined space. Let it mingle with fresh air, flush it out. Save herself, save the other women, who don't deserve to die.

She sucks in a slow breath.

Desley can't mess this up. If Jane is still out there, waiting, then she only has one chance to open this door, to wake Maia and Colette.

If she's not too late already.

No. She screws her eyes shut.

Visualise your success, her counsellor had said in one of their sessions. *See yourself doing the thing. Feel yourself doing the thing. And then do the thing.*

Her fingers tingle as oxygen begins to flow through her body. She thinks of the rock climber who'd cut his own arm off to free himself, after becoming trapped between two boulders. People are capable of enormous bravery under pressure.

If he can cut off his arm, she can stand and open a door.

Desley sees herself stand, feels her hand, slick but capable, on the handle.

But her legs don't share her vision. They refuse to move.

Her breath begins to shorten, quicken. She forces herself to slow down, suck in the air. Deep breaths. Take your time.

Not too long, idiot. Now!

With enormous effort she's on her knees, hands flat against the door.

Leaning a shoulder against the door, she pulls her foot up with her hands.

One, two … no.

She can't do it.

She's too unfit. Her legs ache but are numb at the same time. The room spins around her like a washing machine.

THE FINAL CHAPTER

Her life flashes before her eyes. Only it's not her life. It's the life she could have lived if she was brave.

She could have left Scott.

Alone is better than living with a man that alternates between open dislike and complete dismissal of her. The insults whispered in her ear whenever she appeared too happy.

You're so weird, she's not laughing with you, she's laughing at you. Stop talking, can't you see how much you're boring everyone? Why can't you just shut up and act normal for once?

Even if her books never became bestsellers, she loved writing. It gave her joy.

Before kids she'd worked, and while it hadn't been world-changing stuff, she was good at it. Smart, sensible, honest – a model employee.

A small house on a beach somewhere, her dog, writing in her free time, a happy, loving home for her girls.

Freedom.

With a guttural, primal scream, she pushes herself to standing.

The handle turns.

The door opens and floods the room with fresh, ice-cold, gas-free air.

Desley collapses to the floor in the hallway, lights flickering, red and blue, behind her lids.

Maia

The house is a frenzy of voices, barked orders, shouted requests, machines that beep, lights, clattering boots, and the occasional ringtone.

The nurse monitoring my blood pressure presses a button and the cuff around my arm depresses. She tugs the stethoscope from her ear and smiles. 'You're going to be okay.'

A rueful smile tugs at my lips. How can she be so certain? 'I hope so.'

Slipping away from the clamour, I step outside, longing for some fresh air. The house, windows thrown open, filled with people, still feels oppressive to me.

Colette is huddled under a foil blanket in the back of an ambulance. The foil reflects a silvery light on her, illuminating her like some ethereal warrior goddess. Her mouth is a thin line, and purple bruises shimmer under her eyes.

She's alone.

I wander over.

'Your hair's a mess,' I say.

Eyebrows and corners of her lips raise. 'Can't be perfect *all* the time.' Her voice is Miley Cyrus husky.

My throat hurts too. The gas, or the vomiting, I guess.

'You did almost just die, so I'll let you off. Just this once.'

She huffs a laugh.

I tip my head back. The sky is clear, all signs of the calamitous storm gone. Millions of stars take its place.

'Man,' I whisper. 'What a trip.'

'And I worried this week was going to be boring.'

'Have they said anything to you about Jane?'

The forest is lit up with beams of lights from torches, and rings with the calls of the men searching.

'They haven't found her. Yet.'

Tavis had arrived with the police to discover Colette and me passed out in the dining room, Desley in the hallway. Jane nowhere to be found. They'd called an ambulance, and backup. Vans of dogs and men and doctors and nurses had also arrived.

If Desley hadn't opened the door, we would be dead. The thought makes me shiver.

But almost as quickly as we'd started to feel ill, we'd felt better.

A headache lingers and I totally stink of vomit, but I feel surprisingly good for someone who almost died two hours ago.

I perch my butt on the edge of the ambulance.

'I can't believe Jane killed Laurie and Eliza,' Colette says with a shake of her head.

'I know. This is not what I was expecting from a writers house.'

We sit in silence for a moment, contemplating how close we were to joining Laurie and Eliza. Both unlikeable in their own way, but so vibrantly alive and now …

'Truce?' I gesture for a fist pump.

Her gaze drops to my hand and back to my face. 'I'm too old to understand what you want me to do with your hand.'

We laugh and there's something sweet about the tone. It's like the perfect melody.

I edited an article recently about creating music with AI. Research had proven (or so it said) there is a formula to the perfect beat.

Perhaps it's this.

The sound of two women laughing.

'I'm sorry.' I cringe. There are no words that can undo how I've behaved.

Colette bows her head, it's not quite a nod. 'I didn't withhold payment from Lily. The only thing I was guilty of was not being across everything. It's my career but ... I ... I allowed people too much freedom. Didn't ask enough questions. Was complacent.'

I get the sense she's not just talking about Lily. I think about her husband and the new baby on its way. How badly that must've hurt. I want to cry when I think of how I'd pressed my thumb to that sore, so gleefully.

Memories of Mama baking, sharing what little we had with other women in the community who 'were going through it' flip through my mind.

A true sister to other women. What would she think of the woman she'd raised? Biting my lip to stop the tears that threaten, I gaze around.

Tavis is standing at the front steps, talking to a broad-shouldered policeman. The lights flicker on his face. Our eyes meet and hold.

'I get it,' I say, my gaze still on Tavis. 'It's hard to know who to trust. We don't always get it right.'

I rest my trembling fingers on her hand. It's cold, purple. It makes me think of Laurie. Finally loaded into the back of an ambulance – that surprised me, that the dead took an ambulance as well as the living.

'You should write a book about this.'

'Me?' Colette clicks her tongue. 'Nah. Too commercial.'

We laugh again.

'Actually.' She licks her lips. 'I've been thinking about my next one. Something different. About love maybe. How we think it's one thing, husbands, wives, but it's actually many things. Friendship, motherhood, opening a door for another instead of holding it closed.'

I don't say anything.

'I hadn't written anything since my journo days. I doubted I could do it. There was always a reason not to; kids, a house to run, a husband to manage. But I knew people. Lucinda had been begging to represent me for years. The kids got older, and I had more time so we went for it.'

I nod.

'And then …' She pauses. 'My doctor discovered a tumour in my brain. Benign but aggressive. It was a lot.'

I hiss a breath. 'I'm sorry, I had no idea.'

She lifts one shoulder. 'How could you? But while I spent my days in hospital, trapped in a plastic coffin, radiating my cells, both healthy and otherwise, to death, my husband was making plans to leave me for his pregnant lover.'

Her words strike like a punch to the throat.

'Shit.'

'That's what that is.' She gestures to her face. 'Not a nose job. A second surgery that broke my already damaged septum. A surgery to remove the final cells of an invasive pituitary adenoma.'

'I … I …' But I stop. What can I say? I have no words. I place my hand on her knee and squeeze. Just once.

'I was contracted for the book. The deadline was looming. The radiation took it out of me. So I let my agent arrange a ghostwriter. Lily. I'm sorry she had to fight for the money. I had no idea. Just assumed it was all sorted.'

She turns to meet my gaze. 'So, that's my story. You're under no obligation not to share it, but I would prefer to tell it myself.'

I swallow hard and nod. 'Start it as an essay. I'll find a place for it.'
She side-eyes me. 'Don't you dare say *digital space*.'
I bump her shoulder with mine. 'What's wrong with digital space?'
'It's so pretentious. Just say website.'
'Ah,' I say with a nod. 'You're too old to get it. I see.'
We laugh and she shoulder bumps me back.
'I'll print it in the mag, and on the *website*. I mean it, I'm sorry. I've been an asshole.'
Colette nods. 'You were pretty awful.'
'Just wait until you get my edits on your article.'
We laugh again, longer this time. Not because anything is particularly funny, but because it's a release, from everything we've been through.

We intertwine our fingers and I rest my head on her shoulder.

Thoughts of Laurie still sting. Maybe they always will. I never got the chance to confront him in the way I'd longed for. I'll never have the answer to my questions. *Why? How could you?*

I think of Mama. How she lives on in me.

And how, perhaps, I'm not the last rattling leaf on a tree.

That perhaps my tree is full of leaves that come and go with the seasons. Each as important as the other.

Tavis walks towards me, lit up with a fairy-light blur of blues and reds.

He has a dark woollen blanket over his shoulders, and it dances behind him as he walks. I tilt my face and he bends to press his lips on mine. As he winds the fingers of my other hand between his, the noise, smells, people all fall away.

He says something but I can't hear it. I'm too busy listening to the call of a different future, one without anger and bitterness, recriminations. Torment over things that cannot be changed. Things that will remain unknown.

Mama is not here to tell me the full story, and I'll never believe Laurie's version of events.

And suddenly, it no longer matters.

I don't cease to exist because of Laurie's lack of acknowledgment. I'm not some half beast created by Laurie and Yvonne. Not an abomination created from a vile act of violence.

I am myself. Wholeheartedly, unashamedly myself. Flawed, brilliant, frightened, brave and perfectly me. And I'm just fine.

Or, I think as I tip my face to the sky, I will be.

The wind rustles through all those leaves, and it sounds just like the ocean.

Making Herstory to debut true crime podcast

Making Herstory has released a podcast as part of the pre-publication campaign for Desley Barron's upcoming true crime title *The Final Chapter*. Described as 'true crime meets psychological thriller', Barron's story is based on the grisly events at the writers house Rhamnusia that gripped the nation last year.

Barron herself will host the podcast, and the episode list promises interviews with the writers in attendance at the time of the deaths and locals who knew both the Thorne family and Jane Walker – the Rhamnusia employee accused of the murder of Alan 'Laurie' Lawrence and the custodian of Thorne House, Eliza Jones, as well as the attempted murder of the three female writers staying at the house at the time.

Described by opinion editor for *The Sydney Informer*, Colette Halifax, as 'a shoo-in for the number one spot on *The New York Times* bestseller list', and allegedly the subject of a frantic bidding war, the marketing team behind *The Final Chapter* has devised an innovative worldwide campaign based around the book's true-crime storyline. The book offers the chilling experience of the author through her first-person account of the events.

The Final Chapter podcast will be released in weekly episodes up until the publication date, with the final episode featuring exclusive behind-the-scenes content with Desley Barron.

About Desley

When she is not chasing her loveable dog, a handsome rogue called Crumpet, along their favourite stretch of beach, or travelling with her daughters, Desley spends most of her time reading, cooking and generally enjoying her life.

A proud single mother, Desley supports Empower Women Australia.

The *Final Chapter* is her first true crime book.

Acknowledgements

I live and write on the unceded land of the Jagera and Turrbal people. Aboriginal and Torres Strait Islander peoples are the land's first storytellers and I offer deep appreciation and respect to elders, past and present.

Thank you, Rachael Donovan, for your passion and support for this story and for never spelling my name wrong in our communications (sorry if I can't say the same – that second A trips me up). Laurie Ormond, what a wonderful editor you are. Kind, precise, gentle enough with your suggestions that I understand your point, but don't spiral and become a Desley.

Thanks to the people who had their phones out ready to pre-order this book well before it was even for sale. There have been some real champions of my work and I appreciate you so much.

A huge thank you to Lisa Ireland and the Write Along crew for helping me get to the finish line on this one.

Edwina Shaw and Fiona Robertson for the fantastic retreat that gave me the quiet moments to fine tune this manuscript. Georgina Buckley, Liana Black and Tatia Power for being such great retreat buddies. We have Georgina to thank for the Gandhi/Gandalf line. Sorry I didn't get it as quickly as I hope the readers did.

Clare Griffin and Sarah Fiddelaers – as always, propping me up with the Wednesday Waffle (or the Friday Froth, depending on how busy we are.) I couldn't do it without you.

My favourite readers – Malerie Walker, Erin Fisher, Nicola Storey, Jody Richardson, and the wonderful Madeleine Timbes.

All the incredible bookstagrammers who have supported me and my books over the years, I appreciate you so much!

Kylie Orr, Jo Dixon and Cassie Hamer – thank you for taking time out of your busy schedules to read this book and to write lovely words about it.

This story was inspired by my stay at Varuna and loosely outlined in the lounge over ghost stories and red wine in front of a roaring fire in the dead of winter. Thank you to Laurie Steed for your generosity and good humour. Sorry I kept the name – he's nothing like you at all!

During the final round of edits on this book, the beautiful Linda, also known as Lily Raiti, passed away. Linda was a passionate supporter of Australian authors – spirited, positive, and warm. Talking with her felt electric, like she passed on some of her spark to everyone she encountered. Renaming the only likeable character in the whole book after her felt right. As part of her now lives on in our bookshelves, and I think she would have loved that.

talk about it

Let's talk about books.

Join the conversation:

- @harlequinaustralia
- @hqanz
- @harlequinaus

harpercollins.com.au/hq

If you love reading and want to know about our authors and titles, then let's talk about it.